Plausible Deception

J.B. Millhollin

Grey Place Books—Mt. Juliet, TN
ISBN: 978-1-7358745-4-8
eBook ISBN: 978-1-7358745-3-1
Library of Congress Control Number: 2023918026
Title: *Plausible Deception*
Author: J.B. Millhollin
Digital distribution | 2023
Paperback | 2023

Previous Novels by J.B. Millhollin

Brakus
- Brakus, Book 1
- Everything he Touched, Book 2
- With Nothing to Lose, Book 3

An Absence of Ethics
Forever Bound
Out of Reach
Redirect
Whisper of Hope
To Hide from a Northern Wind:
    Spencer Creek, Book 1
To Hide from a Northern Wind:
    Wilson County, Book 2
To Hide from a Northern Wind:
    Nashville Divided, Book 3
To Hide from a Northern Wind:
    River of Tears, Book 4
I Guess I'll Never Know
When Next, We Meet

Coming soon:

Unacceptable
Life Altered (Book 1 of a two-book series)
Life on Hold (Book 2 of a two-book series)
One More Time
The Reporter
The Prosecutor
My Turn

Chapter 1

Starbucks *Roseville, California*
Early July

The contrast between the man and woman at the table in the far corner of the room was clearly visible. They sat across from each other, he, cool and reserved, apparently without a care in the world—she, doing the best she could to appear calm and collected, but with negligible success.

Patricia Maxwell sat strumming her fingers on the tabletop, while nervously studying all the patrons located within that area of Starbucks in which they were seated. As usual, she was continually involved in some type of non-ending motion. Most of the time, it involved strumming, but, on occasion, she would alter that habit to simply fidget with her cup, the sugar sacks and the salt and pepper shakers.

Finally, her coffee companion, Edward Hall, grabbed both of her hands and held them tightly, which resulted in an unpleasant scowl from across the table.

"What the hell is wrong with you," he asked.

"I need a cigarette."

"Since when?"

He released both of her hands, which she quickly pulled back to the safe shelter of her own side of the table. "You don't smoke. What the hell do you mean you need a cigarette?"

"I have seriously considered starting. You know, this is easy for you. It's *not* for me. I realize this is the third time, but it's just not that easy for me."

Once again, she began to nervously scan the room.

He whispered, "Stop, dammit, just stop! Who the hell are you looking for? No one knows us here. We came here to meet *because* no one knows us in Roseville. Now, if we were in Sacramento, you could worry. In fact, if that's where we were, I would probably be looking around too. But we're not! Relax, for Christ's sake. By the way, you need to back off the coffee. All that caffeine turns you into someone I don't even know. You need to start drinking orange juice."

She stared at him for a moment, clearly considering his comments, then folded her hands, placing them on the table in front of her. She smiled and said, "You're right. You're right as usual. Sorry. Back to business. Give me the details, and let me know how I can help."

"You know, it's not like this is your first time. We have been through this twice before, and it's worked out fine. Your choice in picking the women has been perfect. Of course, then me finishing them off has been, if I do say so myself, exquisite. It hasn't mattered where we have been—Minneapolis, Seattle—it's worked perfectly both times. Just relax. This is just another day at the office for both of us."

"I know, I know, but it still makes me nervous and probably always will. I need another cup of coffee. I'll be right back."

He watched her walk away. Her walk was as sexy today as it was the first day he met her. In addition, as highly as she rated on the 'perfect' scale *out* of bed, she rated even higher on the scale *in* bed. Even though they had just come from a hotel room not an hour ago, he was ready to walk across the street and start all over again. No other woman affected him in that manner.

As she sat back down, she said, "Without going into specifics, just give me the overall plan, will you?"

"Sure. Dorothy and I will head up to Lake Tahoe Sunday morning. When we return the following Saturday afternoon, she is going to meet with a small misfortune. It's that simple. Nothing more, nothing less."

"All the money, stocks, and bonds that were titled in her name, now show both your names as owners, right? Everything?"

"Absolutely. Within a couple of weeks after she's gone, I will give you your share for finding her, and we will move on."

"You make it sound so easy, so effortless, just like you do everything else."

"Come on, relax, Pat. It's fine. I can handle this. Just relax."

"I can't. I need sex. Maybe that will calm me down. Let's go."

As he quickly stood, he said, "Music to my ears."

Home of Mr. and Mrs. Edward Hall
Sacramento, California
Late July

The journey home was uneventful. He drove their Tesla in the driveway just a few minutes prior to 5:00 p.m. As he pulled a suitcase and hang-up bag out of the car, he said, "Dorothy, why don't you go on in and pour us a couple of glasses of wine. I'll join you in a moment."

"Sure will, darlin'," she said, as she walked slowly toward the front door.

He watched as the leg she had injured long ago, was clearly causing her pain. She walked with a noticeable limp.

He closed and locked the car doors, then walked in behind her. He then hung up the hang-up bag and carefully placed the suitcase directly in front of the open staircase leading to the basement.

During the next couple of hours, every time her glass was near empty, he filled it. She was clearly feeling its full effect, when, as it approached nine-thirty, Ed said, "Let's go upstairs. I'm tired. It has been a long day. Maybe we can just fall asleep watching TV. Are you ready?"

She stood, grabbing the arm of her chair for support, as she said, "I sure am, sweetheart."

"Why don't you get the suitcase—it's not that heavy. I need to check on a couple of things in my office. I'll be right along."

Dorothy, with wineglass in hand, clearly unsteady on her feet as a result of only having one fully-functional leg and an overindulgence in wine, moved slowly toward the suitcase. As she did, he quietly followed her. When she finally reached the suitcase, she took hold of the handle as he walked up behind her. She turned toward him and said, "Whatever are you doing, darlin'?"

He gave her a simple sideward shove toward the stairs. He smiled. It was so simple. Yet that simple move of his arm would result in such a reward, such a benefit—and all it took was just a little push.

As he watched, everything seemed to move in slow motion. She first, fell over the top of the suitcase. It followed her along shortly thereafter. She still had wine in her other hand, but she held the glass all the way to the bottom.

Her head first came in contact with a step about halfway down, resulting in a resounding thud. It was clear as soon as she came to rest, she was dead. The suitcase and the remaining wine in her glass eventually landed on top of her, as her body came to a grinding halt.

He quickly raced to the bottom of the steps as he simultaneously called 911. He checked for a pulse, of which there was none. EMS indicated they would be there in minutes, but it was clear to him there was nothing for them to do, except cart off a dead body.

He tore open the front of her blouse and started to pound on her chest, as if it would make a difference. But he wanted the sound of his pounding fist to be the first thing the responders heard when they walked in the door.

They arrived shortly thereafter, he played the part of the grieving widow, and no one suspected a thing. Her fall was clearly the logical result of picking up the suitcase, a bad leg, and too much to drink. She had no children to question any of the issues, and once her funeral was over, so were the questions concerning her death.

Starbucks
Roseville, California
August

Edward had just taken a seat as she walked in the door. He hadn't seen nor talked to her since they last met prior to Dorothy's untimely death. That was the way she insisted it must be. They had further agreed to meet today and discuss business, but this time, it would be discussed *before* they went to the room. This time it would be business before pleasure, so those issues wouldn't linger while they were enjoying each other's company.

She was such a beautiful woman. It was always entertaining to watch her enter a room, then watch the men as she walked by. She was perfect, if one could just move past her paranoia. He almost missed noticing her as she walked through the door. She had her black hair pulled back in a ponytail, wore dark glasses even though it was and had been dark outside for quite some time, and she had one arm in a sling.

As she approached the table, Ed said, "What the hell happened to you?"

She didn't respond immediately, sitting down with her cup of coffee first. "Nothing, nothing, I just didn't want anyone to know who I was, or be recognized on the security camera. Just being cautious."

"Why? Why would anyone be looking for either of us? You are wearing a fricken *sling* to avoid being *recognized*? Are you nuts?"

"First of all, no I'm not nuts. Why would you even say that? Third, I don't know who might be looking for us or at us, but I would rather be safe than sorry. Now, let's talk business so we can get to the room. I don't want to sit here all night justifying my disguise to you. What happened?"

He smiled and wondered how he ever hooked up with such a kook. But she was a kook who knew her business and fit their situation perfectly. As he watched her adjust the sling, he couldn't help but smile as he said, "You know you missed number two."

"What number two? Where?"

"You said, 'First, I'm not nuts, then you said third, I'm…Never mind. Everything went well."

"Details, please."

"We came home, she got drunk, she picked up a piece of luggage by the open basement door, and she fell. She never suffered. She was gone before I could run to her side and respond to her misfortune like the good husband I am."

"So? What about the money?"

"As I already told you, it was all retitled—a little at a time—and finally reached the point a few months ago, where it was *all* jointly titled in both her name and mine. I got it all. I checked yesterday, and I think it all totaled around two mil."

"What about the house? Didn't you say it was also changed to 'right of survivorship?'"

"Yes. I got it too. It's probably worth around seven hundred and fifty thousand. I will get it sold in the next few months and let you know how much I netted."

"So, can we settle up now?"

"Yes. I brought you a check for two hundred thousand which is ten percent of what I received in cash. When the house is sold, I will give you another check for ten percent of the net. Is that okay with you?"

"Sure. Sure, that's fine with me," she said as she took the check, and nervously looked around to, once again, make sure no one was within hearing distance. "Did anyone ever question you about what happened? Do you think anyone ever had any idea what *really* happened?"

"No. The medical examiner determined it was an accident. I never even heard from a cop. We are fine. Don't worry about it."

She took a sip of coffee, then said, "Where do we go from here?"

"Well, we could quit if you wish, but we've been pretty successful. I kind of hate to stop now. What do *you* think?"

She smiled, for the first time since she sat down. "I agree. I don't have as much as I want yet anyway. Let's give it a go another time."

"Where to next? Is there any place you haven't lived that you would like to live?"

She thought for a moment as she again looked around the room for anyone that might be watching the two of them. As she turned toward him, she said, "I've always wanted to live in Colorado. I have been there once or twice, but never lived there. And I would think the mountains would be a lovely place for a long fall resulting in a quick death. Your thoughts?"

He hesitated for a moment. "I love that idea. Figure out which city suits you. Then find us two separate places to live and," he smiled, "start looking for our next victim."

Chapter 2

Conference Room, Tennessee Board of Professional Responsibility
Nashville, Tennessee

"Now Mr. Borkowski, do you understand the nature of the proceedings today?

Clearly nervous, Matt said, "Yes, I understand, but again, you should know I really would rather not be here. I told you he paid me back. This should all be done and over with, you know what I mean?"

The hearing room was dark and poorly lit. The members of the board conducting the hearing, were all seated at a long table in front of him. The only other person in the room, other than Mr. Borkowski, was Paul Thomas, the attorney who was the subject matter of the hearing. Matt was seated at a small table directly in front of the chairperson who sat directly in the middle of the board members stretching to his left and his right.

Paul listened while the complaint was read aloud by the chairman. He sat quietly, waiting for his turn to testify after the complainant was quizzed.

"As I understand your complaint, Mr. Borkowski, you paid Mr. Thomas five thousand dollars to prepare and file a petition for a dissolution of your marriage, is that correct?"

"Yes, that's correct."

"Later, when you checked on whether the petition had been filed, you discovered it hadn't been. In fact, even after repeated phone calls to his office concerning the fact it hadn't been filed, it was *still* never filed, is that correct?"

"Yes, it never was filed."

"I also understand when you asked for your money back, he told you he had used it, spent it, and couldn't pay you back, is that correct?"

"Well, yes that is what he said *then*, but after I filed this complaint, he contacted me about a month later and paid me back in full, plus interest. Then we went and had a drink together. I actually went back to him later for additional work. I like him. He is a good friend. I did *not* want to pursue this. But here I am, unwilling to be here, and testifying about a man I care for and …."

"Wait, just wait a minute, Mr. Borkowski. This man took your money, didn't do any work for you and now you are friends? That doesn't make sense. He, in essence, stole from you."

"Look, I'm telling it to you the way it happened. I should have never, ever filed the complaint. If I could pull those damn papers out from under your nose right now I would. Do you understand what I'm trying to say?"

"Oh, I think you've made yourself pretty clear. By the way, watch that language. Now, anything else from any of the other board members?"

No one indicated they had any questions and, as a result, the chairperson said, "You are free to go, Mr. Borkowski. Thank you for your time. Mr. Thomas please come forward and take a seat."

Borkowski rose, and as he walked past Paul Thomas, who was also now standing, he embraced him and whispered something in his ear, which resulted in a smile from Paul.

Once he was seated, the board chairman said, "Please state your full name for the record."

"Paul Thomas."

"You understand why we are here today, Mr. Thomas? Do you understand the nature of these proceedings?"

"Yes. I've been through this before."

"You understand this is all being recorded?"

"Yes."

"Do you want to tell us, in your own words, what happened here? Do you dispute anything Mr. Borkowski testified to?"

"No, not really. He brought in the money, I deposited it in my trust account, and I later used it for personal purposes. Probably a month later, after he had filed the complaint, I paid him back, with a month's interest. Like he said, we have become good friends since, but as concerns his testimony, it was correct."

"This is not the first time you have appeared before us, is it?"

"No."

"How many times?"
"This is the third."
"The other two were surprisingly similar. You took money from your clients, did no work for them, but paid them back after they filed a complaint, isn't that correct?"
"Yes."
"All the complaints center around money. You have never had one filed against you for your ability to practice law. They seem to all center around money. How long have you practiced Mr. Thomas—for the record?"
"I have practiced in Nashville since I graduated from law school, about 11 years ago."
"Are you still married to the same woman?"
He hesitated before he cleared his throat and answered, "Yes."
"As I recall, you previously testified she was sick. Is that still the case?"
"Yes, she has ALS."
"Is she improving at all?"
Again, he hesitated, before saying, "No. They don't get better with ALS. They only get worse and that's the case with her. She continues to grow weaker by the month."
"Does she need daily care now?"
"Yes."
"Do you have any children to care for, Mr. Thomas?"
"No."
"Do you have insurance that covers her daily care at home?"
"No, I don't."
"Is that where the money is going—to care for your wife?"
He stood up, his six-feet, two-inch frame towering over the small table in front of him. "That is none of your business, sir. That's my own personal issue and I…"
"Stop right there, Mr. Thomas. Apparently, your personal issue is lapping over into your practice. I should advise you that if you hope to continue to practice your profession in this state, you better answer *every* question asked of you and do it truthfully. Your right to practice is at stake here. *Do I make myself clear?"*
He ran his fingers of one hand nervously through his jet-black hair, then sat down.
"I understand. I apologize, but she's an important part of my life. I

watch her slowly slip away every day. I can't keep up with the money issues. My house is mortgaged to the max, I work as hard as I can, but it's just difficult to keep up."

"I understand, but you can't continue to finance your personal issues with other people's money. This is the third time this has happened and every time it ends up the same. You take their money, use it for your own purpose, and then after they file a complaint, you pay them off. This is not acceptable. Even though the people, on all three occasions, wanted their complaint dropped, that's not how it works. You know that. You know fully well that's not how it is supposed to work."

"I understand, I do, and I think I've got it figured out. My practice has grown and grown quickly. I am still involved in civil litigation *and* I'm starting to pick up some criminal work. Lately, I have clients knocking down the door. That's not bragging, that's a fact. I can't keep up. So, what I am saying is I really think I have this all worked out. In fact, I'm considering taking on at least one more attorney."

"Be that as it may, I have no idea what the board will want to do, but I can tell you one thing. You need to stop the activity which continues to give rise to your appearance before this board. Whether this time they reprimand you, or suspend you for a time, you can't appear before us again, *for any reason*. The next time you are here, I can assure you this board will show you no mercy whatsoever. *If* you appear before us again, I have a feeling the only conclusion this board will reach will be disbarment, regardless of the facts surrounding the complaint. Do you understand what I'm saying?"

"Yes sir, I do."

"A ruling will be issued within the next week or so. You will get it in the mail. Remember what I told you, sir. Not again. *If* you are allowed to keep your license this time, do not appear before us again for any reason. You are free to go."

Paul rose and turned to leave the room. As he did, the chairperson, said, "Oh and Mr. Thomas."

Paul turned and said, "Sir?"

"I am sorry about your wife, I truly am, as are the other members of this board. We wish you both nothing but the best."

Paul hesitated, looked down, cleared his throat, and said, "Thank you sir. Thanks to all of you."

Law office of Paul Thomas
September

Paul sat in his office, trying to figure out which case to handle first. The office had been insanely busy lately, and the extra hours spent at his desk were not enough to keep up.

He continued to occupy the same office he opened when he graduated from law school, but he was afraid it was about time to find another larger space *and* something he could afford. That would most likely be a major issue in downtown Nashville. He probably also needed to hire at least one more attorney. It had reached the point for the first time since Anna had been diagnosed, that his income and his expenses, including Anna's medical and home-care costs, were approximately the same each month.

He figured her home-care costs would remain relatively constant now, since he had to have someone with her all the time when he wasn't home. But at least he knew, in advance, how much he was going to need for the next month, a luxury he hadn't had a chance to enjoy since she became sick.

"I got the mail, Paul. Hate to tell you, but I had to sign for the one from the bar association."

He slowly looked over Hanna Parks from top to bottom. She was an excellent secretary, which is why he had increased her wages every time she asked. But her clothes were clearly purchased from another planet. Today she had on some kind of purple top that made no sense whatsoever, with a short orange colored skirt. Complimenting that, were a pair of tall high-heels, and a brightly colored bow stuck in her hair. Apparently, her off-colored pink lipstick was intended to bring everything together. He needed to have a talk with her. The clothing she wore had to adversely affect people walking in the front door. She really needed to tone it down just a touch.

"Thanks, Hanna. I was expecting it. By the way, do you pick out your own clothes anymore or does someone do it for you?"

Hanna smiled as she leaned against the door frame "You know Paul, you've asked me that before. I pick them all out myself. Don't you just love this collection I have on today? I call it my *early-American ensemble*."

"That's not exactly what I would call it, but yes, you look fine." He reached for the envelope. "I hope after today, you can continue to show off those appealing articles of clothing in this office. I just hope I've received a reprimand and not been suspended or disbarred. Keep your fingers crossed."

He slowly opened the envelope while she stood by. He looked at the four-page document which started with a full statement concerning the factual issues. He started to read aloud. "This hearing concerning Paul Thomas is being held pursuant to…"

"Stop. Stop right there." Hanna stepped inside his office and walked up to the front of his desk. "Go to the end. I don't give a shit why the hearing was held. I just want to know if I still got a job. Go to the end and tell me how they ruled."

He looked up at her and said, "Good idea. I can read the rest later." He then placed the first three pages on his desk, proceeding quickly to the end. Once there, the only word he read was, "Reprimand."

Hanna smiled, turned and walked out of his office. He put the last page down, stood and walked to the window. He was lucky this time. He knew it. This could never happen again. He needed every penny he had to take care of the woman he loved with all his heart. Without this practice bringing in the money for Anna's care, the one that could possibly suffer the most was her. From now on, he would do whatever he had to do to insure this never happened again *for any reason whatsoever.*

Chapter 3

Sam's Coffee Shop *Denver, Colorado*
November

Edward Hunt and Patricia Maxwell sat as far away from everyone as they possibly could. Sam's Coffee Shop couldn't hold a large number of people, but at midnight, there weren't many looking for a cup of coffee anyway. Edward was able to find a table near the back wall which suited him.

Pat had just taken a seat as she said, "How did the move go from your apartment to the house?"

Ed was in the process of dumping two small sacks of sugar into his coffee as he said, "Good. Some of the guys I met at the apartment complex helped me move."

"Is it a nice home?"

"It's all right. It will suit our purposes, anyway. I hope I'm not there long. What have you come up with?"

"Well, first of all, I want you to know, I don't particularly care about not seeing or talking with you other than at these little meetings which are infrequently held. Do we have to keep meeting like this?"

He smiled, as he said, "Unfortunately, yes. It has worked well in the past, and I'm not much into altering a successful formula. It's difficult for me too, you know. Tonight, is the first time we have even had a cup of coffee together for quite some time. But I do think it is best we remain apart until the job is done and we either quit or move on."

She looked around nervously, before she refocused on Ed and said, "You know, it's not natural for a woman to go this long without sex. It creates bad hormones which will eventually kill a woman. You know that don't you?"

He smiled as he set his coffee cup down. "No, I didn't know that, but I *do* know you are full of shit…I *d*o know that. Now, let's get down to business. What have you got for me? Who are the contenders for this project?"

Pat had already finished her first cup of coffee. "Just a minute, let me get another cup."

Here we go again, Ed thought. She gets nervous, she drinks coffee. The coffee puts her on edge, she gets more nervous. It was a vicious cycle he watched each and every time they discussed a job. If for no other reason, you had to love her for her predictability.

As Pat sat down, she said, "We have three to choose from. The first one is Jacki Howard. I met her through the church I started attending here in Denver. She is about 50, attractive, very religious, sweet, and she would never expect to meet, let alone marry, someone like you. She's, as best I can tell, loaded. Her husband died about two years ago, so she should be pretty lonely by now."

"Go on."

"The next one is Verlene Nelson. She's about forty and I met her at a singles club meeting. She's attractive, has a little money, but I'm not really sure how much. She has a beautiful home, but the car she drives is an older vehicle, and she never wants much to do with paying the bill when we go out to eat. I get mixed signals from her."

"Who is the last one?"

"Her name is Samantha Arnold. I met her at a widow's club meeting. She too, is around fifty. I know she has a lot of money by the way she dresses and by the appearance of her home, along with the vehicle she drives. By the way, I checked the recorder's office in the court house. None of these women have mortgages on their homes and each home is assessed at well over a million. This woman is pretty bold in her approach to most anything. She would probably ask a few more questions than the other two before she married you."

"Are they all looking for a husband, or do you know?"

"I wouldn't have included them as part of the 'potentials' if I felt they were happily single."

"What about family issues?"

"Two of them have kids, but they don't live in Denver. The third one doesn't. She has no children, and from what I can tell, no relatives living in Denver at all."

"Who is your pick?"

"My pick would be Jacki. She's the one with no children, she's looking for a man, and it appears to me she has a ton of money."

"What does she look like physically?"

"You mean, does she have a bad case of warts?"

"Come on, you know what I mean. But in response, yes, it would take a lot more effort for me to have sex with her if she wasn't physically appealing. I'm going to have to do that you know. It's a hell of a lot easier if she is attractive and not covered in warts. Now, what is she like physically?"

"I hate this part. You're with her, *doing that,* as many times as makes her happy, and I *don't* enjoy knowing that. I always have to sit on my ass waiting for you to knock her off before I get my turn. There's not much I like about that part of this job."

"You know, you're a pretty rich lady today because you *waited your turn,* and, I might add, soon to be even richer. But I will stop whenever you wish. When we quit, as we have previously discussed, I'll marry you, and we will live on an island somewhere in the Caribbean. You know that. We have discussed it before. Now, how do you want to proceed?"

She looked around the room for a moment, and as she reengaged in the conversation, she turned toward Ed, and said, "She is tall, sexy as hell, short black hair in a pixy cut. Believe me, you will have absolutely no problem having sex with her."

"Sounds like she's the one then. What's the best way to meet her?"

"Start going to church."

Sam's Coffee Shop,
Denver, Colorado
March

"Do we have to keep meeting at midnight?"

"Yes."

"End of the discussion?"

Ed said, "Okay, *why* don't you want to meet at midnight?"

"Well, because I am always so tired the next day. It takes me two days to recover. Can't we meet like normal people, maybe during the day, or midafternoon or something?"

"Yep."

Pat said, "Yep what? Yep mid-afternoon?"

"Nope. Yep, we *can* meet like normal people, but nope the discussion's over. *We meet at midnight.*"

"Fine, whatever." She looked around at the patrons still enjoying a cup at Sam's, which consisted of very few people, mostly transients and travelers, as she softly said, "How are things with miss rich bitch?"

"Whoa, you *really* got up on the wrong side of the bed. You have a really bad attitude. But in response, everything is fine. Today was somewhat of a bore since I spent most of it making plans for the wedding, but that's fine. It's just the next step in the process."

"When is it?"

"June 15, at 8:00 p.m. Everyone in the church is going to get an invitation."

"Is she as rich as I thought she was?"

"She has a lot of money, yes. I'm not sure yet how much. She is already talking about commingling mine and hers. I hate to do that with mine, but if they ever investigate anything, it would look a hell of a lot better if my money had her name on it, as hers did mine."

"What's the family situation?"

"She has a sister in New York who also has plenty of money. I don't think they're real close. Other than that, she has no one—but me." He smiled the smile that had captured the hearts of so many women in his life, and which, of course, later helped in eventually bilking the same women.

She reached across the table and placed her hand over his.

He quickly pulled his hand away. "We can't let our guard down now, Pat. We don't have all that far to go with this one. We have both worked too hard on this to have issues come up now, and that's what could happen if the wrong person saw us holding hands. Just wait a few more months."

She pulled her hand back, as she said, "Have you settled on a plan yet?"

"Not really. I want to wait until at least a year after we marry, so we are looking at June of next year before I even think of making the move."

"Do you think it will it be difficult to get her to fall for whatever it is you come up with?"

"No, I don't think so. Even now, I pretty well have her wrapped around my finger. I really don't think there is going to be a problem. By the way, you did a great job finding her, as you always do."

"So, do you have any preliminary thoughts about her sad demise?"

"Well, she did say she liked to hike and that she especially liked to hike around Estes Park. I did a little research, and based on that research, I do know there are a couple of trails in the back country that aren't heavily traveled in the early fall. I'm thinking she's probably going to take a header off one of those trails, leaving nothing at the bottom but a mess for someone to clean up. That's what I'm thinking right now."

Patricia reached over, and again placed her hand over his. She smiled, squeezed his hand and winked, as she whispered, "You're the best, Ed. You are just simply the best."

Chapter 4

Office of the Associate Dean of Law
Vanderbilt University
May

"We know something went on, Miss Andrews, we just aren't sure what it was or who exactly was involved. We *do* know enough, however, to know *you* are somehow involved. Why don't you just tell us what happened?"

Ruth Andrews, a Vanderbilt senior law student, sat before the associate Dean of Law, Mark Haskins. He wasn't about to see her sweat. She would say nothing—nothing about her or about the other students that were involved. They had discussed it prior to the hearing today. They had all cheated concerning a test involving international law. But all those that had the answers, all those that had cheated on the test, had remained tight-lipped and said nothing. She wasn't about to be the one to spell the beans and tell this guy what they had done.

"I have no idea what you are talking about."

"It was pretty easy to figure it all out. Eight of you gave identical answers to the questions. It was like you used a copy machine. We know something went on; we just need your help to establish exactly what happened. Now, can we expect some cooperation from you?"

She had been here before. Not while in law school, but there had been other times, while she was a juvenile, in which she found herself under investigation. Some money missing here, some merchandise missing there, but nothing anyone could ever prove. She never admitted anything then: she wouldn't today.

"Sir, I swear, I have no idea what you're talking about. We did nothing but study together. I have no doubt no one, and I repeat *no one* in that group I studied with, ever cheated."

"You know, you come from a great family, Ms. Andrews. I know your daddy. In fact, he and I went to school together right here, right here at Vandy. I know your momma too. She's a great woman—just love her to death. They are good, honest, hard-working people. I've never known either of them to be dishonest, or lie about anything. I expect the same from you. Now, give me a little information concerning exactly what happened here, would you?"

She thought about her parents—they would not take no for an answer when she told them she didn't want to attend law school. They insisted. Life as a law student had been about like she expected. It was more than difficult for her from day one. When parental pressure was included with the difficulty of just trying to grasp the subject matter, the result was cheating to succeed, and that's exactly what had happened. She had cheated to make it through.

"You know, Mr. Haskins, I can't make stuff up. Nothing went on and I can't tell you it did when it didn't. I'm sorry, but that's the truth. Now, is there anything else?"

"We are going to make the whole class take the test over again. We're also going to make sure the whole class knows why, and who we feel was involved in this scheme. How do you think the rest of the class is going to feel about that?"

"Probably not the best. I understand your frustration, but I wasn't involved in anything nefarious, and I doubt my father's going to be very happy with you—with the school—if you start throwing my name out there indicating I cheated on a test when you have no proof I did. That probably would not go down well with him, since it's clearly slanderous." She stood, "If that's all Mr. Haskins, I have a couple of finals I need to prepare for. I'm really sorry this has happened, and if I find out who was involved, I'll surely let you know."

"Oh, we know who was involved Ms. Andrews, we just can't prove it—at least for now. Get out."

Later that morning, she had coffee with Harold Vorhies, a classmate, and one of those involved in the group of students under investigation.

"How did it go, Ruth?"

"Good, it went good."

"Did you tell them anything?"

"Hell no. He did, however, tell me that the whole class was going to be retested. He tried to intimidate me by telling me they would tell the class why, and who was involved, but I suggested that might be a problem, since it would be a slanderous statement. I think he'll reconsider that move, but we'll see."

Harold smiled, as he said, "Good job. And by the way, if they do retest us, it won't matter. I'll have the questions then too, so don't worry about it."

"I figured."

Later that day she considered her involvement in so many of these incidents. The rush was always there—the rush that came with getting something for nothing.

Then, to get away with it provided an even greater sense of pride and accomplishment in a job well done and adequately concluded. To do anything in a conventional manner just didn't seem to be enough for her. She simply needed to feel she held the upper hand—to succeed in her own way. Her *own* way was to succeed by pulling the wool over their eyes. That was all that mattered. This situation was no different.

Law Office of Harsh and Armstrong
Nashville

"How long have you been with us, Ruth?"

"Since right after I graduated, Mr. Harsh. Since about June of last year."

"We've been very pleased with your work since you've been here. But let me ask you a question. Do you ever handle cash in this office? Do your clients pay you in cash?"

"Very seldom. If they do, I just give it to the front desk and let them handle it like I'm supposed to. Why do you ask?"

"You know, I am personally acquainted with your parents. Love them both. Good people. Honest, trustworthy to a fault."

"Thank you, Mr. Harsh."

"As I recall, you are an only child, isn't that correct? You have no siblings?"

"Yes, that's correct."

"What's your relationship with your parents, Ruth?"

"It's fine. It's good. What is this all about? Why do you ask?"

"Well, I saw your father the other day, and he mentioned you were on the outs with them. He said the three of you had a slightly different philosophy about life and that your relationship with them wasn't very good right now."

"Oh, that's nothing, Mr. Harsh. We've had our issues through the years but no different than most parents and their kids. No different than what we see in this very office every day."

"He made it sound pretty serious, Ruth."

She stood, "It's really not a problem. I'll work on it though. Anything else?"

"Yes, there is something else. Please be seated."

She took her seat as she said, "What else do we need to discuss?"

"Do you have a client by the name of Streeter?"

"Yes. I represent him in a dissolution of his marriage. Why do you ask?"

"How long have you represented him?"

"I think about two or three months. The dissolution hasn't yet been completed. I think it's set for trial in about sixty days or so. Why, what's the problem?"

"Did he pay us a retainer?"

All of a sudden, Ruth didn't care for the direction this conversation was heading. "Yes. He gave me a check for twenty-five hundred dollars which I gave to the front desk."

"Was that all?"

"Yes."

"Well, that's not what he says. He says he had five hundred in cash which he gave you too, but it never showed up as a credit on his bill. Do you know anything about that?"

She thought for a moment and finally said, "You know I believe he did make the payment, but I thought I gave that to the front desk for deposit. Did you ask them?"

"I *know* he is correct in that he gave it to you, because I saw the receipt you gave to him. The front desk never saw the money. They never received it from you."

"Maybe they are mistaken."

"Gladys handles the money. She's done that now for almost twenty years and never made a mistake. I don't think she made one this time either. What happened, Ruth?"

She was caught, and she knew it. She had told accounting not to bill him until the case was over. That would have given her time to come up with the $500 which she had 'borrowed' to help pay for new furniture in her apartment.

"I only intended it to be a loan, Mr. Harsh, and that's the truth. I was going to replace it before the case was concluded. I really needed the cash. I can promise you it would have been replaced before the dissolution was final."

"You have been here less than a year, and we already have problems."

"I can promise you it will never happen again. I love it here, Mr. Harsh. I made a mistake. One for which I am deeply sorry. It will never happen again."

"The only reason you are sorry is because you got caught. We have never in all the years since I formed this firm, had this type of problem."

"Again, I'm so sorry. I promise it will never happen again."

"Not *here* it won't. I expect a letter terminating your employment, on my desk no later than tomorrow morning. I will give you a break in that no one in this office will say a word about why you quit. That will at least give you a chance to start over somewhere else. I am doing that as much as anything, because I don't want anyone knowing what a fool I was to hire you in the first place. Do you understand?"

She lowered her head and said, "Yes, sir. I'm sorry."

She left his office and walked down to her office to type up a termination letter. As she walked, she thought this would never have happened if the billing department had followed her instructions. This was the first time she had actually been caught. One good lesson learned—if someone else is directly or indirectly involved in your scheme, make sure you can rely on them to do what they say they are going to do. This would have all worked perfectly if the billing department…

As she typed, she concluded what's done was done. Time to move on. Time to find a new job and hopefully *keep* it this time, in spite of what some might consider a small character flaw.

Chapter 5

Starbucks
Denver Colorado

He watched her as she walked across the parking lot and approached the front door of Starbucks. In spite of the fact that she was a beautiful woman, her attitude and approach to life was, at times, hard to handle. Through the years, they had spent time together on numerous occasions, and found, at least for short periods of time, they enjoyed each other's company in many ways.

But he had no doubt a long-term relationship with her was problematic. He just felt, at some point in time, each of their own individual personality traits would clash, and someone would get hurt—probably him. They would never make it in the long run. He knew it—she hadn't yet figured that out.

"Ed, why did you change our meeting location?"

He stood as she approached. "Does it matter?"

She reached over and removed a small dollop of chocolate stuck near his mouth. "When did you start eating chocolate croissants? You never eat sweet stuff, at least not when I've been around you. I wonder how many other things you've kept from me."

He smiled as he said, "Did all these issues come up because I changed our meeting place—and now, I'm eating a chocolate croissant? Whoa. I'm glad I didn't have a cup of tea. That could have *really* resulted in an inquisition."

"Whatever. Forget I said that. How's everything going? Are you ready to make this work? I am getting tired of living here, I know that. I don't like the people, I'm tired of looking at those damn hills out west, and I am *not* ready for cold weather which will probably be here in a week. I need new surroundings. Oh, and before that, like right now, I need a cup of coffee."

She stood and walked over to order a cup while he finished his croissant. As she returned to the table, he said, "It won't be long. It looks like we are going to Estes Park on the fifteenth, and return the twenty-second. Hopefully, the right opportunity will arise and only one of us will come home. Hopefully that 'one' will be me."

"How is everything between the two of you?"

"Good. Couldn't be better."

She looked at him, and took a short sip of hot coffee, before she said, "Is everything alright? You're not getting soft on me, are you? Do you have feelings for this woman? Something's not right. Something's changed. What's going on here?"

He hesitated, before he said, "She is a nice woman. She's just a really good soul. This is going to be a little more difficult than the first three. Don't misunderstand. It's going to happen. But this one will… be… just a little more difficult."

She looked at him sternly and said, "You know there are only two options here, don't you? It's either murder her or live with her. There is no in-between."

"I know that. I'm fine. I will take care of business, but this one is difficult. All of the other women had so many issues. The loss meant nothing to me. But this woman is a good Christian woman, and a good friend too. She will definitely be missed. This one just isn't quite so easy."

"So, is she still going over a cliff?"

"About as far over as a person can go. I got one all picked out. I went up there and checked out the area last week one day when she was in church. Perfect area. Lightly traveled even during midsummer. We aren't going until after the Labor Day crowd goes home, so there should be absolutely no one around. It should work out well."

"Are we meeting here again next time?"

"Yes. Let's meet here the evening of the twenty-seventh around ten. We would probably be more than safe even if we meet during the day, but let's continue to keep a low profile until this is completely over, and we know it's a done deal all the way around."

Estes Park, Colorado
September

The day was magnificent. The trail up the mountain had been devoid of other hikers. Ed had planned on that being the situation.

Jacki was athletic and had no trouble with the altitude issues, nor climbing the trail. She had mentioned how he had done such a wonderful job in selecting this particular path at this time of year. The trees were just starting to turn, the air was crisp, and the sky was blue. Perfect day for a walk in the mountains.

They had just reached one of the highest points on the trail when Ed said, "Why don't we take a break here. I'm a little winded. I just want to look out over the valley and observe what God has given us."

"Good idea, sweetheart. How right you are. What a beautiful world he has made for us."

She sat down on a large bolder which was on the mountain side of the trail and away from a drop off that appeared to approximate five or six hundred feet at a minimum. He sat next to her, and for a few moments neither moved, neither said a word, content to look out over the valley which stretched for miles. Finally, he pulled out a small canteen of water and both took a drink.

As he put it away, he said, "What an incredible view."

She took his hand, and said, "Thank you."

"For what?"

"For making this the most wonderful time of my life. I had a great first marriage, as you know. But my time with you has been so much fun, so full of energy, so enjoyable in so many ways. Just, thank you."

"God brought us together. I didn't have a thing to do with it. Let's both just thank him."

"Amen to that."

"Are you ready to move on?"

He stood, and as he did, he moved slightly closer to the edge. "How about one more kiss before we reach the top?"

She walked to where he stood and kissed him, then said, "You know how much I love you. You are just the best. Thank God for you Ed, thank God."

With that, he gave her a push, and she fell over the edge. He watched as she tumbled head over heels, without a sound, and continued to watch as the dust flew when she finally touched down.

As he continued to view the area, making sure no one had watched, he said, "Honey, I did you a favor. Now, you can thank God in person. Tell him hello for me if you would."

Starbucks
Denver, Colorado

"We about had a problem this time, Pat."

She had just sat down. She almost dropped her cup of coffee with his remark coming before they even said hello.

"What do you mean, 'almost had a problem.' Do we have one or don't we?"

"We don't, but we almost did."

"Okay, okay, quit giving me the runaround. What the hell happened? No wait, let me structure this conversation to make it easy for you to explain and much easier for me to understand. First of all, is she dead?"

"Pretty much."

Pat rolled her eyes, and said, "You see, there you go again. I hate it when you are like this. *Is she dead—yes, or no?"*

"Yes, she's dead."

"Was it investigated, again, yes or no."

"Yes."

"Are you being charged with anything?"

"No."

"Is the investigation over?"

"Yes."

"Is the money ours?"

He smiled, and with a slight hesitation thrown in for effect, finally said, "Yes."

She stood, walked around the table, leaned down, and kissed him. "Now you see how easy a conversation can be, you bastard." She walked back to her chair, took a quick sip of coffee and said, "*Now*, give me the details."

"Well, I shoved her over the edge, she fell about six hundred feet, and that was that. I went back down the mountain, told them what had happened, played the grieving widower, took her body home and cremated her. Her funeral was uneventful. I finally got rid of her sister, and I checked out all the money issues yesterday. It is all jointly held with me, as is the house, which I already knew. The cash totals around three mil, and I'm thinking the house will bring about eight hundred thousand, give or take a few thousand. Here's your cut for now. I'll give you the rest once the house has been sold."

He handed her a check for three hundred thousand dollars.

“Holy shit.”

“Ironically, that’s probably exactly what she said as she was falling.”

“What’s the story on the investigation?”

“Initially, I was a little concerned. I figured they probably felt I might have had something to do with what happened, but there were no witnesses and nothing to establish anything but the fall. They wrapped everything up shortly after her funeral and I’ve heard nothing since. I don’t think I will. I have no doubt it’s over.”

They both sat in silence, she looking at her check, he watching her.

“So, what are your thoughts, Pat. One more, two more, or done now?”

“I was thinking about that before we met up. I really think I want to try one more, maybe make it a good one, then retire with you permanently. What are your thoughts?”

“I agree completely. One more will put me in a position to never have to worry about money again.”

“You mean, *we* would never have to worry again.” After no immediate response from Ed, she said, “Don’t you?”

“Absolutely. That’s absolutely what I meant. So—where to next?”

“You know, we were going to end up on an island in the Caribbean anyway, why don’t we just keep moving in that direction. Ever been to Nashville?”

Chapter 6

Judge's Chambers, Davidson County Courthouse,
Nashville, Tennessee,
January

Paul Thomas sat, waiting patiently for the judge to finish a short hearing before walking into his chambers. His mind wandered, as he considered the many years of friendship the two of them had enjoyed. Paul and Judge John Dimmler had gone through college together. Not so many years after they both started practicing in Nashville, John decided to run for judge in Davidson County. Paul remembered all those countless hours he had worked with him on his campaign. It all paid off though, as John ultimately won his bid for the judgeship.

He took a deep breath as he remembered it hadn't been long after the election, that all of Anna's health issues, along with Paul's ethical issues, began. Of course, if his ethical issues had been a problem at the time of the election, John would not have wanted his help or his endorsement.

Since the election, they had remained the best of friends, to the extent that John had even offered to help with the financial issues.

Paul thought how lucky he was to have him as a friend. Even though they were both involved in the legal profession, there were times in which their legal positions were in conflict. But, through the years, they continued to respect each other's status and maintain a close relationship.

As John walked through the door, he said, "Morning, Paul. How's Anna? Is there any sign of improvement at all?"

Paul sat in one of the old, hardwood chairs which surrounded the judge's desk, and which should have been used for firewood during the 20th century. Nothing in the room had been updated for years, those in authority citing a lack of public funds for such 'foolishness.'

"No, she is about the same as she's been for the last six months. She won't improve, Judge. As you know, it's not good, and it's only going to get worse."

"I don't know how you do it. I've watched you take care of her for the last few years and make her the center of attention in your life every single hour of every day. I really don't know how you do it. You have more compassion in your little finger than I have in my whole body. You never say much about caring for her. You seldom complain. I really admire you—more than you'll ever know."

Paul looked away as he said, "It's been tough. Somedays I wake up and before I even get out of bed, I wonder how I will ever make it through the day with her health issues, with the money issues, and with an ever-increasing office practice." He turned toward the Judge, smiled and said, "But then, I look over at her, look at what she's going through and quickly realize I have no problems at all."

"Speaking of your practice, I know it's getting larger all the time. I know how much you work to stay on top of it all. But don't you think it's about time you got some help—maybe hire someone to come in with you. Have you thought about that?"

"I have. In fact, Hanna and I are going to discuss that very subject later today. I know at this point in time, paying a new attorney will hurt financially, at least for a while. But with all the new business I have, I don't think it will take long until an additional attorney will easily be paying their own way. At least I hope that's the case."

"How long has it been since you've been over home. You need to come over one of these evenings, have supper with us, relax, drink a glass of wine and take a deep breath."

"Thanks, but that's hard to do. I let the caretaker leave as soon as I get home, so I would need to make arrangements for someone to care for her during the evening too. That's another expense. Nothing is easy anymore, John, nothing."

"Like I told you, I have no idea how you do it, but again, I sure as hell admire you for what you are doing. By the way, what are you doing here, at the courthouse, today?"

"Oh, I've got a sentencing before Judge White. Shouldn't take long. I am a little concerned about the sentence he's going to impose. This kid's got a horrible record." He stood as he said, "I guess I better move along. Let's get together in the near future, John. We have a lot to discuss."

As Paul walked in the courtroom, he noticed Jennifer Gordon the prosecuting attorney was already seated. Paul dropped his file on the table and took his seat next to Jimmie Pratt, a nineteen-year-old habitual offender that had pled guilty to breaking and entering and was now waiting to be sentenced.

"Everyone ready to proceed?"

Both attorneys answered, "Yes, Your Honor."

"Ms. Gordon, what's your position concerning sentencing?"

She stood and said, "Your Honor, this is the third time this young man has appeared before you since he turned nineteen. He was placed on probation the first two times and violated it both times. He is now before the court again today, for an offense similar to the first two, and the state no longer believes probation is a viable alternative. We feel he needs to serve some time. Maybe this young man will think twice before he does this again. That's our position."

"Thank you. Mr. Thomas?"

Paul stood and said, "Ms. Gordon is right in that this is Jimmie's third violation since he turned nineteen. This is the first time I have represented him. We've had some long talks about where he has been in life and where he is headed. I think he finally gets it, Judge, I really do. He's ready to start contributing to life rather than continuing to take. He has a job. For the first time in his life, he has a job. I helped him find one, and it's certainly nothing big, but it's a start. He will lose it if he goes to jail."

He looked down at his client for a moment before he continued. "Simply put, he needs a break. He knows this is it for him. If he screws up this time, he knows he is done. You might notice, Judge, that none of his offences involve a crime against another person, nor are they drug related. They are just all about money—money he needed to help his family get through day-by-day. With this job, he can bring home that money without violating the law. This kid is a good kid, Your Honor. I would ask the court to give him one more chance to prove himself—just… one… more… chance."

Paul took his seat. The judge sat back in his chair, and nervously cleared his throat. He leaned forward and thumbed through some of the paperwork, finally just closing the whole folder.

"Stand up, Mr. Pratt. I thought I had this figured out. You were going to jail. That was before your attorney, Mr. Thomas, made his comments—before I knew you now had a job. You know, you're pretty, darn lucky. You ended up with the right person representing you. He cared enough about you to help you find a job, to go the extra mile, to put you in a position to succeed rather than just fail again as you did the last two times you were before me."

He sat quietly for a moment before he continued. "I'm going to give you that one last chance to prove yourself. You screw up this time, you are done—believe me, you are done. You're young, you have your whole life ahead of you, none of your crimes involved violence, and you have a good man, your attorney, that believes in you. I'm sentencing you to probation for a year, Mr. Pratt. Don't screw up this time. Don't blow this opportunity. You'll not get another."

Later that day, as Paul sat reviewing employment applications, Hanna walked in his office and stood in the doorway, leaning against the frame, watching him as he reviewed the applications.

He finally looked up and said, "What?"

"How did you get that done? How did you get that kid probation?"

"Oh, I don't know. I really felt the job was the key to the whole thing. Once he got the job, I figured he might stay out of jail. He is really not a bad kid. He just has no direction. The job will help take care of that problem."

"You stuck your neck out getting it for him, didn't you?"

"Might have. Yes, I might have a little. I just hope it works for both employer and employee."

"You know, your compassion, your desire to assist, to help, is going to get you in trouble one of these days. I know it's a good thing to be kind-hearted, to help your fellow man and all that bullshit, but you kind of go overboard sometimes."

He smiled. "I really hope your choice of wording is better in those letters I don't dictate—that I just ask you to compose, sign my name and mail. I understand what you are saying, but this kid needed a break. I helped him get one. End of story. Now, what are we going to do with all these apps?"

"Don't ask me. You are the one that thinks we need another attorney in here. I hope you're ready to hire another secretary too. I can only do so much you know."

"I hope it comes to that, Hanna. I am going to start interviewing these applicants next week. There aren't many that have applied. Why don't you call each one and set up times for them to come in. Hopefully, one of them will work out and we can spread the work load between two of us, instead of me trying to do it all myself."

Chapter 7

"Your appointment is here. She's older than both our ages combined, she can't hear, she can't see, she walks with a cain, and she's still—*surprise*—alive," Hanna whispered. She smiled and said, "Good luck," then turned and walked out of his office.

He waited for a moment, then stood and walked to his doorway to see if she was still on her way. About halfway down the hall, an older woman, white hair, with a colorfully patterned umbrella she used as a cain, crept her way toward his office.

"Might I help you, ma'am?"

"Oh no sir, no sir, I'm fine. I'll just be along shortly. You never mind. Go back in your office. I will be right there."

Paul walked back through his office door and stood while she continued at a snail's pace.

She finally sauntered in, a short step at a time, and took a seat in front of his desk, at which time, he too, sat down.

"Good morning. My name is Martha VanArsdayle. Your name is Paul Thomas." She hesitated. "Am I correct, or am I in the wrong office…again?"

Paul smiled and said, "No, Ms. Martha you are indeed in the correct office. I don't believe we have met before, have we?"

"No sir, we haven't. But you come highly recommended, by whom, I shall not say. I need a little legal work done. Now can y'all do it for me or need I go elsewhere?"

"Well, it depends. What do you need done for you today?"

"I need a will. I need a simple will just leaving a few particular items to certain people and then the remainder divided equally between my two worthless children. Can you handle that?"

Paul smiled as he picked up a pen and said, "Yes, ma'am we certainly can. Can you give me the names of your children?"

"Yes. His name is Steven VanArsdayle and he lives in Phoenix. Her name is Rhonda Collins and she lives in New York City. By the way honey, they're both as worthless as it gets, just so you know."

He smiled as her description caught him by surprise.

"I wish I was just joking with you, I really do, but it's as true as true can be. They are both just totally worthless children. They visit 'bout once a year, and to be honest, by now that's once too often. And those idiot children of theirs, my grandchildren, they aren't much better. I see them whenever it's convenient *for them*, and that's about once every two years. They are grown up and I would love to have a close relationship with them all, but they're just so busy, you know, so busy."

"I'm sorry, Ms. Martha. Do you want to leave everything to just your two children or do you want to include your grandchildren too?"

"Let them take their parents share if the parent is already gone. Put it in the will that way. I'm also not going to leave anything to either of my children's disgusting spouse's."

"I understand. Now, can you tell me what assets you have, how they are titled and where they are all located?"

She reached in her purse and pulled out a few sheets of paper, handed them to him, and said, "Here. That's all of it and where it's all located."

He took the paperwork from her old, withered hand, and reviewed each page, before he said, "There is well over a couple of million dollars in cash accounts and property value here. It shows it is all titled only in your name. Is that the way you believe it to be?"

"Yes. That's the extent of the cash, and it's all in my name only. It is to remain that way until after I'm gone. I don't want any of my money-grabbing relative's names on any of my accounts until I am dead. Same way with my house and accompanying land. It too, is all in my name. By the way, sir, it was recently appraised at over two million dollars."

"Now, I'm assuming your husband is already gone. Is that correct?"

"Oh yes, Paul. He died twenty years ago. He made quite a sum of money in the record business, but he's been gone for some time now." She moved forward in her chair, placing one of her arms on his desk, and smiled from ear to ear as she said, "Are you asking about him because of the will, or did you have another reason for asking me about my marital status?"

The question caught him totally off guard. He dropped his pen, leaned back and laughed. "You know, you are without doubt, the woman I would think of first if I weren't so committed, but I'm an old married man and very committed to my wife. Sorry."

She smiled, and said, "Oh that's fine, that's fine. I would probably be a little slow for you anyway. Now, what else do you need from me?"

"Can you provide me with a list of items you want to pass on to other people?"

"Got it right here." She pulled an extensive list of names with designated items of property which she wished to pass on to each individual.

He reviewed the list, and said, "Okay, this looks fine. I'll put everything together for you, including a living will, and you can review it all the next time you come in. If you wish, I can give you a call and let you know when everything is ready. How did you get here?"

"Oh, I have a driver. Yes, that would be fine. Just give me a call, and I'll come right in. I don't have much else to do these days."

Over the course of the next three days, she called five times with minor changes concerning many of the small specific bequests she made to individuals. Each time, Hanna would tell her it would take but a moment to make the change, and to come in the following day. Then, the following day, she would call in with another change.

On the fourth day, she expressed a desire to meet with Paul again.

She arrived at his office around 3:30 p.m. By 3:45 p.m. she had finally navigated the hallway to the door of his office.

He stood as she started to walk through the doorway, and said, "Good afternoon, Ms. Martha. Might I help you to your chair?"

She motioned at him with her free hand to remain seated. "No, no please remain seated. I'll be along. Just don't you worry, I'll be along."

After she finally took her chair, he said, "Are you ready to sign? I have the completed documents right here for you."

"Just let me ask you one question, Mr. Paul. Do y'all think I'm doin' the right thing leaving half of everything I have to each of my children? We don't get along that well. Should I just leave it to charity? Those kids got enough anyway. What should I do?"

Paul sat back in his chair and considered her question—certainly not an unusual one based upon her circumstances.

"I guess, if it were me, Martha, unless they have really done something to hurt you, or harm you in some way, I would leave it to them. They are still your children, and unless they really did something to intentionally hurt you, I would give what I had to them."

She looked down, and after a few moments, looked at Paul and said, "I think you're right. Give me the papers."

Paul pushed the paperwork across his desk for her to review and asked Hanna to come in.

"What do we need anyone else in here for? Why did you ask her to come in?"

"Because in Tennessee, Ms. Martha, two disinterested people must witness you signing your will."

"Oh, okay, I understand. Where do I sign?"

As Hanna walked in the room, Paul turned to the last page and pointed to the signature line. "You understand this is your last will and testament you are signing, correct?"

She whispered, "Yes," as she signed her name. Paul and Hanna witnessed her signature, placed the will in an envelope, then gave her a copy. Hanna took the original to place it in their safe.

Immediately after she walked out the front door and left with her driver, Hanna walked back to Paul's office. She leaned against the door frame as Paul finished up with the first of many calls he needed to return.

As he hung up, he said, "What?"

"You know she is going to be a repeater, don't you? And I mean repeater with a capital *R*. She's going to be back here, and back here, and back here."

Paul leaned back in his chair, then laughed as he said, "I'm thinking the same thing, but if that's the case, we will just keep billing her and billing her and billing her. She's really a nice lady—certainly worth a little money. But I have the same feeling. She has plenty of time on her hands, and there will always be 'just a small change I want you to make'. No doubt in my mind about that."

Two weeks later Paul checked his calendar. Ms. Martha had been in four of the ten business days contained within those two weeks, and each time she needed 'just a small change.' Each time she wanted to see *him* before she made the change, but shortly, he was going to tell her just to give the needed information to Hanna. Each time he saw her, she was with him for at least an hour. Hanna would handle the situation in much less time. The fee he charged would remain the same no matter who saw her. Unfortunately, he had already had enough of Ms. Martha's, 'I changed my mind,' and they had only just met.

Chapter 8

Nashville, Tennessee

February

They had reserved a table for supper at a small upscale restaurant in the Gulch area, near her apartment. The afternoon had been spent discussing past jobs, their relationship and their future—the future *after* they were finished with Nashville and the project they would shortly discuss.

Now between bites of ham-wrapped scallops and hickory-grilled red snapper they would fine-tune the specifics concerning the job at hand. It was time to get down to business and try to successfully conclude their *last* job.

Edward said, “So, you have an apartment rented in *your* building for *me*? Is that a good idea? We have never really lived that closely together while preparing for a new job.”

“It is ten floors away from me. I think as long as we are careful, and only see each other occasionally, we’ll be fine. It was easier for me that way too. I didn’t have to spend weeks finding a place somewhere else for you to live. Besides, I was able to rent it for only six months at a time. You shouldn’t be living there that long anyway, if you do your job right.”

“Speaking of doing my portion of the job, who have you lined up for me?”

“Well, the first one is Janice Hardy. I met her at church. By the way, using a church seems to be a fairly productive method of meeting widows. I started going to this particular church when I first arrived here and met her almost immediately. She has had me over to her house for coffee. I can tell you the woman is definitely loaded. Nice looking to. She is probably a few years older than you and has no children.”

"That sounds like a good start. Anyone else?"

"Sure. You know I always have three for you to choose from. Next, there's Rebecca Hawley. I met her at AA."

He looked up, smiled and said, "You started attending AA?"

"Anything for you, Ed, anything for you. She's about our age. She used to be a raging alcoholic. But after her divorce, and her generous settlement, she decided she was done with the booze. She has been attending AA for about two years. Nice woman. She is a little unconventional, but nice. I'm never sure what she is going to say or do, but I like her. She has two children, both of whom live in Nashville. She's pretty close to them."

"And the third potential victim?"

"Her name is Carolyn Crawley. She's a dead ringer for Barbara Streisand. I met her at a singles club. She is a little pushy, but I know she's looking for a man, and I mean really looking. You can't believe how much money she has, but she might be a little tough to live with after the initial glow wears off. She's a bigger woman too. Not fat, just burly—kind of strong looking, if you know what I mean. She might give you a tussle if you tried to hurt her without really having the upper hand."

Ed took another bite of snapper. "I don't want to try to murder someone that might actually be stronger than I am. She's out. Between the other two, which one do you think would make the better mark?"

"I would think church lady would be the easiest of the other two. We've had pretty good luck with other woman who were 'of the faith' and this one seems to fit the mold quite well. She has no children, she's very trusting, and she's a devout Christian. She would seem to me just what we are looking for."

"Well then, church lady it'll be. What church?"

"It's near us. Maybe we can take a drive around the area, since you don't know it yet. I will point out the church, and we can drive by her house."

"I'll wait a few weeks before I introduce myself. Hopefully we won't need that lease for my apartment much longer than the initial six-month term. Is her home big enough for the two of us?"

"It's big enough for *22* of us. It's huge. What are you planning for her, and more importantly, when?"

"You know, there are lots of lakes around here. I've become interested in fishing." He smiled. "Did you know that? Did you know

I love to fish?"

She looked at him for a moment, then started to smile as she figured out what he was actually saying. "Really? You…fishing? Is *that* what you're going to do—take her fishing and drown her?"

"That's the plan for right now. What are you smiling about? I can fish. I got some fishing skills. I'll need to play it by ear, but for now, I'm thinking one of those larger lakes around here, shortly after dusk some evening is going to find itself with an extra body."

"What if she doesn't…what if she doesn't like water—or fish?"

"Let's take it one step at a time, sweetheart. You need to place me in a position to meet her first. Then we can plan her unfortunate demise based on her likes and dislikes. But for now, let's share a dessert, and head back to your place."

Great. Once we solidify the plan in a little more detail, perhaps Mr. Hall, you and I can spend a few…or maybe many minutes getting to know each other again, in a physical sort of way. In fact, I just might have some extra rope laying around—or maybe even a pair of handcuffs…"

Chapter 9

Nashville, Tennessee
March

Months had passed since Paul had made it known he needed an additional attorney to work in his office. He figured the recency of his bar association reprimand, which was disclosed just prior to the commencement of his search, might have been the reason he had heard from so few applicants—none of which were satisfactory.

Because of the reprimand, he had somewhat reduced his aggressive search. But that approach had done nothing but exacerbate the inner office issues. He had reached the point where he simply couldn't handle all the business by himself. Paul dreaded the thought of interrupting the flow of his office—taking time to meet with the applicants, interviewing, then training them. But he had put it off as long as he could. In addition, he desperately needed the additional income a new associate could eventually provide.

After making it known, once again, that he needed an attorney for his office, this time the result was completely different. There had been 17 applications filed—17 young graduates, all requesting employment in his one-horse operation. That, to him, was a surprise. His reputation in the community, because of the complaints filed, wasn't that good, and certainly he wasn't considered one of the 'big shooters' as concerned the legal community in Nashville.

Early this morning, he had been reviewing applications for an hour prior to Hanna's arrival. Actually, he had been reviewing them all *again*, already having dissected all of the applications a number of times prior to today.

All 17 multipage applications needed to be reviewed prior to the commencement of interviews. He wanted to personally interview all of them with as much advance information about them as he could acquire both from the application and from outside sources. It was important their employment with him resulted in a good fit from day one.

Unfortunately, their remained a nagging, inherent problem with his role in this process. He was completely inept at determining the worth or integrity of an individual as a result of a first meeting. Yesterday, while assessing his upcoming role in determining the merits of a prospective employee, he had concluded if he had interviewed Attila the Hun as a potential employee, he probably would have hired him on the spot, feeling there was a good chance no opposing attorney would ever walk over him. He just wasn't very good at this sort of thing.

He heard Hanna walk in and begin preparing for the morning's activities. Before long he heard her start down the hallway, toward his office. Upon reaching his door, she leaned against the doorframe, and said, "Well, y'all ready for today. We have one every half-hour starting at nine and running until six tonight. Are you going to be able to handle all of these young, vibrant, out-of-work wannabes?"

He smiled as he not only looked at how ridiculous she looked, but also considered her assessment of the day's activities. She was hard to take serious in her five-inch heels, pants that stopped six inches short of her ankles, and a blouse that appeared four sizes too big, everything in mixed colors of red, green and purple. If someone had placed gifts under her, and she stood very still, she could have been mistaken for a human Christmas tree. He wouldn't tell her. He had tried that, and the next day it had been worse—much, much worse.

"I guess. I'm not much good at this, so I may ask you for your first impression of each of them. After the interviews, by the way, when the applicants call every hour wondering whom I selected, make sure they understand I'm going to need a little time to assess *all* of them. Maybe I will be ready to make a decision next week sometime. I'll just be glad when it's over, when we have a new attorney working with us and we can move on."

After interviews all morning, and half the afternoon, he had heard all he wanted to hear. The most important issue with most of the applicants was 'how much are you going to pay me.' After the fifth one asked the same question, it became somewhat difficult to accept. There were few that asked about the type of work, the hours, or the working conditions. It was mostly, 'what can the firm do for me.'

He sent Hanna home at five. He had two interviews yet to conduct. The applicant scheduled for five-thirty never showed up. Paul tried calling his cell, but the call went unanswered. He left a message asking him to return his call as soon as possible, but a few minutes later, when he still had not heard from him, he threw his application in the trash.

Paul heard the door open for the last applicant. Knowing Hanna had already left for the day, he walked down the hallway to the lobby to introduce himself and walk her back to his office.

He extended his hand as he said, "You must be Ruth Andrews. My name is Paul Thomas."

She shook his hand, as she said, "Yes, I am. Nice meeting you."

"Come with me."

As they walked back to his office, he considered her physical appearance. She was certainly dressed for business. She had on a dark business suit, with a white scarf for accent. Her long jet-black hair was pulled back in a pony-tail. She was almost as tall as he was, and her dark eyes helped complete an attractive young woman, who appeared extremely focused.

Once they were seated, he said, "I've had a brief opportunity to review your application. It looks like you've been out of school for a couple of years, but it doesn't appear as though you've had much experience. Is that correct?"

"Yes. After I graduated, I went to work with the firm of Harsh and Armstrong. That didn't work out very well. About a year later, I was hired and I still work for the firm of Bailey and Bailey, but that's not working out the best either."

Paul hesitated while considering her unsuccessful efforts at prior employment. "As you might imagine, I'm somewhat concerned about the fact you haven't been successful with either of your prior employers. Can you tell me what happened with those firms and why it hasn't worked out?"

She looked down for a moment, before she said, "Well, as concerns the first firm, I can tell you, but I don't want it leaving this office, if that's okay with you."

"Absolutely. Nothing leaves this room."

She looked down again, and hesitated. She never looked up as she said softly, "Mr. Harsh touched me inappropriately. I objected. He fired me. There were no witnesses. I wasn't going to start my law career off with a lawsuit against my first employer. I just walked out and never looked back." She looked up as she said, "Working at Bailey and Bailey is fine, but they never give me anything very important to do. I've been there well over a year now and all I do is research. I'm simply tired of it. I want to be involved in litigation—that's why I became a lawyer."

"That sounds like an unfortunate start for you. Don't your parents live here in Nashville? I believe I've met them somewhere along the way."

"Yes, they do. They have been here for years."

"What are your thoughts about salary?"

"Whatever you think is fair."

"The hours are long. Sometimes you may need to work into the wee hours of the morning."

"I'm fine with that. I'm not married, I have no children. I expect my career to be my life, and that's exactly the way I want it."

"You know, we aren't entirely involved in litigation. Much of our work is in litigation, but we also handle estates, set up trusts and things of that nature, so I don't want you to think every day you'll be in the courtroom. That's just not the case. This office has an extensive office practice too. Are you okay with that?"

"Absolutely. Don't get me wrong. Right now, I'm extremely interested in working in the courtroom, but that doesn't mean along the way I may not change my primary interest to some other aspect of law. I'm very flexible in that respect."

"If I were inclined to hire you, when could you begin?"

"I would need to give the Bailey firm two weeks' notice, unless they don't care and allow me to leave immediately. But I imagine two weeks from now would be my best guess."

The talk from then on centered upon his practice and a 'normal' day at the office. She asked a number of questions, but all of them concerned what he did and what his practice actually involved. Not one of her questions concerned what the firm could do for her. They eventually discussed salary, time off and hours of employment. He initiated the discussion concerning each subject, and she never made any attempt to alter any term of employment he suggested. She finally left the office around seven-thirty and he locked up.

The next morning, after Hanna arrived and had an opportunity to prepare for the day, Paul yelled at her to come visit for a moment before his first appointment.

"Do you think you could work for a female attorney?"

"Last I knew, they weren't much different than male attorneys—just one or two small anatomy issues. Why? Did you find one you liked?"

"Well, the applicant scheduled for five o' clock never showed up, but the woman at five-thirty made an impression on me. I want to look everything over again, but I'm thinking she may be the one."

"Have you checked references?"

"For reasons I won't go into, she won't have one from the first firm. She didn't work for them very long anyway. The second firm hasn't been having her do much so they won't be able to tell me much about her legal abilities. But I know the family, and they are good people. She got good grades in law school. She never once, contrary to what all the others did, asked what *I* could do for *her*, which was certainly a mark in her favor. She's just ready to start a career and excited about it. I liked her."

"I don't like not having any references."

"I know, that bothers me too. But I believe she at least deserves a chance, Hanna."

"You know, that little streak of compassion running vertically, the length of your body is going to get you in trouble someday. Do whatever you think is right. I'll have no trouble working with her."

Later that week, he called Ruth Anderson. "You ready to go to work?"

"Oh… my… God…yes. When do I start?"

After the call ended, he only hoped once again he hadn't been a bad judge of character. He just figured if he was wrong, it wouldn't take long to find out, and he would just have Hanna fire her. She would most likely be better at that than he.

Chapter 10

He really didn't give a damn what the new guy thought, or said, or did. He didn't like partners. In fact, he *hated* partners. He didn't like working with anyone. He had made it clear many times, but they just keep giving him partners. The last two partners he had, were both shot and ended up with desk jobs. Now they give him this new kid—this piece of shit new kid that was still wet behind the ears.

Sam Harvey sat at his desk sorting through paperwork, old and new. The department had just named Terry Oswald as his new partner. He had been with the police department for a number of years, but was just recently promoted to detective.

"So, you're the infamous Sam Harvey. Nice to meet you. Heard a lot about you. Glad to be working with…."

"Yeah, yeah, whatever." The kid was standing behind him, and when Sam turned around, he had his hand extended for the obligatory 'new friend, new partner handshake.' Sam slapped his hand without shaking it and said, "Go sit down."

His desk was immediately in front of Sam's desk and situated so they faced each other. Terry's desk was clean except for a lamp, a pen and a short stack of files. The opposite was true concerning Sam's desk. It was impossible to see the top of his desk—to much paper, to many files.

"I've heard a lot about you…Sam. Is it okay if I call you Sam? I assume it is if we're going to be partners and all."

Sam pulled the stub of a cigar out of his month, the one he had been chewing on since the last one fell apart an hour ago. "I don't give a shit what you call me, as long as you do your job."

"Okay…Sam… thanks. Can you bring me up to date concerning what we are working on right now? I have copies of some of the material, but maybe it would be easier if you just told me what we're working on. Is that okay with you?"

"No. Review the goddamn files. When you're done, let me know. *Then* we'll talk. Not until then."

An hour later, Terry looked up over the top of a pile of paperwork, and said, "You have been a cop now what, about 20 years?"

Sam continued to chew and write.

Terry waited for another 30 minutes before he said, "You been a cop about 20 years now?"

Sam looked up and said, "Yes, yes I've been a cop for *about* 20 years. And every day, of every month, of every year, I just keep telling them and telling them I want to work alone. But they continue to shove punks like you down my throat. Now shut up and let me do my work will you?"

"Sure, sure. Sorry."

About 15 minutes later, Terry said, "In those 20 years, have you ever not solved a case?"

Without looking up, Sam said, "One."

"You failed to solve only one case in all that time?"

"One."

"All the rest you've solved?"

Sam never answered.

There was another pause in the one-sided conversation until Terry asked, "I understand you don't believe in computers. Is that right?"

"Correct."

"Is there some reason?"

"Ever been hacked? Ever had your identity stolen, all your bank accounts compromised, your whole life turned upside down because of some prick that's broke, computer savvy and has nothing else to do but steal from you? Ever had that happen to you?"

"No, I haven't. Have you?"

"Once."

"Catch the guy?"

"I told you there was only one that got away. That was him. I don't trust a computer for anything. I write all my notes out by hand. Takes more time, but at least they're safe that way. The department don't like it, so I might make a few notes on the computer just to appease them, but other than that, all handwritten. Leave me alone. Not one more question until this afternoon. Understand?"

"I do. Yup, I surely do."

Sam took his lunch break at twelve-thirty and left by himself, without saying a word to his new partner. He ate where he always ate when he was in the office. He had eaten at Puckett's downtown for a number of years. The food was always good and he could eat at the counter.

Terry apparently had never left for lunch. When Sam returned, he was still seated at his desk, with paperwork spread from one end to the other.

As soon as Sam sat down, Terry said, "Were you ever married?"

Sam looked at him and said, "Why?"

"Oh, no reason, I just wondered. I got a wife and two kids. Love them to death. I just wondered if you were married."

"Yeah, I got a wife, I guess. I never see her. We kind of go our own way. I see her when I have a little extra time—I'm married to my job, period."

"What time do you normally go home? Do you have any regular hours?"

Sam once again looked up from his files and said, "What do *you* think? I never quit. Sometimes I go home at five, sometimes I sleep in this chair. And, by the way, I expect the same from you. You can tell that little woman of yours there may be nights you are never home. That's what I expect from any partner they assign to me, and that's sure as hell what I expect from you."

"I understand."

About an hour later, Terry said, "Sam, can I ask you about a particular file—apparently one you've been working on for a long time?"

"Which one?" Sam asked without ever looking up.

"Oliver."

Sam lowered the paperwork he was reviewing, and said, "What do you want to know?"

"I've heard about this guy—guess about everyone has. Oliver's his name. He's been in and out of trouble for as long as I've been a cop. Nothing much ever seems to happen to him. Everyone tells me he's a murderer, but he gets charged, he gets off. Looks like you have a couple of files on him. What's your take on the guy?"

"Interesting question. Let's see, 'What's my take on the guy'? '*What's my take on the guy?*'" He leaned forward against his desk, and elevated his voice a couple of levels as he said, "He's a dirty, rotten, lying son-of-a-bitch that I just can't quite get my hands on. Does that adequately answer your question?"

Terry laughed and said, "Tell me how you *really* feel."

The look on Sam's face never changed, as Terry stuck his head back in the file and again whispered, "Tell me how *you* really feel."

Near 5:00 p.m., Sam looked up at his new partner who by now had loosened his tie, and had finally been able to make his way through all the casefiles Sam was working on.

Sam said, "Before I leave, just so you know, of all the people whose files you reviewed today, by far the most important case I'm working on is the Dean Oliver case—the guy I mentioned earlier. His wife turns up missing. His girlfriend turns up missing. Anyone that appears as though they might infringe on his territory ends up missing. A couple of the girls that prostituted themselves for him, but left for some other job, end up missing. We all know what's going on with this guy, we all know how dangerous he is, we just can't catch him. But we, you and me, we're gonna get him. And you and me, we ain't gonna be in very good spirits until we do. You get what I'm trying to say?"

"Looks like we got our work cut out for us."

"They all screw up. Just give him time. They all make a mistake eventually."

"Perhaps you and I could go over his file in depth tomorrow morning?"

Sam got up to leave, and as he did, he said, "Yeah, maybe you and I'll just do that. Maybe that's just what we'll do tomorrow morning." He turned around and walked out the door with briefcase in hand.

Later that evening, after an abbreviated supper and a quick look at the evening news, he opened his briefcase. It was full of files and handwritten notes all concerning one individual—Oliver. *He* could read his notes—no one else could. Sometimes, even he had trouble reading his own handwriting, but sooner or later he figured it out.

Sam thought about the many hours he had spent trying to determine the best method of apprehending the man, but every time he tried a new approach, Oliver seemed to counter it. He knew Sam was after him. He had even threatened him—*"stop or else."* Sam had told no one, figuring if and when his boss determined this case had become so personal for both the cop and the crook, he wouldn't let him continue to work it.

Sam had to smile as he continued to review his notes. Everything just might have recently changed. Now, he had someone inside.

Someone that was willing to help him. The informer had been talking with Sam for almost a month, and it was through him, Sam found out Oliver had considered killing him, feeling he might be getting too close. No one knew of the informer, not even within the department. This could be the break they had all been waiting for, and no one would know about the man 'inside' *until* he had provided the information they all needed to convict.

He continued to review his notes until he reached the point where he was so tired, he just couldn't read another line. He leaned back in his chair and shut his eyes. He would get this guy, this prick, Oliver, if it was the last thing he ever did as a cop. No doubt about it. He would get this…this…

Chapter 11

It had been a long week full of pressure from each and every direction. But now perhaps he could consider the future with somewhat of a smile—at least as concerned his practice. Paul had finally hired someone to take over some of his extensive work load, and perhaps eventually be productive enough to remove some of the financial pressure.

Hanna had closed down her desk for the week and walked back to his office to tell him she was leaving.

"So, what's going on in your life this weekend?"

He hesitated, finally smiled and said, "I'm just staying home and looking after Anna. There's not much change in what I do from week to weekend to month to year, as you know."

"I know. I'm sorry, Paul, I really am."

"I'm not complaining. She would do the same for me in a heartbeat. I know that, which is why it makes my job easier."

"It's *not* easy though, is it? I mean on a day-to-day basis it's got to be incredibly difficult."

"It is certainly an emotional roller coaster. Today, I feel guilty. Tomorrow I may feel overworked. The next day maybe I feel I simply cannot lose her. Every day I feel different about her situation. But today, today I feel guilty."

"Why? You have handled it all so well. Many people know what you've done to care for her on a daily basis, and they admire you so much for that. Why do you feel guilty?"

"Because for the first time, today, *for the first time*, I really don't want to go home. I *hate* myself for that. I just don't want to walk in that front door."

"I completely understand. What an incredible burden for you to…"

She said no more. He finally looked up at her, smiled and said, "See you Monday."

As he heard her close the outer door, he pulled out his phone and punched in the judge's number. "John, have you left work yet?"

"No, why? I'm just getting ready to."

"Do you want to meet me for a drink?"

"Absolutely. Where?"

"What about Jack's on West End? It's on your way home."

"See you shortly."

Paul was waiting when John arrived. Each discussed their day, Paul detailing his office activities, John discussing the hearings over which he presided. Finally, as the conversation concerning work began to wane, John said, "You must have been able to talk the caregiver into staying a little later today. You've told me in the past how difficult it was to get away after work because she leaves as soon as you arrive home."

"I called her and asked if she could stay until eight or so. She said she would be glad to."

"Was it just time for a break?"

"Yes," Paul said softly. "You know, I have such conflicted feelings. I feel so guilty sometimes. I know what I have to do, what I need to do when it comes to caring for her on a daily basis, but…but sometimes it just gets so hard, so difficult. No doubt she would do the same for me if the tables were turned, but sometimes that doesn't much seem to matter."

"I can't even imagine how you must feel—how difficult this all really must be. Has anything changed since the last time we talked—is there any chance of a recovery, or is it just a slow downhill slide?"

"At this point, there is no chance. That's what makes it even worse. If there was just *any* chance of recovery, only the slightest hope, it would make it so much easier for both of us. But she knows. She understands. To look in her eyes and see that look of desperation every morning before I go to work—*it is so difficult.*"

"Is there any letup at the office? Is business good? Are the fees coming in so at least there is not such a financial burden anymore?"

"Yes, that's not such a problem anymore. I don't know what I would do without that income. We have gone through all our savings and the house is mortgaged to the hilt."

"Do you have any idea how much time she has left?"

"No. She's actually already lived longer than the average. She can't hardly do anything but blink any more. That's the only way we really can communicate. Worst disease ever. To remember her as she was, and to see her this way now…"

Their discussion lasted only a few more minutes. It was approaching the time when he knew he would need to leave the bar to make it home in time to relieve the caregiver.

On his way home, he formed a new mental resolve. He would handle this and handle it as she would have with him—he would give her all he had until she died or he could physically give no more.

She was sleeping when he arrived. Paul sent the caretaker home. He concluded he wasn't hungry and would forego supper, instead pouring himself a large glass of bourbon on the rocks.

He checked on Anna, who appeared comfortable. He then walked out on his deck and sat down. It was dark—no moon tonight. The late April air was crisp, but comfortable. There wasn't a cloud in the sky.

He remembered all those cruises he had taken with her, when they would sit out on their balcony aboard ship and look up at those same stars he was looking at tonight. How many times they would have a drink and sit out under this very sky, later to walk inside and make love before she fell asleep in his arms.

They had always wanted children. They wanted to enjoy life, as a couple, together, before children came into the picture. They were only getting serious about having a child when she was diagnosed.

He remembered all those discussions concerning saving money for the future, which was an important factor for both. It too, was all moving in the proper direction, until medical and caregiving expenses got in the way. Now, they had exhausted all their savings and every line of credit they had available.

He noticed the caretaker had received a call from Anna's parents and one of her siblings—a brother in California. Her parents lived in Atlanta. When she was first diagnosed, they would travel to Nashville nearly every weekend. Lately, not so much. He understood. They still called, maybe every other day, but the trips to Nashville were becoming less frequent.

He could not condemn them for their infrequent contact. It was so painful to watch, especially by someone that knew her as well as they did…as well as he did.

He took another drink. The air was turning chilly. He needed to walk inside—back to reality. He needed to check on her, which he did at least twice each night to make sure she was still resting comfortably.

As he stood, he remembered the last thing the doctor told him the last time he saw her. He felt her life could now probably be measured by weeks—not by years or months as before—but by weeks.

What would he do with her gone? She was the only thing in this world he loved without reservation, without exception. He would need to move on. But without her with him, he just wasn't sure he could do that—or, for that matter, whether he even wanted to try.

Chapter 12

Ruth stepped off the bus and immediately felt the late spring sun warm her all over. She looked at all the traffic, listened to all those car horns blaring, and felt fortunate she was able to use public transportation to travel to the office.

While employed with the Bailey firm, she had quickly learned all about how difficult it was trying to reach the office driving through morning traffic in downtown Nashville. She had no choice with that job—they wanted her to have a vehicle ready and with her. But today was a new day. It was her first day of work at the law office of Paul Thomas, and today she *did* have a choice. Not having to handle morning traffic was worth the price of the bus ticket many times over.

Bailey and Bailey had allowed her to give them only one week's notice, further verifying that her employment status with them was unimportant and unnecessary. She knew it anyway. They just verified what she had already confirmed by allowing her to quit without the normal two-week notification.

She was early. The office was locked. She sat outside waiting for someone to show up and unlock the door—in more ways than one.

Hanna arrived shortly before 8:00 a.m. and let her in. She led her down the hallway to a small office directly across the hall from Paul. They had previously moved a desk, some file cabinets and a new computer along with a few necessary supplied, into her new office. She would need to make the office her own. It would take some time, but she would personalize it during the next few weeks.

As she sat, visualizing how she wanted it decorated, she heard Paul walk in the front door. He walked down the hallway, stopped in her doorway, and said, "Good morning. I hope those items we put in here for you will at least get you started. Are you comfortable? Will this work for you?"

"Absolutely. I am so, *so* excited about getting started. Is there anything I can do for you now, this morning, today? What do you need me to do?"

Paul laughed. "No, no I'm fine. I think we will have a short office meeting with the three of us in a few moments, and then you and I can talk about the specifics of our practice. I blocked off the morning so we could have an opportunity to talk and organize. I have appointments starting this afternoon. I took the liberty yesterday of setting up your first appointment. It's set for tomorrow morning, and I'll discuss it with you later.

As he started to back toward the doorway, he said, "Maybe this afternoon we can drive to the courthouse. I can introduce you to a few people there that can make your life much easier during your practice. Just sit back, think how you want to decorate your office, and in a while, I'll have Hanna come in."

Later that morning she met with both Paul and Hanna. They discussed office policy along with office procedure concerning the flow of work to be completed. Her first impression of Hanna, as seemed to happen often with Ruth, was completely wrong. Hanna's physical appearance was deceptive.

Today she actually dressed the colors of a watermelon. Based on that, Ruth figured she was probably one loopy broad. But once the discussion began between the three of them, she soon determined she had made an error in judgement. Hanna was clearly a professional. She knew the business of administration as concerned the practice of law, better than Ruth would most likely ever know it. Instead of discarding her comments, as she did at the beginning of the conversation, she found herself actually taking notes whenever Hanna spoke.

Immediately after Ruth returned from an abbreviated noon break, Paul took her to the courthouse. There he introduced her to a few of the employees in the clerk's office, telling Ruth which one to see for which purpose. Together they walked down the hallway to see if the judge was in his chambers. He was, so Paul introduced her to him. After a short visit, they drove back to the office.

Paul was anxious to discuss the specifics of her day-to-day responsibilities and more thoroughly define her areas of practice. Once back in her office, he sat down with her, and said, "Let's talk about what I am thinking I need you to do."

She picked up a pen, grabbed a legal pad from the corner of Paul's desk, and prepared to take notes. "I'm ready," she said.

"As concerns litigation, anytime you visit with anyone concerning filling any type of lawsuit, do not promise them anything or take a retainer of any amount until we visit about it. In addition, as concerns money you receive for any purpose whatsoever, it is to be given to Hanna. She will set up the appropriate paperwork and an interoffice account for the individual once she receives it from you."

"Got it."

"Concerning criminal cases, if I need to be in court for a hearing of any consequence, I'll probably want you to second-chair me. If *you* have a hearing of that nature, I'll probably want to second-chair you."

"Now as concerns the day-to-day office practice we have here, I'll have Hanna initially just set you up with some fairly easy issues. The more complicated problems, she will set up with me, until you are a little further into the practice. Do *not* hesitate to walk across the hall if you are having a problem with someone, or with their issues. I will be glad to sit in on the rest of the appointment with you. Don't feel embarrassed if you need help. We all do, believe me, we all do, at some point in time."

"What about continuing education?"

"The office will pay the fees. I want you to involve yourself in as much of it as you can, as soon as you can. Bring all your materials back here when finished and we will discuss everything they went through. Now, at times there will obviously be some people you have appointments with you just can't handle. For some reason or another, the two of you just aren't a good fit. When that happens, discuss it with me, and we will either transfer the client over to me, or get rid of them."

"Does that happen often?"

"No, but when it does, it can create a very difficult situation for both attorney and client. For instance, I've set you up with a client tomorrow morning I just can't meet with one more time. She's an old lady, plenty of money, and she had us draw a will for her. That was six weeks or so ago. Since then, I checked a couple of days ago, and she had been back in 16 times to have the will altered, in mostly insignificant ways—just small things. We get a fee every time she walks through the door. She never complains about paying, but I am getting so damn sick of seeing her I could scream. When she comes in tomorrow, she's to see you. I will introduce the two of you and then she's all yours. Those are the types of issues I'm talking about."

"I understand."

Their discussion lasted but a few more minutes, until Paul had a client walk in for his appointment, at which time he left her office and met with the gentlemen in his office.

As Ruth continued to review all he had told her, she couldn't help but consider how she might somehow find a way to increase the amount of money she was receiving through the office more quickly than simply a bimonthly paycheck. It would be difficult, because all the money went through Hanna, and she sure as hell didn't want to lose this job because she misappropriated a measly sum of five hundred dollars this time. She had traveled that road once—not going back.

She closed her door and called an old friend she hadn't talked with since law school.

As soon as he answered, she said, "Harold, how the hell are you?"

"Well, well how's my old partner in crime? How is everything going?"

"Good. How about you? Have you ever heard anymore from Vanderbilt? I assume the investigation is over. I figured it ended as soon as we graduated."

He laughed. "It actually ended when you basically told them your old man would sue them for slander if they mentioned any names. That was a great move, Ruth. Who are you working for now?"

"Actually, this is my first day with Paul Thomas. How's everything with the Blake firm?"

"Good, good. I'm getting along good here. Right now, I am a little bored but I'm sure everything will pick up."

"I really have nothing of importance to discuss, but I do want to remain in touch. You and I worked pretty well together when we were in school, and you never know when one of us might just need the other…for something or other."

"Good idea. I got your number now. If something comes up that looks like it might be a fun and I need a partner that's not afraid to get a little dirty, I'll give you a call."

She laughed, and said, "And I'll do the same."

After the call ended, she didn't know if remaining in contact with Harold would ever amount to anything, but she knew it wouldn't hurt either.

Remaining in touch with someone whose thought-process paralleled hers, would most likely never be a problem, but it certainly could be a benefit. Something might come up at this office that could set her up, financially, for the rest of her life. She would remain vigilant, continuing to look for the right situation, then simply make a determination as to whether the ultimate *risk* was worth the ultimate *reward.*

Chapter 13

Starbucks
Murfreesboro, Tennessee
July

Ed continued to wait patiently. He had arranged to meet Patricia at three p.m. It was now three-thirty. She was late. She was never late.

Finally, at three forty-five he saw someone who appeared to be Patricia walk across the parking lot, toward the door. But whoever it was had a baseball cap pulled so far down over her face, it was difficult to determine facial features. Perhaps the hat was to fend off the hot, July sun, but knowing her, she wore it to remain *incognito.*

Once she reached the doorway, it was obvious it was her.

She walked to the counter and ordered a cup of coffee. Upon picking up her cup, she walked toward his table. He stood as she approached.

"First of all, where the hell have you been, and second, *really*? You *really* think that hat is necessary? Leaving Nashville and coming here to meet you was probably an unnecessary precaution anyway, but now the hat. Come on."

"Just shut up and sit down," she said quietly.

She took a seat across from him, not even acknowledging his attempt to embrace her as she approached.

He took his seat and said, "Okay, what's the problem. This is the first time I have seen you in months and you are like this. What is going on?"

Softly, she said, "You tell me. You tell me what's going on. That's what I want to know. What the hell *is* going on?"

"I just felt it might be best to meet here instead of somewhere in Nashville. We have both lived there now for over a year, and we both know people. I just thought it best to get out of town. If I would have known it would upset you like this, we could have figured something else out. Next time, tell me you don't want to leave town, and we will work it out. Sorry!"

"Don't play games with me, Ed. You know what I'm talking about."

"Rather than make me guess, just tell me what's on your mind, will you? And take off that stupid hat. I can't even see your face with that thing pulled down that far. Take it off or I'm out of here."

She removed the hat, and said, "What the hell is taking so long? Why don't you just kill her and get it over with. Like you say, it's been well over a year, and she's not even dead for Christ's sake. I'm getting tired of Nashville—of living in limbo. I want to move on, move on to an island. Get this over with and move…."

She started to cry. She reached down, pulled a tissue from her pants pocket and started to dab at her eyes.

He waited until she stopped crying and had put the tissue aside. He then reached out and took her hand, which she didn't resist. "I'm sorry, Patricia. I know how you feel. Really, I do. But this one has been a doozy. It's not been like any of the others. This one has been the most difficult. But it's all good. We are not far away, and it should all be worth the wait."

Ed watched as she took a couple of deep breathes, composed herself, then placed both hands around her coffee cup.

Apparently ready to discuss rather than complain, she said, "Tell me about the process with her. We have hardly discussed it. What about the wedding and what happened after that? I was at the actual wedding, of course, but I haven't seen you, or had a chance to talk to you in detail, for way too long. What the hell is going on?"

He reached out, pried one of her hands away from the coffee cup and held it as he said, "Calm down, Pat. I'm sorry this is taking so long, but the process with her has been difficult. Even getting close to her after we were introduced by you, was tough. She just didn't seem to want to let anyone back in her life. Obviously, I was finally successful, but it took all I had to get there. She was resistant to becoming involved with someone again."

"I understand that and I know we briefly discussed that the last time we were together. But, what about the wedding? Relatives? Resistance from her? What the hell happened?"

"We knew she had no kids, so thank g od I didn't need to worry about that. I knew the only thing I had to worry about were shirttail relatives. There's only one and that 'one and only' was and continues to remain a problem. Her name is Marsha Dawson. She is a cousin who lives in Knoxville and she's a total bitch. At least she has been to me."

"What's her story? What's her motivation? What reason does she have to be that way? Does she think…."

"Stop. Let me finish. Then you can ask all the questions you want. First, she didn't want us to get married. That's why there was a delay. Otherwise, we would have been married just a few months after we met, in spite of how cautious a woman she is. But then, even after we married, she is constantly visiting us or calling Janice on the phone. It doesn't seem to bother Jan, but I get so tired of her I could wring her neck."

"Okay, again, what's her motivation?"

"I thought they might be really close, until one day Janice let it slip that she had her named in the will. Then it all started to make sense. She obviously thinks Janice will leave everything to me and exclude her. That's the only thing I can figure out."

"So how are you handling the situation?"

"I'm not. I just devote all my energy toward Janice and let the relationship between us take care of her relationship with Marsha. As our relationship has improved and continues to develop, Janice has taken care of the issue involving her cousin with no help from me whatsoever."

"Have you had any outside interference from anyone else?"

"No. She has no other relatives that she hears from on a regular basis. Her friends have accepted me, because she asked them to."

"What about that house? It looks huge."

"Oh, it is. It is also just full of antiques. I don't know what they are worth, but I'm thinking the house is worth a million. I have also determined that she's got about two million in the bank, in her own name only."

Patricia hesitated, looked away and whispered, "I miss you. I miss you so much."

He again, reached out and took her hand. "I know. I miss you too, and I'm hoping it won't be much longer. But it just seems to be taking her a lot longer to adjust than it did the others. We really haven't even discussed combining our assets. That's the next step, and, as you know, a pretty damn important one."

He looked away, as he said, "You *know* I have never wanted to use a will to transfer funds and other assets to me, because they can be contested. The best way has always been a joint tenancy bank account or joint certificates and that's the path I'm trying to take her down."

He released her hand and said, "But unfortunately, so far she's not going down that path with me. I need a little more time. I've told her how much money I have and that I want to combine it all together so that either of us can benefit if something were to happen to the other."

"Did that help? How much longer is this all going to take?"

"I don't know. I'm thinking maybe another few months. I can't push too hard or she'll become suspicious. We just can't let that happen. I'll let you know. That's all I can do. I really think, during the next six months or so, I will have this all cleaned up and be ready to finish her off."

"Have you come to any conclusions concerning how you're going to kill her?"

He smiled. "I guess I haven't had a chance to tell you how much I now *really* enjoy fishing. I've learned a lot about it from the experts at Piercy Priest Lake just east of Nashville. They have seen plenty of me. I have continued to tell them I'm going to get my wife interested in fishing, so the stage has been set. I just need to get both participants on the lake at the same time in the same boat at dusk. That's all I need."

"Have you been around the lake? Are there places that are quiet enough and private enough for you to finish this?"

"The lake is huge. Yes, there are a number of little coves, many of which should be empty about 8:00 p.m. some weeknight this fall. She's going to fall out of the boat as I drive across the lake. At least that's going to be my story. I think it will work just fine. No witnesses will help. I'll make plenty sure she's dead before I drive back to the marina to ask for assistance in finding her."

She looked down into her coffee cup as she asked, "So, how is your relationship with her?"

"She's a good woman. She is clearly much more cautious than the others have been, but we're making headway, albeit slowly. I like her. I think if you had the opportunity, she would also be a good friend of yours. But obviously, in this instance, it's not *friends* either of us are looking for. She needs to die. I'll take care of it, but first we need to make sure all the funds are titled correctly. Then I'll finish the job."

"How is your *personal* relationship with her?'

"Why don't you just ask me how the sex is and get it over with? It's fine. She's not very imaginative, like you are. She doesn't do to me the things you do. She's pretty bland, but other than that we are fine. Most importantly *she* enjoys it."

"I do so miss you, Ed. This last year and a half have been hell. Not seeing you but a couple of times, combined with very little telephone contact, has really been hard on me."

"I know, but it shouldn't be much longer, *and* since this is the last one, with as much money as this woman has, we should be fixed for life. Believe me this one is worth waiting for."

"Is there any way we can spend the rest of the morning together? Is she gone or with someone else, where maybe she wouldn't miss you for a morning?"

"No. Sorry. That can't happen today. I'll call you, and maybe we can work it out later. I've got a burner phone that I can use if the right opportunity comes up, but we are too close to take a chance—just to close."

"So, this is it, again, until I hear from you?"

"Yes. You want to leave first?"

"Okay."

She stood, and started toward him. He held his hand up to stop her as he said, "You will hear from me soon. I love you."

She stopped, nodded once, then turned toward the door as she once again pulled the baseball cap down low over her face, to hide who she really was.

Chapter 14

Ruth leaned back in her office chair and smiled. What an exciting couple of months it had been! On her desk were stacks of paperwork concerning a number of upcoming criminal and civil cases waiting for her review. She had just finished trying a criminal case involving a drug possession charge, with Paul second-chairing her. It was her first jury trial. It was her first acquittal!

What a rush—almost as exciting as getting something for nothing. Paul told her how well she had done. He had assisted, but she had been responsible for preparing and trying the case.

She heard Hanna walk in the front door. She walked down the hallway to Ruth's open office door, leaned against the frame, smiled and said, "Hey, congrats. I heard about the acquittal last night. You guys work pretty well as a team. That was a nice way to start your courtroom experience, for sure."

"Thanks. Paul is a good teacher. He was right there with me all the way."

"It sounded like an interesting case."

"It was. The facts really were in our favor. There were two runners. One got away—our guy got caught. The one that actually had possession threw the drugs away while being chased. They pinned it on the one they caught, our guy, but he wasn't the one in possession."

"Paul and I had a chance to discuss the case with some of the jurors after they rendered their verdict. They just basically said either of them could have possessed the drugs. They weren't sure, after reviewing all the evidence, which one actually 'possessed' and they weren't about to base a verdict on that much uncertainty. It ended just the way we hoped it would. The cop wasn't very happy about it, but the charge shouldn't have ever been filed in the first place."

"That all sounds pretty logical to me. What's next?"

"I'm not sure. There are a number of cases he wants me to look over. I am just waiting for him to get here this morning and figure out which one he wants me to work on. By the way, you look great. Love that color combination. I always liked black and gold together."

Hanna smiled and said, "Well, thank you very much. I'm always getting those smartass remarks from the boss about how I look. It's nice to hear from someone with a discerning eye for once. Here comes Paul. I better go to work."

Ruth nodded. She heard him say 'good morning' to Hanna, make a sarcastic remark about how she was dressed and start his walk down the hall.

"Morning, Ruth. How does it feel to come out a winner in your first start?"

She smiled and said, "Really, really, good. Thanks for all the great advice. You're the best teacher I ever had."

"You have a good natural instinct for handling people—for handling situations like that. You need a little more experience, but you're going to get along just fine in the courtroom."

"Thanks."

"We will see how you handle Ms. VanArsdayle. When it comes to office practice, that will be the real test for you. She's tough."

"I think she comes in this morning around ten or so."

"Expect her a half-hour early and for it to take her that same half-hour to walk from Hanna's desk to your doorway. Have patience. You'll need all you can muster."

"What is she wanting this morning?"

"The same thing. She needs to change her will. That's all she ever comes in for."

Ruth continued to review files until around 10:00 a.m. when Hanna walked back to her office and informed her that Ms. Martha had just departed her vehicle and was in the process of walking through the front door. She told her to expect her new client to arrive at Ruth's office door about ten-thirty. Ruth smiled, and continued to review files as she heard her next appointment slowly open, then walk through the office door.

Twenty minutes later she saw a hand grab her door frame. Ruth got up and walked to the doorway, then noticing a short, old, crooked body attached to the hand. She said, "You must be that sweet Ms. Martha everyone has told me about. Let me help you to your chair."

"And you my dear, must be that new young lawyer in the office that everyone has told *me* about. You know, I was somewhat concerned when Mr. Thomas said he wanted me to see you today, instead of him. But I do believe this is going to work out just fine, just fine indeed."

Ruth helped her to her chair. Once both were seated, she said, "You look very nice today, Ms. Martha. Love your dress."

"Why thank you. I've had this dress for years, but I just don't wear it much anymore."

The conversation subsequently wound its way through a myriad of topics, from clothing, to weather, to life in Nashville. She also had an opportunity to include a few acrimonious remarks concerning her two 'idiot' children. Finally, it reached the subject of her purpose for the visit—her will.

"Ms. Martha, I understand you needed to see us concerning your will. Now, what is that all about?"

"Well, it's not too complicated really. In my will, I bequeathed a small figurine, actually it was a figurine of an old cow, small and precious, that has been on my mantel for years, to my only daughter, Rhonda. But I want to change that. She's an old cow herself. She doesn't need to be reminded of that every time she looks at her mantel. Besides, I imagine she'll just throw it away as soon as she gets it anyway. I want to change that. I want to give it to my friend and one of my neighbors, Mary Robbins. She will appreciate it a lot more than that daughter of mine and that's a fact. Can you make that change for me?"

Ruth smiled as she said, "Oh certainly, we can make that change without a problem. Now, while you're here should we just discuss your financial situation a little more in detail?"

"Why of course, if you wish. What would you like to know?"

For the next hour, Ruth went through her finances, making sure each certificate and bank account was titled properly and would pass in accordance with her will. If Ms. Martha didn't know the answer to one of Ruth's questions, Ruth would place a call to the financial institution for her and Martha would request the information she needed.

Once finished, Ruth said, "Everything you have indicated you own, as concerns your finances, is properly titled. You need not worry about that. Why don't we go ahead and make the change to your will, and have that ready for you in a couple of days. I can call you and let you know when it's ready."

"That would be just wonderful, my child. Let me ask you, do you ever make house calls? I mean like doctors used too? I use a driver, and sometimes he isn't available when I need him. If need be, could you just bring that to the house? I understand I would need it witnessed when I sign, but you could witness it, and I could get one of the neighbors to witness also. Would that work for you if I just can't get that driver lined up to pick me up when I need him?"

Ruth thought for a moment, and finally said, "Sure, sure, we will get it to you one way or the other."

"Thank you so much my child." She leaned back in her chair, becoming much more comfortable, as she said, "Now, tell me about your family, Ruth. You just tell me all about your family."

Chapter 15

Ruth thought about Ms. Martha and the changes in her will a number of times during the week. But she had so many other issues occupying her time, she failed to follow up with Hanna as to whether the changes had been completed. Once she checked, she found out the changes had just been finished. Martha had called an average of five times a day every day including today.

"Ms. Martha, this is Ruth."

"Who? Who is this? Is this a crank call? I've had enough of these you bastard. I'll see you in hell!" She hung up.

Ruth smiled and hit redial.

Again, Martha answered, and said, "If you call here again, I'll find out who you are you bitch and send someone to stop you *permanently* from making calls again. ...*forever.* Do you understand me? I have people that will do that for me."

"Martha, this is Ruth. Ruth, your attorney. *This is your attorney.*"

Martha hesitated, while letting that statement settle in. "Oh, oh Ruth. I'm so sorry. I'm so very sorry. I've been getting these calls and...never mind. So nice to hear from you. Is my paperwork done?"

"Yes, it is. It's all ready for you. When would you like to come in and sign?"

"As soon as possible. Today or tomorrow would be fine. But I have a small problem. My driver is off both days."

"Well then, let's just wait until the following day. How does that work for you?"

"It doesn't. No, I want to get this done as soon as possible. Let me ask you, would it be too much of an inconvenience for you to come here, to my house?"

"Sure, I can do that, but we do need a witness. Is there someone there that could witness your signature?"

"I could get my neighbor. She's a widow woman. She could come over. She has nothing else to do. I'm sure she would come right over if we need her."

"I'm checking my schedule as we speak. What about around three today? Would that work for you?"

"Certainly. That will be just fine. See you then."

A little before three, she was knocking on Martha's door, briefcase in hand. The house was old, but well maintained. It was situated on a parcel of land near the outskirts of Nashville. Ruth figured before long, Martha's house would be in the way. Development had already started to edge in this direction. Her home and acreage would soon be worth a considerable amount of money to some developer who wanted to build in this area.

She could hear her walking toward the door, but it took a full five minutes for her to reach it.

"Come in, come in, Ruth. Please come in. I have a desk over in the corner there for you to review everything with me. Please come on in."

Ruth walked into a home one could only describe as decorated pre-world war—didn't matter which one—first or second. *Pre-either war* would have been an accurate description.

The antiques located around the room had to have been worth thousands of dollars. The home was beautiful and well-kept, but had just never been updated.

Ruth walked toward the desk and as she did, she said, "My, what a lovely home."

Martha walked slowly, but surely, to a chair positioned directly in front of the desk, where she finally sat, long after Ruth had been seated and had removed all the appropriate paperwork from her briefcase.

Once comfortable, Martha said, "Oh thank you, thank you so much. I love it here. I've had so many offers to sell, but I don't want to leave. This is my home. I'm staying here as long as I can. The offers just keep going up, but I just keep telling them no. Wouldn't you Ruth? Wouldn't you just tell them no? I don't want to move to some damn townhouse or apartment in Nashville."

"Then I would stay right her, Ms. Martha. I would do exactly what you're doing, no question about it. Now, here's where I made the changes you requested. Right here."

Ruth pointed to the line where the beneficiary's name had been altered. "How does that look to you?"

Martha took out her glasses and slowly read the paragraph that had been amended.

"That looks fine my child, just fine. Now might I ask you a rather personal question?" She didn't wait for a response, before she continued. "I have left my children in the will as primary beneficiaries of all I have. I really don't want that. I just plain don't care much for either of them. Should I take them out? And if I do, who should I leave it to? I don't know what to do."

"You know, Ms. Martha, let's discuss that another day. Maybe after you and I have had a chance to talk and I know you a little better we could talk about such issues. Is that alright with you?"

She smiled. "That's a wonderful idea, my child. Now should I have my neighbor come over to witness my signature?" She picked up the pen and started to sign.

"Certainly, but don't sign that until she gets here. Give her a call and let's get her over here before you sign, okay?"

Her neighbor came over immediately. After an explanation as to why she was needed, Martha signed the will and both Mrs. Grafton and Ruth witnessed.

It was clear Mrs. Grafton wanted to read the will. She tried more than once, to move pages around and review the contents, but Ruth kept her focused upon the only issue for which she was needed.

Once she left, Martha informed Ruth she had prepared a plate of small sandwiches along with a pot of tea. She asked Ruth to stay and visit for a spell. When Ruth said she would, Martha then asked her to go to the kitchen, and bring back the tea and sandwiches so they could talk while enjoying a midafternoon snack.

When finished and as they were enjoying a second cup of tea, Ruth said, "Now Ms. Martha tell me about your problem involving your family."

"Well, I really don't have any problems with them. They just don't care whether I'm alive or dead. I haven't seen a one of them since Christmas. That's not unusual. I'll go months and not hear from any of them unless they need something. If they need money, you can damn well bet I'll hear from them. I just hate to reward them when I clearly mean nothing to them. That just doesn't make sense to me."

"But who *would* you leave it to? You asked *me* that question, now I'll ask *you*. Would you leave it to a charity? Is there some charity you believe in? What are you thinking, Ms. Martha?"

"I don't know, I just don't know. No, I have no particular cause I support. I have no church. I would rather leave it to someone…someone that would appreciate it…and that appreciated me while I was alive. I just don't know."

"Let me think about that, Martha. I'll give it some thought and maybe we can discuss it again before long."

Ruth tried to leave three times. Each time, Martha would show her another area of the home. Each time their tour would take almost an hour to complete. It was after seven when Ruth finally approached the office door. The front door was locked, but as she turned the key, she noticed a light emanating from Paul's office.

"Hi. What are you still doing here?"

Paul had removed his tie which was now situated across one of the chairs, and had piles of paperwork extending from one end of his desk to the other. "I'm getting ready for that Amos trial. It starts in a few weeks. I had the caregiver just stay with Anna an extra couple of hours so I could prepare here." He leaned back in his chair, and smiled. "So, how did your little trip go today? I understand you made a house call."

"I did. It went fine. She's a nice lady—just a little lonely. I was there for over four hours. I intend on billing her accordingly. Is that alright with you?"

"Certainly. I am just glad it was you and not me. I don't handle that type of client very well. I'm glad you're here to do it. Did you get the change signed?"

"I did. I'm sure I'll see her again in a few days. We had a long talk, and I doubt the talk we had—about her kids—is over. It seems she has had enough of them."

Paul leaned forward and started looking for something situated amongst all the paperwork on his desk. "Just take care of her. Do what she needs done. I'll be out of here in a few minutes."

Ruth walked in her office and sat down, reviewing a number of phone messages that had come in while she was gone.

She shoved them all aside and leaned back in her chair as she thought about her field trip to the home of Ms. Martha. She was an old woman with lots of money and disgusted with her family. Based on that scenario, she wondered if this might be an opportunity she should consider.

She concluded it might take a little time and extra effort, but she would make trips to her house as often as was necessary, staying as long as Martha wanted her there.

Maybe somewhere along the way, Martha might consider another option as concerned a possible heir to her fortune. This client's problem, might indeed be the perfect situation. Tonight, after Paul left, she would begin putting together a course of action that could end in a successful resolution of not only Martha's goal, but also her own—a win/win situation all the way around.

Chapter 16

"Ms. Anderson, you may cross-examine."

The Amos trial was in its third day. Mrs. Amos, represented by both Paul and Ruth, had already testified. Direct examination of Mr. Amos was completed, and it was now up to Ruth to pull the truth out of the one Mrs. Amos had labeled, 'a lyin' son-of-a-bitch'.

"Might I approach, Your Honor?"

"Certainly."

"Are you in charge of all the family finances, Mr. Amos?"

"Absolutely. My wife didn't *'get it'*—she didn't *'understand'* any of that."

"Are those your words or hers?"

He hesitated. "Mine. She handled the house; I handled the money."

"Apparently, you handled it, but not very well."

"What do you mean?"

"Just what I said. You have a great dental practice, but after ten years in the practice, you don't seem to have put away much money. Do you normally review all of your money issues with your wife?"

"Sure. She knows what we have."

"And are *all* your finances, your assets, your accounts, your business information, part of what we are discussing here today?"

"Well, they most certainly…."

"Hold on there, Mr. Amos. Keep in mind you are under oath. If you are less than truthful the penalty might just be a little jail time. Keep that in mind. Now, answer the question."

"You really don't need to be so condescending. I know how this all works. Yes, to the best of my knowledge everything has been included."

She walked slowly toward the empty jury box, leaned back against the front partition, folded her arms, and said, "You've got an old college friend by the name of Walter McDuff, don't you?"

"Yes, I do. But what's he got to do with any of this?"

"We subpoenaed him. He's outside in the hallway, waiting for us to call him to come testify on our behalf. Would you like to change your story about all your financials being disclosed and included as part of the proceedings here before the court today?"

He cleared his throat, changed positions in his chair, and looked away for a moment before he answered. "Hell no, I don't want to change my answer. Why should I? He has no information concerning my finances."

"Oh, come now, Mr. Amos, you really want to take that kind of chance? Come on—reconsider your position here. He owns and operates a dental supply company, doesn't he? He does a considerable amount of business all over middle Tennessee doesn't he?"

"I guess, yes. I guess he does business all over the area. So what?"

"Let *me* ask the questions please, Mr. Amos. You do a considerable amount of business with him don't you?"

"I guess. I have a large practice. I use a considerable amount of his product."

"And is everything you pay him actually for a product, or do you give him money, or his company money for which you get nothing in return?"

"I…I pay him for…product. That's what I pay him for…product."

Ruth looked out the window. It was early summer, but hot. However, inside the courtroom the temperature was very comfortable. She turned toward the witness, and noticed Mr. Amos wore a tie, but no suitcoat. However, it was obvious the pressure was getting to him, as he was literally starting to sweat through his shirt.

"You ever pay money to him for nothing in return?"

"Certainly not."

"Last chance. Wanna change your story?"

He said nothing.

"No? Would it surprise you to know that he's ready to testify, under oath, that you have been laundering a great amount of the cash you receive in your business through his firm for years? He has decided, no matter how good a friend you are, he's not going to go through an audit by the IRS or law enforcement, and suffer the potential penalties he could be subjected to, just because you are a friend. And, of course, all that laundered money he received, he then transferred to that Mexican shell corporation you set up. *That* money you deposited in the corporate account without your wife's name never shows up in any of your joint accounts nor has it been included as part of these proceedings has it, Mr. Amos?"

She walked toward the witness, and now stood nose to nose. Her voice grew louder and more intense. "None of it, not one penny, is included as part of your assets in this proceeding. From what we can determine, over the last few years it amounts to well over two hundred fifty thousand dollars. Wanna change your answer *now*, Mr. Amos?"

He quickly said, "Oh no, there's not that…"

He turned and looked out the courtroom window. When he reengaged in the conversation, he whispered, "I would like a moment with my attorney before we go any further."

"Probably a really good idea, Mr. Amos. We'll hold on to your college buddy until we hear from you or your attorney. Judge could we take a short break?"

"Yes, by all means. Court will be in recess for a half hour."

After the judge, Mr. Amos and his attorney had left the room, Paul looked at Ruth and said, "Well done. We got him right where we want him."

"I'm thinking we'll get a little better offer this time—maybe about a hundred and twenty-five thousand better. I guess I would hold out for two hundred if I were Mrs. Amos. What do you think Paul?"

"I agree—hold out for two and see what he does. In return, we'll guarantee his attorney that none of the information concerning his illegal activities goes to law enforcement or the IRS."

The parties settled mid-afternoon. Ruth arrived at her office just before 4:00 p.m. The paperwork for the new change in Ms. Martha's will was prepared and lying on her desk for review.

She started to look over all the other messages and notes she had lying on her desk, and as she did, Hanna came to her doorway.

"Paul gave me a call from the courthouse. He just went on home from there, but he told me you did well today. He thinks you have a great future in the courtroom. You have certainly impressed him, that's for sure."

"Thanks, Hanna, that's nice to hear. The trial went well after we got the bastard's attention. Now, to this mess on my desk and Ms. Martha.

"So how are you handling *this* change in her will? Do you want me to call her, and have her come in, or what?"

"Actually Hanna, I'll handle it. She wants me to come over with it and sign it at her house. The neighbor is ready to come over to witness I guess."

"So how many times in the past three weeks have you been over there, about ten?"

"Hell, I don't know. Plenty that's for sure. But I just keep charging her. She doesn't seem to mind paying the fees. It seems more comfortable for her to do this in her home, so I just try to keep her happy."

"When are you leaving?"

"Shortly. Could you put the changes in an envelope for me? I'll go now. Maybe I can get home before dark and still enjoy some of my evening."

Hanna got everything ready for her. Ruth arrived at the VanArsdayle home shortly before 5:00 p.m. They called Ms. Grafton. She arrived shortly thereafter and again, witnessed the change to Martha's will.

Martha had fixed supper for two, and wouldn't take no for an answer. The food consisted of a number of old family recipes. Once the meal ended, and each had a cup of coffee before them, Martha again brought up the issue of distribution of her funds at her death.

She could not decide what to do, but *had* decided she wasn't going to leave it to her children.

"What about just spreading it amongst a number of charities, Martha? That would benefit a number of different people and causes."

"Yes, I guess that's an option. What about just spreading it amongst all my friends? I could do that too, couldn't I."

"Certainly, that's an option. Do you have a lot of friends, Martha?"

She thought for a moment, and finally said, "Not many that I would want to leave anything to, I guess. Oh, there's Ms. Grafton, but I don't know that I like her enough to leave her anything. She's really kind of bitchy most of the time, if you know what I mean."

Ruth laughed and said, "I know exactly what you mean."

The conversation slowed. Martha was in deep thought.

Just as Ruth stood and prepared to leave, Martha said, "What if I were just to leave it to you? Could you distribute it as you thought appropriate? Could you distribute it to charities that really need it, to my kids if you felt that was appropriate and to other friends, if they came to my funeral and such? Could you do that for me?"

Ruth looked away for a moment before she said, "I could I guess, but I really don't like to think of you as being gone, Ms. Martha. You and I have become so close, I don't know what I would do without the trips over here to your house. Surely, I'll do whatever you want me to do. Should we have a new will prepared along those lines? What do you want me to do?"

She smiled, "Yes, of course, make one up that way, and let me think about it. I feel better about that problem already, knowing that you'll handle all that for me. Just takes it right off my mind. I'm so glad you would even consider taking on that responsibility, Ruth. It just eases my mind so."

Later that night, long after she arrived home, Ruth still tingled with excitement. What an opportunity. She would need to think it all through, plan it out, and then strike while the iron was hot. She couldn't prepare the will *and* have her own name on it. This would need to be well- planned. It would make no sense to prepare the will, have Martha kick off, and then have the will overturned later. She might need some help for this project—and luckily, she knew just the one to call.

Chapter 17

Sam Harvey watched his partner saunter across the precinct floor, heading toward his deck. His suit and tie, combined with his obvious swagger, would in another time, another place, clearly indicate he was the owner—that this place and all in it belonged to him. His appearance conveyed everything Sam wasn't. It was definitely going to take some time to get used to this guy, if he ever did.

"Morning, slick. Glad you could make it."

Terry Oswald sat down across from Sam and said, "Hey, I asked you not to call me that. Call me prick, idiot, or even Terry, but lay off the 'slick' will you?"

"*Mr.* Slick, better?"

Terry never responded. As he reviewed the prior weekend's activities, he said, "Looks like a lot of murders over Labor Day. I see Hack Green went down. Didn't he work for Dean Oliver?"

"Yup."

"You heard anything?"

"I heard a while back that Green had started out on his own. He apparently put a few girls together and was going to operate in competition with Oliver. I heard the relationship between the two of them wasn't good, but that was the last word I got concerning either of them."

"How was he murdered?"

"Couple to the back of the head."

"Isn't that Oliver's signature?"

"My, don't you learn fast."

"C'mon you old fart, just answer the question."

"Yes, yes that's how Oliver normally takes care of his problems."

"So, what are you thinking?"

"Well…*Mr.* Slick…I'm thinking maybe a trip to Mr. Oliver's office is warranted later today—maybe late afternoon, after we are sure he's at his office. I wouldn't want to show up in advance and while he's still at home, sleeping. I know he never gets to his office before two. Do you want to go?"

"Hell yes, I want to go."

Later that afternoon, Sam looked around the office for his partner, but couldn't find him. He picked up his file and started for the door. Just as he reached for the doorknob, he heard his partner yell, "Hey, old man, stop right there. I'm going with you." He ran across the office floor, and as he did, he said, "Were you *really* going without me? *Really*?"

Sam never stopped. He turned the knob and walked through the doorway, never acknowledging his partner, or his partner's question.

They drove to Oliver's office building in Germantown and walked into an older, single-story building, housing the office of Dean Oliver, where his secretary stopped anyone from gaining access to Mr. Oliver's office until approved by him.

Sam pulled his badge, flashed it at his secretary and said, "We need to talk with Mr. Oliver. Please understand we need to talk to him *now*, not later, not somewhere else, but here and *now*. Please convey that message to him, *now*."

While she starred at him, she picked up the phone, and said, "Police are here. They wanna talk to you. No.... Yes.... No.... Okay."

Sam heard the door click and his secretary said, "Go on in."

Oliver was seated behind a large oval desk. His office was half the size of the whole precinct. Built-in cabinets, custom designed out of oak, lined the walls all around the room, with the exception of that area where floor to ceiling windows looked out over the street below. The cost of improvements and furnishings in the office were clearly worth more than Sam's salary for a couple of years.

Oliver stood and extended his hand as the officers walked in.

"Good afternoon, gentlemen. Dean Oliver. Have a seat."

Neither officer shook his hand, both electing to simply sit.

Oliver withdrew his hand and as he sat, he said, "Can I see both of your badges please? How can I help you? I have a prearranged call in just a few minutes, so we need to hurry this along."

Both officers showed their badges, as Oliver wrote down their names.

"Thanks, boys. Now who's, in charge here? Both of you...neither of you? Who's the boss here?"

Terry said, "He's the oldest. I guess he's the boss."

Sam glared at him, then turned toward Oliver and said, "I'm the senior partner. You know a guy named Hack Green?"

Oliver leaned back in his chair, smiled and said, "Sure. Everyone knows Hack. Why? Great guy. Known him forever."

"*Knew* him forever. He's dead," Terry said.

Again, Sam glared at his partner, as Oliver dropped the smile, leaned forward and said, "*No.* You have to be kidding. What happened?"

Sam, once again in control, said, "He took a couple to the back of the head."

"Really. When did that happen?"

"Saturday night over Labor Day weekend. Mind telling us where you were that night?"

"Me? *Me*? I was at a party with friends all night. Well, until about midnight anyway. I went with my wife. She was with me all evening. After we left the party, I went home and stayed home with her the rest of the night. Now, come on boys. You don't think I had anything to do with this, do you?"

"It kinda smells like something an asshole like you would do, Mr. Oliver. You two weren't getting along the best, were you?"

Again, Oliver leaned back in his chair. "Harvey, Harvey. Sam Harvey. I think I have heard of you Mr. Harvey. You been after me, haven't you? I think I heard somewhere you been after me. Am I correct?"

"Just answer the question tough guy. Were you two getting along?"

"Sure, sure we got along okay. I'm going to miss him that's for sure. You know, you got no evidence that indicates you should be looking at me for his murder. In fact, you got *nothing* to go on as concerns me *or* my whole operation, for *anything*. But I keep hearing these rumors you're after me. Is that right…*Sam*? You chasing me?"

"Is it true he was starting his own little operation and that he was in competition with you?"

"Not that I know of. Never heard that. Now, answer my question, cop. You after me?"

Sam leaned forward and motioned for Oliver to do the same. He then said softly, "Yup. I'm after you. And you know what? I'm going to getcha. Mark my words you asshole. I'm going to getcha."

"Watch yourself cop. Just watch yourself. A few words of advice?

Get off my ass if you know what's good for you."

Sam sat back, smiled and said, "You didn't just threaten me, did you? Is that what you just did? Because I'm really thinking that's exactly what you did."

"No sir. That was no threat. I was just trying to help. Trying to redirect your efforts in a more productive direction." He stood. "Now, gentlemen, I have work to do. Thanks for your time. I enjoyed the visit. Doors right behind you. Have a good day."

Both stood. Terry looked at Sam and said, "You going to let him get by with that? He threatened you. I heard him."

Sam smiled and said, "He just fueled the fire, Terry. That's all he did. Before I'm done with him, he'll have one hell of a lot more to worry about than some stupid childish threat." He turned to look at Oliver, and pointed his finger at him as he said, "And that my friend *also* isn't a threat, that's a promise."

All the way back to the precinct, Terry tried to make conversation with Sam. But Sam remained silent, writing notes as Terry drove. Once they walked in the precinct, again Terry tried to engage Sam in conversation concerning their approach in apprehending Oliver. But he was given no response whatsoever, Sam electing to walk silently to his desk, where he continued to make notes.

Terry sat down at his desk, and while reviewing other files, occasionally looked up only to find Sam deep in thought and continuing to write.

Finally, about two hours after they returned, Sam looked across his desk at Terry and said, "That guy's a prick."

"Well, yes that's one way to describe him, I guess. What's our next step here? I mean it's pretty clear he knocked Green off. How do you wanna approach this?"

"You got any proof? Because *I* don't have *any* proof, he did it. Do you?"

"No, but..."

"Well then, maybe Einstein, that's our next step—to get a little proof."

Terry said nothing. He went back to reviewing other files. A few moments later, Sam looked at Terry and said, "But I'll tell you one thing. We are going to get that murderin' son-of-a-bitch. You and me...us...we're going to get that son-of-a-bitch if it's the last thing either of us ever do."

Chapter 18

It had been a slow, tedious day—and it had gone exactly as Ed had planned. Saturday afternoons in mid-September, were set aside for the sole purpose of watching football and that is exactly what he had done. Meanwhile, Janice cleaned house all day, which included cleaning around, over and behind Ed.

Finally, after picking up his legs to vacuum the floor under them, she shut the vacuum off and said, "Honey, y'all want to do something tonight, or are we just gonna sit here and watch football the rest of the day and all evening too?"

"No, no sweetheart, you want to go out to eat?"

"I guess. I want to do something other than this, I can tell you that."

"Beautiful day out. I can get a boat lined up at Piercy Priest, and we can take a spin around the lake—fish if you wish or just go for a ride."

"Maybe we could stop for supper somewhere after the ride?"

"That will work for me. Let me call the boat club and see if we can get something lined up. Maybe leave about six?"

"Sure, I can be ready by then."

Ed had lined the boat up the day before, wanting to make certain they had the type of boat he needed for this particular spin around the lake. They did, and he reserved it, telling them he would be there about six.

On the way to the lake, he listened to her talk…and talk…and talk. The woman could carry on a one-sided conversation better than anyone he had ever met. The subjects ranged from cooking to sewing, to travel, to relatives. He was tired of her. Regardless of his wife's religious beliefs and charitable work, he had convinced himself the world would be better off without her.

Ed took his fishing gear with him, telling Janice he may want to fish for a short time if the opportunity presented itself.

Once they arrived, their boat was waiting for them. He made certain, even though it was a power boat, it had a set of oars, which it did. They were to be used in case the engine died and couldn't be restarted—at least, that's what they told him to use them for—he actually had another use in mind.

They rode around the lake until near dark. He had already found a cove which was secluded and small enough people didn't find it interesting to frequent on a regular basis. He had no doubt at this time of day, they would find the shoreline and the cove vacant.

Janice was facing the back of the boat, and as he came to a stop, she said, "What are we stopping for?"

There was still enough light to see her, but barely enough to see the shoreline. As she started to turn to face him, he picked up one of the oars and swung at her with the flat side of the oar, so as to stun her but not make a deep gash, which would have happened if he had hit her with the oar's edge.

The blow nearly rendered her unconscious. She fell backwards, off her seat and to the floor of the boat.

Ed picked her up, to which she offered no resistance. He lowered her into the water, and put his hand on top of her head holding onto her hair so she couldn't move out from under his hand. Ed then shoved her head under the surface and held it there. The coolness of the water was enough to bring her back to consciousness, and she started to struggle. He held her head under water until she quit, until the bubbles stopped and until she started to sink. When he could no longer see her form, he moved the boat a few feet away, and continued to watch the surrounding area for a few moments, making sure she didn't surface and again start her incessant chatter, explaining how she still had some cleaning she had yet to do, or that there was a trip she still wanted to take.

When he was finally convinced she was gone, he lowered himself over the edge of the boat and completely submersed himself in the water, climbing back in using the small ladder attached to the rear of the boat.

Once he was back on board, he used some liquid soap he brought with him in a small plastic container, to thoroughly clean off the blade of the oar. He then started the engine and drove out of the cove across the lake as fast as the boat would carry him, discarding the container of liquid soap once he reached the middle of the lake.

Upon arriving at the dock, he ran into the office and informed everyone his wife had apparently fallen out of the boat. He told them he had started the engine and left the cove at a high rate of speed. The last he knew she was located near the back of the boat. But a few moments later, he turned to visit with her and she was gone. He said he immediately returned to the point where he last saw her and dove into the lake. He searched the waters in that area, but simply could not locate her.

The manager immediately called law enforcement, and within minutes four boats belonging to management were flying across the lake to the cove where Ed believed everything had happened.

Shortly thereafter, they were joined by law enforcement, which included divers. Ed told them he wasn't exactly sure which cove they were in when he last saw her on board, so the location he gave them might not be completely accurate. They searched for hours, but it was just too dark. Law enforcement would wait until morning to resume the search.

After returning to the dock, they wanted to discuss the specifics concerning exactly what occurred. Wrapped in a blanket, Ed sat down with an officer to review the facts.

The officer was large to say the least. He could fill two chairs, and Ed was a little concerned the one he was sitting in wouldn't hold him. He had a small mustache and found it difficult to look at Ed as he talked.

"What happened—in your own words?"

"We were just enjoying the evening. I told her it was time to leave and she said, 'fine.' I turned around to talk to her as we approached shore and she was gone."

"Neither of you were wearing a life vest?"

"No," Ed whispered. "Wish we would have been. This could have all been avoided."

"You went in after her?"

"Yes, but I wasn't exactly sure where she fell out and I knew I needed help."

"Did you two have issues before? I mean, was everything okay between the two of you?"

"What are you asking me?"

"Let me ask you this. How long have you been married?"

"Long time…year and a half I guess."

"Long time?"

"Okay, what are you trying to say?"

"Nothing, nothing. Do either of you have any children?"

"No."

"Had she ever been in a boat before? Have you had her out here before?"

"Yes. Many times."

"But she didn't know enough to sit down when you took off?"

"Officer, I don't know what happened. It all went on behind me. One minute she was there, the next she was gone. I have no idea what happened."

"You didn't hear her yell out?"

"No, the engine was way too loud for that, and I don't know if she ever had a chance to yell out."

"Was it completely dark when you decided to come back to shore?"

"Pretty much, yes. Why?"

"So, there most likely were no witnesses?"

"Probably not. It was just too dark."

"Do the two of you normally come out by yourselves or do you bring other people with you?"

"No, we normally come alone. I don't know that many people yet and there really aren't many people my wife knows that also enjoy boating and fishing."

"I take it she's a long-time resident here?"

"Yes."

"And I take it you're not?"

"No. I've been here awhile, but I just don't know that many people yet."

"Where did you come from, Mr. Hall?"

"Colorado." He really didn't want to discuss his back history, but he also didn't want to get caught lying to him concerning something as seemingly irrelevant as his prior address either.

"Okay that's enough for now. Are you staying around here tonight?"

"Yes, of course. I'm staying right here until I know what the hell happened—whether she's okay or not. I'll be here if you need me."

The next morning, they were out on the lake shortly after dawn. The morning was crisp and cool—the lake as quiet as it was the night before. But it took another couple of days for her body to float to the surface. She initially sank under the surface, but her body had now floated to the top. They found her as soon as all the divers fully searched the area. She was as dead as he hoped she would be.

After returning to the dock, they took her to the morgue. The officer told him there would probably be additional questions, but they would wait until after her funeral to ask him. They also told him not to leave the area until they had a chance, in more detail, to determine exactly what happened. Ed told them he would be available whenever they needed him.

He drove home and changed his clothes. Before he started to contact her friends and make funeral arrangements, he took out a burner phone he had hidden under the seat in his vehicle. He sat down, leaned back and dialed Pat' s number.

"Hi. It's done."

"What happened?"

"She drowned."

"And tell me again—everything is jointly held, correct?"

"Yes, yes everything is jointly held. We are fine."

"Any problems."

"I don't think so."

Pat hesitated. "What do you mean 'you don't think so?' There either are or there aren't. *Are* there or *aren't* there?"

"There was a cop that was asking a lot of questions. I don't think there will be a problem, but he told me they might want to visit a little more. I told him I would be around whenever they need me."

"What's your gut telling you?"

He smiled. "It is telling me it's done. It is telling me the questions might not be over, but that they can't prove a damn thing."

She breathed a sigh of relief. "See you soon?"

"I'll let you know."

Chapter 19

Since Ruth's first day on the job, Saturday morning had become the highlight of her week. Ruth had no social life. She actually had plenty of opportunities—she just wasn't interested.

Her job—practicing law, preparing for trial, preparing an estate plan, or simply doing legal research—was her life. She didn't have time to date, or to socialize. Saturday morning, with a cup of coffee in hand, practicing her chosen vocation, without the hassle she normally handled during a busy weekday, was for her, as good as it gets.

As she reviewed her court appearances for the coming week, she heard Paul enter the office door. He walked down the hallway, and as he appeared in her doorway, he smiled and said, "You are here pretty early, aren't you? Or maybe the questions should be, 'What the hell are you doing here this early on a Saturday morning? Don't you have a life outside this office?"

"I guess I could ask you the very same questions."

"True." He plopped down in one of two chairs in front of her desk. "Well, you've been here almost six months now. What do you think?"

"I love it here. Thank you for allowing me the opportunity to work with you. I absolutely love it."

"You're doing well, Ruth. Hanna enjoys working with you. A couple of the judges you appeared before, have even commented on your abilities in a positive manner. I think you've even made friends with old Mrs. VanArsdayle."

"She's a good soul. I like her. Lord knows I've been with her enough—I better like her." She hesitated. "Paul, I think you should know she's mentioned leaving me something in her will. I know that's not ethically correct, at least with us drawing her will, but I did want to tell you she has discussed it."

"Well, you know of the potential ethics violation if that were to happen, especially if you or anyone in this office drew the will. Believe me, you don't want to go there with her. The bar association watches those types of issues very closely. Besides that, it's just not morally proper. The undue influence issue is always present both legally and morally. But I'm sure I'm not telling you something you don't already know."

She considered his remarks long after he left her office that morning, and the issue now was whether she should cancel the appointment she had already made across town. She finally concluded it wouldn't hurt to honor the appointment and at least talk—at least discuss the issue.

At precisely 2:00 p.m. she walked into the reception area of the office of Harold Voorhies. He apparently heard her close the outer door and he walked out to meet her.

"Been a while, partner."

He embraced her as she said, "It has been. How's everything going here?"

She looked around the reception area as he discussed his current employment status. The office was bare. There were few pictures on the wall, the carpet was worn, and the furnishings appeared to be early 20th century. Not impressive to say the least.

He motioned for her to follow. While walking down the hallway she had an opportunity to look in the offices of other partners along the way. They appeared shabby, and certainly not what she would have expected from a law office which appeared to be held in such high esteem by other members of the bar.

His own office was small and poorly decorated. Certainly, no more than three or four people could sit in front of his desk at a time.

As she shut his door behind her, she said, "Nice office, Harold." Ruth lied as she continued to look around.

"It's okay. It was the only job I could find. Hopefully, I'll be able to move on from here, but that law school cheating situation followed me after we graduated. I was considered the ringleader even though they couldn't prove anything. It affected my employment status, although no one would ever tell me that to my face."

"I'm sorry, Harold. You were a good student, with a great mind. I hope this all works out for you."

"Thanks. It will. Now, I'm curious. What brings you here to see me and on a Saturday afternoon?"

"Are these offices soundproof? Is what we discuss here this

afternoon completely confidential?"

"Absolutely. Why?"

"First of all, I have a client I need you to see."

He smiled. "Great. Sending me business already. Love it."

"Well, it's not quite that simple, Harold."

"Why? What does this client need to see *me* for? Is it something you can't handle?"

"Not really. It's just a simple will."

"What complicates the issue?"

"She's my client and she wants to leave everything she owns to me."

Harold leaned back in his chair, clasped his hands behind his head and said, "Well, that isn't going to work now, is it?"

"It might—if you draw the will. If you do your research with her and make a good record as to what happened, I think it might work just fine."

"I don't understand. How's this all going to 'work just fine.' Explain."

"You prepare the will, have her sign it, get paid for your work, and along the way, maybe even make a carefully worded recording saying this is what she wants. Then hold the will until she's dead. Pretty simple. I'm not involved in any way, except bringing her here in the first place."

He thought for a moment. Finally, he said "I guess that might work." He sat back in his chair and thought for a moment. "Now, let's just take it a step further. What's in it for me?"

"Well, you'll get paid for drawing the will, and you'll get paid for probating her estate. Of course, you may have to testify if her family files an action contesting the will, but you will be paid if you do."

"And you get…?"

"She is probably worth in excess of two mil."

He leaned forward and said, "Bullshit. Are you kidding me? And you end up with it all?"

She said nothing.

Harold remained quiet, as he considered her proposal. She sat, waiting for him to think it through, to process all she had just told him. Finally, he said, "I'll tell you what. I want $100,000 paid to me at some point in time after you get your money. This all needs to be worth my time and effort. I figure that's about fair."

"What about half of that if this all works out?"

"Nope. A hundred thousand!"

"You know, there are others I could go to that would take less."

"Can you trust them? You can me. What's that worth to you?"

For effect, she sat quietly considering his proposal. "You're right. A hundred thousand it is."

She relaxed slightly, leaning back in her chair as she said, "Now, I'll bring her to you initially, then leave it up to her to get here on her own whenever you need her. After the first visit, I'll make sure my presence is noted wherever I am, when she is with you, so there will be a record of the fact that I didn't come with her each time she saw you."

"That will work fine. Do you want to see the draft of the will, before she signs it?"

"Yes. She has told me she might leave the money to me to distribute to other people as I saw fit. If she brings that up, off the record, just tell her it has to be left to me unconditionally—that's just the way the law is. Of course, the only one that's going to end up with anything is me, but she'll never know that."

"When do you want me to see her?"

"This week. She is really old. We need to get this done. I'll pick her up and get her here. I can probably sit in on the initial conference, but then I'm done. I am anticipating a will contest. She hates her kids, and I don't think they much like her, but I have no doubt they won't go down without a fight."

Ruth hesitated, then continued as she said, "But I guess that will be your problem. I'll testify, but in the end, it will be you that needs to win the will contest, not me. Why don't we set her up for Wednesday at about ten?"

"I'll make that work."

Later that afternoon, as she drove back to her office, she thought how remarkably well her time with Harold had gone. She was even happy with the amount she would need to pay him. When Ruth initially concocted the plan, she figured he wouldn't give in for anything less than half of everything she got. Luckily, she played her cards right and would get by for a mere hundred thousand—certainly peanuts compared to what *she* should net from the demise of dear old Ms. Martha.

Chapter 20

Milo's Bar
Portland, Tennessee

Again, he waited. This was quickly becoming a habit he would find hard to accept. Ed had moved their meeting location out of town. Patricia was already 20 minutes late. He had gone through one cup of coffee and was walking up to the counter for a refill, when he noticed her.

He continued to watch as she approached the door. No disguise this time. Ed motioned to her while she scanned the room, trying to locate him. He walked toward her as he said, "Do you want me to get you a cup?"

"Yes."

"I have been sitting over there next to the wall. I'll bring both cups when they're ready." He nodded towards a table for two, located in the corner, away from any of the other tables.

She walked away from him as he watched her every move. Her walk was enough to excite him. She wore nothing but jeans and a sweater. He figured the no bra look was for his benefit, but this time, that look wouldn't be enough. Hopefully, their time apart would soon end, but based on what he now knew, unfortunately it wouldn't end as soon as he hoped it would.

He picked up both cups of coffee and walked to the table. As he sat down, she said, "Okay, why here? Good God this is half a country away from Nashville. Do we *really* have that much to worry about?"

He smiled as he said, "Glad to see you, too."

She looked down, as she mumbled, "I'm sorry. I *am* glad to see you, but it's *over*—why the need to meet you in another city—almost in another *state?* Is there a problem here you haven't told me about?"

"I don't think so, no."

"You know, that's the second or third time you've waivered

concerning your answer to that very question. Obviously, something is different this time. You are always so confident. Whether it's good or bad, right or wrong, you are always certain of your response, your answer. That's not the case this time. Tell me what's going on, Ed."

"Okay, okay, just relax. Everything is going fine, except for this one cop who's having a little trouble letting this all just die. He has called me twice for additional information, and the last time he said he would probably have a different cop, a detective I guess, give me a call later this week."

"What's the issue? What are they looking into?"

"I really am not sure. He just doesn't act like he believes me. I told him the whole story twice. Apparently, there's some element of what I'm telling him he just isn't accepting. That's why I moved our meeting here. This is the first time since we've started that I am actually somewhat concerned about what's going on. If I knew what he was specifically doubting, I could try to put the issue to rest, but he just keeps asking about different issues—there doesn't seem to be anything he is specifically concerned about. I'm sure we are fine, but we need to really be careful until this is completely over."

"What about the money?"

"It amounted to a little over two mil. I think I better hold your share in my name for a while so it can't be traced to you in any respect if the investigation goes any further. We haven't had this issue before so cash transfers to you haven't been a problem. We can settle up later after this has all calmed down. Eventually, I'm going to put the house on the market. With that cop watching everything I'm doing I didn't want to do that too quickly. As strong as the real estate market is in Nashville, I don't think it will take long to sell. Once it does, we can get out of here, but until then we need to just lay low."

"That's fine. How much longer?"

"I don't want to put the house on the market until he seems satisfied. Probably another couple of months."

"And I suppose during that time, we shouldn't be together?" she whispered.

He reached over and placed his hand over hers. "No. That would not be a good idea. Patience, Patricia, for just a bit longer."

"You mentioned she had a relative you said continued to remain a problem. Is she causing issues?"

"Yes. She is raising hell with me. She told me she spoke to the investigating officer at least twice. I have no doubt that is fueling the investigation. I wish I could have sent her to the bottom of the lake with Janice. She is definitely pushing the investigation further than I believe it would have gone if she would have remained silent."

"So, what's next?"

"The cop said he would call me later today or just stop by the house, so I need to be there when he arrives. I guess we just move forward until it's safe to leave. My plan, as I said, is to list the house, most likely, in about 60 days. If they have anything on me, I'll certainly know by then, and if they don't, listing the house, in and off itself, shouldn't raise any red flags. They already know I'm not a lifelong resident of Nashville. Leaving the city after the death of my wife shouldn't be a stretch for anyone."

"Should I go ahead and see if I can find us a place somewhere in the Caribbean?"

He thought for a moment, then said, "Yes, that would probably be a good idea. That will give you something to do, and help both of us when the time is right. In fact, if you want to fly down there and look at a house or two, I certainly have no problem with that."

"Any idea what Janice's house is worth?"

"I think it's worth at least nine hundred thousand, but I'm going to list it at seven hundred and fifty, hoping it sells quickly. With all we got from her, I'm not going to be concerned about losing a measly hundred and fifty thousand, especially when I got that cop sniffing around."

She looked down, cupped her hands around her coffee and whispered, "I miss you so much."

"I know you do, Patricia, but it's just a little while now. Why don't you start looking at homes, maybe first on Aruba and then the Caymans? If you find something that interests you, fly down there and take a look. We can meet every couple of weeks now, since I don't have Janice hanging around my neck."

She seemed to accept Ed's plan, and they agreed to meet in two weeks, same time, same place. This time before she walked away, he kissed her—nothing to draw any attention, but with enough passion to placate her for the moment.

Later that day, once he returned home, the phone rang. He had been waiting.

"Good afternoon, Officer Cobb, how can I help you today?"

"Just one or two questions, Ed. Just routine. Did you have any life insurance on Janice?"

"No, not a penny."

"Was she a wealthy woman?"

"What do you mean by wealthy?"

"Oh, I don't know, I guess anything over half a mil would be wealthy to me. Was she worth more than that?"

"Yes. But to be honest, so was I. About six months after we married, we just put all our money into the same accounts. It was much easier to keep track that way. The money was in joint tenancy certificates and checking accounts. It was to pass to the survivor if one of us died."

"So, you got all her money?"

"Yes, and she would have received all of mine if I had died first. That's the way we both wanted it. Why are you asking these questions, officer? Is there something going on of which I am not aware?"

"No, not really. I am just trying to finish up my investigation. Do you happen to know a woman by the name of Martha Dawson?"

He laughed. "Oh, my, yes. I know her well. She's related to Janice, and she has called me numerous times since her death. Apparently, she was in Jancis's will and feels she's entitled to some money. I just let her ramble on. Is she the reason you're pursing this?"

"She thinks you murdered Janice for her money."

"You know, that's insane. I already had plenty of money. I think I had more than she did when I married her. If I would have been the one that hadn't made it off the lake, Janice would have received everything I had. That just seemed like the fair way to do it."

"I understand, I understand. I just need to follow up, that's all. By the way, have you ever been married before?"

Paul swallowed hard. "Yes, I have. Ended in divorce though. Long time ago. She was a good woman, but the marriage wasn't for either of us."

Officer Cobb was silent, until he said, "Just give me a moment to finish my notes."

After a delay of a couple of minutes, he said, "Okay, that's it for today. Do you have plans for leaving the area, Mr. Hall?"

"You mean permanently?"

"Well, that or even for a shorter time in the near future?"

"No. I plan on being right here."

“Okay. That’s all I have for now. I’ll be in touch.”

Ed terminated the call. This was all starting to become somewhat uncomfortable. He wondered if he should employ an attorney. The cops had nothing, yet they continued to push. And the lie about the divorce might have been unnecessary, but he couldn’t tell him about all the dead wives.

He would wait before employing an attorney. That might appear to be an indication of guilt. He would wait and see what Officer Cobb’s next move might be, or if this was the end of the investigation. He had never walked this road before—and it was certainly a road he had no desire to continue to walk much longer.

Chapter 21

Ruth could only hope this case ended as well as the Amos case. She had settled that case during trial and it had settled well—both client and attorney ended the day with a smile on their face. This case was, however, slightly different. The woman she represented was crazy. Well, maybe not literally, but pretty damn close.

The offer opposing council had made to settle the case was fair. She had explained that to her client. She also told her that if they went to court, and a judge listened to all the evidence, he might not be as generous as opposing council. Ruth told her in no uncertain terms to take the offer, but to this point she had refused—and even refused to counteroffer. 'Her man' had another woman—she wanted her day in court to tell the 'whole story' come hell or high water.

This case was unlike any she had tried before. It had come down to the client completely controlling the situation—the flow of the case. She refused to accept Ruth's advice concerning any aspect of the proceedings. It was time to discuss how they should proceed from here with someone having more experience with this type of client than she had. Ruth had no idea how to proceed with her going forward. She finally concluded it was time to discuss the problem with her boss.

She walked across the hall and said, "Morning, Paul. You have a minute?"

"Sure, sure, come in, have a chair. I'm just getting ready for that Bronson criminal case next week. What's going on?"

She walked in, took a chair in front of his desk, and said, "This damn Winthrop case is what's going on. I cannot seem to get through to her. As you know, they made a great offer, but she just doesn't seem to care. All she wants to do is rant and rave about his 'new woman.' And she wants to do the same thing in court. I really don't think the judge will be nearly as generous with her as her husband's offer was, and I've told her that. It looks to me like her husband is letting his guilt associated with that other woman, influence his offer to her. It's definitely working to our benefit, but I just can't get her to accept it. I don't know what to do with her."

"I have been there many times, Ruth. Sometimes you don't have a choice. You just try the case. But you need to make sure everything between the two of you is in writing. Set out the offer in writing, show that she rejected it and have her sign it. No sense having this 'I said, you said' problem with only oral statements to reconstruct what happened. Get it in writing just in case the trial all goes south on us, and we end up with a shit decision. Before you do that though, let me talk to her about it the next time she comes in. Maybe I can get her to think about the offer with her future in mind, rather than who her husband has or hasn't been sleeping with."

"Great. I would really appreciate that." Ruth rose to leave.

"By the way, whatever happened to Ms. Martha? I don't see her around much." He smiled and said, "You must really have her under control."

She hesitated. She figured now was as good a time as any. "Paul, I sent her to another attorney. She kept telling me she wanted to leave everything to me. You told me we couldn't draw a will that way. I didn't know what else to do with her. I haven't seen her since she went to him."

"You're kidding. Who did you send her to?"

"An old classmate of mine, Harold Vorhies."

"So, what happened? Have you talked to him since she went to see him?"

"Just briefly."

"What did he say about her will?"

Just then, Hanna walked down the hallway and stopped at Paul's doorway. "You two talkin' 'bout Martha?"

Paul said, "Yes."

"I haven't had a chance to tell either of you yet, but I just got a call from her daughter. She told me Martha died last night. They are looking for a will."

Ruth wanted to smile, to laugh, to scream *yes,* but instead she held it all in and said, "What did you tell them?"

"I told her I'd get back to her."

"Tell her to call Harold Vorhies. His number is in the attorney registry you have."

"Did he prepare her current will?"
"Yes."
Paul said, "Ruth, did she leave everything to you?"
Ruth lied as she said, "I don't have any idea. I haven't talked to Harold since he prepared it." She had in fact talked to him a number of times, but it had always been on her own personal phone—nothing anyone would ever see if they were to view previous calls made on the office phone.
"You better hope she didn't. That could affect your practice, my practice and everything else. You better hope she left it to anyone *but* you."
Ruth left at noon indicating she would return around 1:00 p.m. She normally just picked up something down the street and ate lunch in her office, but today she needed to make a call. It was important no one else listen in.
"Harold, did you hear about Martha? I understand she died last night."
"I'm not surprised to hear from you—I *am* surprised you waited this long."
"I couldn't get free. What's going on? Have you heard from her daughter?"
"Oh yes, I certainly have. She's coming in this afternoon to review her mother's will. You will probably hear her yell at me from your office. She is *not* going to be happy."
"Did you change anything in her will since we last talked?"
"Nope, everything is the same."
"Well buddy, if it all goes as it's supposed to, before long, you are going to be a hundred grand richer. And it's not going to need to be split with partners or reported to the IRS. It will be free and clear."
"Oh, I know, and *you Ruth,* are going to be a very rich woman."

Later that afternoon, Paul returned from court and walked in her office. "Have you heard any more about Martha's will?"
She figured now was as good a time as any. "Yes, I talked to Harold. He indicated he had prepared her last will and was meeting with the family later this afternoon."
"Who got the money?"
She hesitated.
"Who got the money, Ruth?"

"I did."

"Jesus Christ, are you kidding me? You got it all?"

"I think so."

He said nothing. He stood looking at her briefly, then turned around walked out her door and into his office, slamming the door behind him.

Later that night, she phoned Harold. He answered almost immediately.

"Hi Ruth. Well, we are in a hell of a mess here. You were right. She is a bitch. She's going to sue me, you and everyone else that is involved in this. I'm looking up cases involving undue influence as we speak."

"I told you about her, so it should come as no surprise."

"I showed her a copy of the will, and I thought she was literally going to piss her panties. I have never, ever seen anyone that mad—that upset."

"Did she take a copy?"

"Certainly. She was going from my office to some other lawyer's office. She already had a name. She said she had been to see him before about her mother and that firm would be handling everything for her from now on. She left so fast she never even gave me his name. I don't even know who to contact."

"I have no doubt you won't have to wait long. Are you the executor?"

"Yes. She left me in as executor. As you know, I made a recording of the conversation with Martha when she told me what she wanted. In case her daughter runs over me with her car and fricken kills me before this is all finished, the recording is in my safe."

"Are you still okay with all this? You're not getting cold feet on me, are you? Are you really concerned she might be violent? You're really not that not worried about how this is all proceeding, are you?"

"Okay, let me answer all those questions as best I can—yes, no, no. Does that adequately answer all of them? Yes, I'm in this for the long haul. I'm not worried about her being violent, although it's been a long time since I've seen anyone that mad, and no, I'm not that worried. Is your boss okay with what's going on here?"

Ruth said, "No, not really. But what can he do about it? What can anyone do about it now? It's done. He will have to live with it just like everyone else, unless a judge sets the will aside."

"Well, I can't see that happening, at least not based on what we've done to make sure it *doesn't* happen. Let me ask you one question, so I know how to answer if I'm asked. What if she wants to settle—what if she wants you to, for instance, take half, and give the other half to the family? What would your answer be to that?"

Ruth thought for a minute, and finally said, "Would telling her to go to hell, be appropriate? No, Harold, I'm not settling anything with them. Martha gave what she had to me, and I'm takin it all."

Harold considered her response, and finally said, "Okay, Ruth. So be it. I'll be in touch."

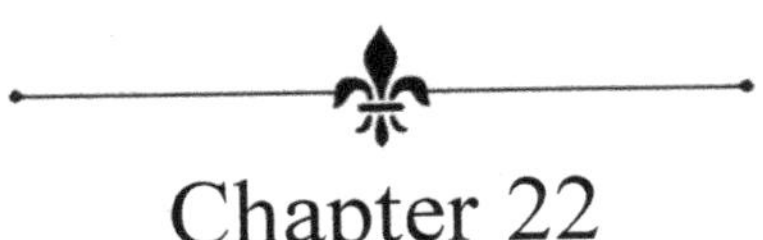

Chapter 22

Ed waited patiently, for a knock on his door. But he had already waited much longer than he had originally anticipated. The cop told him he had additional questions and would arrive by 10:00 a.m. It was eleven-fifteen. He still hadn't appeared.

It had now been over a week since he and Officer Cobb had last discussed his wife's death. He assumed the investigation was over. But apparently that was an invalid assumption. It seemed so simple to him—he didn't understand why it didn't seem that way to them.

Finally, he got the knock he was waiting for. He opened the door to find a man, short and stocky, in a shabby raincoat, with a soggy cigar, half chewed to the end, starring at him through bloodshot eyes.

"Morning sir, my name is Sam Harvey. The department turned the investigation involving your wife's death over to me to finish it all up. Mind if we visit for a moment?"

"No, no certainly not. Please come in." Ed extended his hand, and Sam shook it, weak grip and all.

As he walked past, Ed couldn't help but notice how strongly he smelled of cigars. He hoped the smell wouldn't somehow transfer to his furniture, making it less marketable.

Ed led the way to the living room, where they both had a seat while Sam reviewed the notes he had concerning his current understanding of the situation. He looked around the room, said, "Nice house," then resumed reviewing his notes.

Finally, he looked up and said, "You know they did an autopsy on your wife don't you?"

"Yes, they told me that was standard in cases of this nature."

"Yes, yes, it is. They were exactly right on that. It *is* standard in this type of situation. Did you know they found a mark on her face, on her forehead, which occurred before she died—as if something had struck her in the face before she passed away? Did you know that?"

"No, but I guess it's no surprise. She could have hit the boat, or hit something when she fell in, who knows."

Sam continued to review his notes. He looked up and said, "I tried to take a look at the boat and have someone determine whether her DNA or anything from her body might still remain on the boat and if so where it might have been located. But they had already rented it out multiple times—and cleaned it after it came back in—multiple times. Of course, at the time it happened, no one was looking at the situation as a crime."

"Are you now?"

"Am I now, what?"

"Looking at this situation as a crime?"

"No, not really. I was asked to tie down some loose ends and that's all I anticipate I will do. You know, she's got this relative that's pretty upset. She thinks you killed her. She calls me almost every day."

"Is that why you continue to investigate?"

"Mostly, yes, mostly. Now, as I understand it, you had all your money in joint accounts, and you ended up with all of it, is that correct?"

"Yes, as she would have if that had happened to me."

"How much was that? Just round it off. I don't need actual amounts."

"Around two million."

"And you got it all?"

"Yes."

"And the house?"

"Yes."

Sam again looked around, "Nice house."

Ed never responded.

"Now, why did you decide to go out on the lake at dusk? Any reason?"

"No, not really. I was watching TV. She had been cleaning all day. She said let's go take a buzz around the lake, and that's what we did."

"You hadn't planned this the day before?"

"No."

"Well then why did you rent the boat for Saturday night, the day before?"

Ed got a lump in his throat. He smiled and said, "Well, to be honest, I actually figured *I* would use it Saturday night. I had anticipated *I* might use it, but not the two of us, if that makes sense to you."

“Oh sure, sure that makes sense.” He continued reviewing his notes, as he said, “You don’t have any other lady friends, do you—that you are seeing?”

“No, no of course not.”

“What are you going to do now that she’s gone? Are you staying here or moving on?”

“For now, I’ll probably stay put, but who knows. I don’t really know that many people around here. I might move to where I have a little more family.”

“Why did you come here in the first place? Did you meet Janice on line or something?”

“No, no I just had always wanted to live in Nashville. Exciting town. I moved here, met Janice through the church, and we married.”

“That’s that little Baptist church not far from here? Is that where you met her?”

“Yes.”

“Are you a religious man?”

“I’m not exactly sure what that means, I guess, but I do attend church.”

“Have you been back to church since Janice died?”

“Oh sure. Yup, I surely have.”

“She’s been gone a month now. How many times have you been back?”

Ed paused and considered the question. “I don’t know, I guess. Everything has been kind of a blur since she died.”

The truth was that he hadn’t been back once. Janice was dead—why go back?

Sam continued to write.

“What day were you married?”

“I can’t...remember…right off the top of my head. We had been married about a year and a half.”

Sam peered over the top of his glasses, and said, “You only been married a year and a half and you can’t remember the date?” He laughed. “I been married forty years. Everybody, including my wife—no, especially her—knows I can’t remember jack shit, but she would kill me if I forgot the day we were married.”

Edward smiled and cleared his throat, but said nothing. This was clearly not going as he had planned.

“Now, let’s talk about your life prior to Nashville. You said you had been married. How did those marriages end?"

Ed hesitated just a moment before he answered, uncertain how to avoid this particular issue. Finally, he said, "I have been married a couple of times. Both ended in divorce. I finally thought I had found the woman I could spend the rest of my life with here—and now this."

"And I believe you told Officer Cobb you were from Colorado, correct?"

"Yes."

"Where about in Colorado, Ed?"

Shit, he really didn't want to get into this, but he was trapped. "Oh, around Denver. Around the Denver area."

"You got kids, Ed?"

"No."

"Never had none?"

"No."

"Never married other than to the woman in Colorado and to Janice?"

Time to lie. "Nope."

"You have her body cremated?"

"Yes. That is what she wanted?"

"When did you combine all this money together? How long had you been married before you did that?"

"Probably a year. It was her idea by the way."

"So, what's that make you worth now, Ed?"

"I don't know exactly, I guess."

"Just take a guess. I assume the house went to you too?"

"Yes. Probably including the house maybe five million."

"Rich man. How did you make all *your* money, Ed?"

"Oh, different things. Stock market, real estate, different things."

"Did this all happen in Colorado?"

"Mostly, yes."

"You never lived anywhere else?"

That question didn't sound like a question. It sounded like he knew the answer and just wanted it verified. This conversation had reached the point where it could go no further. This interrogation was entirely different than the one handled by Officer Cobb, and it seemed to have reached the point where the officer was no longer investigating him. It seemed he already had his mind made up and was just seeking more information to confirm his conclusion.

"You know, Sam, I can call you Sam, can't I? Or do you prefer I call you officer, or Mr. Harvey, or something else?"

"No, Ed, Sam is fine."

"You know, Sam, I think we've gone about as far as we're going. I think I need an attorney. You probably better leave now, unless you are ready to charge me with something."

"Now wait. I'm really almost finished. I just have a few more questions for you and then I'm done. How was your relationship with your last wife? Could you give me her name and number? If I could just visit with her a moment maybe we could end the investigation."

Ed stood. "Time to go, Mr. Harvey."

Slowly Sam got to his feet. As he turned to walk toward the door, he said, "You're not going anywhere are you, Ed?"

"No. I have no plans to leave the area at this time."

"Just call and let us know if your plans change, okay?" He turned and extended his hand.

Ed shook it and said, "I will. Either I will or my attorney will."

He watched as Sam walked out the door, finally ending his review of his notes as he opened his car door, sat down and drove away,

Once Ed could no longer see the vehicle, he walked in the garage, and pulled his burner phone out from under the seat of his car. He autodialed Patricia, who answered immediately.

"How did it go?"

"Not well. He asked way too many questions. I finally ended it when I told him I was going to see an attorney."

"Oh shit. What are we going to do?"

"Now, just relax, Patricia, just relax. I'll find an attorney. Hopefully they'll be able to put this all to rest quickly and without any further problem. Let me get back to you."

"Did he continue to poke around in your past? You said the last one did that—did this one do that?"

"Yes. He wanted to know all about my prior marriage *and* wanted to visit with my prior wife. I had previously told him I only had one. I didn't want him knowing there were others. It got pretty sticky for a while."

"So, what are you going to do?"

"I'm not sure. I told him I was going to get an attorney, just like I told you, but I may wait a bit and see what he does with the information he has, *if* he does anything."

“What attorney are you going to, if you do go to one? You don’t know anyone around here. How are you going to find one?”

“When I do employ one, *if* it becomes necessary, I want a woman lawyer. I think I work best with women. I read an article a while back about some woman lawyer who got a guy off a drug charge. She took the case to trial and won it. I might try her first.”

“Who is she? What’s her name?’

“Andrews is her name, I think. Yes, that’s it—Ruth Andrews.”

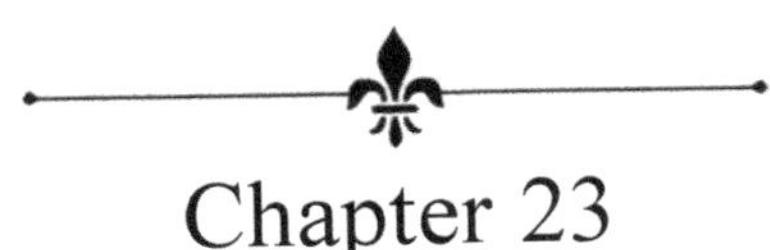

Chapter 23

The last couple of weeks at the office had been difficult to say the least. Ruth knew Paul was upset—he didn't try to hide his disgust with the situation involving the VanArsdayle will. But she just didn't understand why he remained so upset to the extent he had an issue even responding to her 'good morning.'

There was no question but what he had concluded that Ruth should have somehow made *certain* she received nothing from Martha. But when it happened *anyway,* you would have thought he would have wanted to know the particulars—why it happened and whether there remained a possible violation of the cannons of ethics.

He had remained unusually quiet since the will had been made public. It was difficult to discuss *anything* with him. He simply didn't want to communicate with her. He had made that perfectly clear.

She heard him walk through the outer office door and start down the hallway. As he approached her office she said, "Paul, do you have a minute?"

He stopped at her office door and said, "What?"

"We need to talk. It's time the silent treatment ended here one way or the other."

"Just a minute."

When he walked through her office door a few minutes later, he had removed his jacket and left his briefcase in his own office. He closed the door behind him.

He sat down, as he said, "What do you want to talk about, Ruth?"

She leaned back in her chair and said, "You know what I want to talk about. I understand you are concerned about the VanArsdayle will, but I'm not sure why. I told you I didn't prepare it. I told you I had nothing to do with it. Why are you so upset?"

He thought for a moment, crossed his legs, and said, "Did you know I've had prior issues with the bar association?"

"No, not really. You have never mentioned anything about it, and…no, I know nothing about that. What kind of problems?"

"It doesn't matter. The specifics are irrelevant. But I've been before them twice, and the last time they told me if I ever appeared before them again, they would most likely suspend me, or disbar me. Since the last hearing, I've tried to be careful, no matter what I was doing, to stay under the radar, to stay well within the rules. Every penny I make from this office I use to take care of my wife. I don't have any leeway here. I'm strapped. Then, at this point, to have an employee of mine do something I told her specifically not to do, and place this office right square dab in the middle of the spotlight again…"

He stopped in mid-sentence.

It was clear he was extremely angry and beyond frustrated.

She let him cool off for a moment before responding.

"Okay, first of all, I knew nothing about all of your prior problems. But, what does her last will and testament have to do with those problems anyway?"

"I have no doubt the bar association is going to look at this as a possible violation of the rules. You, after having dealt with her as her attorney, are now the sole beneficiary of everything she has. Regardless of how that came about, there is no doubt in my mind her kids will file a complaint against you and against this office. Now, I assume there will also be a lawsuit filed to set that will aside. If you lose, if the facts support their position, you and I will both most likely be disbarred. And I don't know about you, but I really need money right now, as does my sick wife."

"But what if we win the will contest, Paul? What do you think the situation will be then as concerns the bar association?"

"I don't know. They may still go after us. But certainly, if it's determined you *are* entitled to the money, the chance of a bar association problem is much smaller."

"I don't understand. Why does this involve you? You had nothing to do with it."

"I have no doubt they will look at me as well as you. I will end up before them, which is just what they told me not to do. To be honest, I have no idea what they will do if you win the case. All I know is that you've put me, this office, and your career, in jeopardy."

"I knew nothing about all the prior issues. I'm sorry, Paul. I didn't mean for all this to happen."

"Needless to say, I'll be hoping for a successful conclusion concerning the litigation issue. I have no doubt the bar association will wait until the trial has concluded before they come to a conclusion concerning what they are going to do. I'll be available to help concerning the trial in whatever fashion I may be needed. Obviously, I have a substantial interest in the outcome."

Once he got it off his chest, Paul was a different person. During the course of the day, they discussed many of the trials that were scheduled in the near future. He appeared to be his old self. She had no idea there were collateral issues which would now involve Paul and the contents of Martha's will.

Hopefully, everything would turn out well for both of them—she certainly wanted to continue to work in his office, regardless of the eventual size of her net worth.

Later that afternoon, as she considered what she might potentially be 'worth', and the impending, inevitable litigation, she figured it was time for an update. She auto dialed Harold. He answered immediately.

"Hey, Ruth. I was just thinking about you. I just got a copy of the petition they're getting ready to file. They don't like you. Martha's kids—they don't like you—at all. They call you every name they can get away with and still get by with putting it in the petition. Do you want me to fax a copy to you?"

"Why did they fax it to you in advance? Why didn't they just file it?"

"Why do you think?"

"Are they wanting to settle?"

"In the worst way. I think you could probably offer them a quarter of Martha's net worth and they would take it."

"I've already told you how I feel about that, I still feel the same way."

"I have told them that. They are getting ready to file it. There shouldn't be much discovery, so I'm thinkin maybe an early trial date. I will talk to the attorney that represents them and let you know his thoughts. I'll fax a copy of the petition to you."

"By the way, who represents them?"

"George Grisham."

"What do you know about him?"

"I don't really know him at all. I've checked with my partners though, and they say at one time, he was a pretty good trial lawyer. But they say now his has age has taken its toll. I will give him a call and tell him you aren't interested in settling. Then I will give you a call and let you know what he says—what his approach might be."

Later that evening, after Ruth reviewed a copy of the petition, she thought about Paul and those issues that involved his profession along with his livelihood. But she ultimately concluded that wasn't her problem. His problems obviously started long before she was even employed.

It didn't matter anyway. The facts were as they were, and she had an opportunity to become rich as a result of the will. She didn't care who got in her way. She wanted the money regardless of who got hurt, even if it meant neither she nor her boss ever practiced law another day.

Chapter 24

A cold November wind blew him off the street and through the precinct door. It was early, before dawn, and Sam Harvey couldn't sleep. So, he did what he always did when he had a case on his mind—he got up and went to work. The Hall case was bothering him. He needed to review his notes—for the fourth or fifth time.

Something was wrong. The whole 'situation' just didn't feel right to him. It was like building a new home which looked fine upon first glance, but then after walking through the front door, you discover that the only bathroom is in the attic. Something was just plain wrong.

He had been at his desk reviewing the file for a couple of hours before he noticed Terry walking toward him. He peered at him over the top of his glasses as his partner reached his own desk, and said, "Morning, Slick. Glad you could make it."

"Go to hell. How long have you been here old man? Did you just spend the night here? You know, normal people have lives beyond their jobs. I know that's a difficult concept for you to understand, but that's the one I live by—I do have a life beyond this office, and that isn't ever going to change. What are you looking at inside that folder—pornography?"

Sam never said a word, content to laugh on the inside and irritate the living hell out of his partner on the outside.

Terry pulled the files he needed to review before he left to interview a couple of locals concerning a murder. As he did, he said, "Did you hear John Barkley was shot last night? Took two to the back of the head. It looks like another Oliver hit to me."

"Yeah, I heard that too. It does sound like his work. I also heard that the two weren't getting along, so we might want to look into that one ourselves. I don't want that investigation assigned to no one else, that's for sure."

"Does it bother you at all that he's threatened you? I mean, there are other people that can work on this, you know. You sure as hell have your hands full with other cases. It just seems to me as personal as this one has become it might be best for you to distance yourself from it. We got other good people that could handle it. What do you think?"

Sam never even looked up.

After a few minutes, Terry said, "Okay then. I guess we can look into that murder too. By the way, what the hell are you so involved in? You've had your nose stuck in that one file since I got here. What are you looking at?"

Sam said nothing, continuing to shuffle papers and study notes.

Terry waited for a response. He finally went back to reviewing his own files, content to let silence rule the moment.

Thirty minutes later, Sam finally put the folder down, looked at Terry and said, "This Hall case just isn't right. Something is wrong."

"You mean the drowning case—the one you investigated when I was out of town?"

"Yes."

Terry laid his file down, and said, "Do you want to talk about it?"

"Sure. There were no witnesses. She drowned after dark while on Piercy Priest Lake. He says she fell out of the back of the boat. It just seems to clear cut."

"Could she swim?"

"No one seems to know."

"Is there a lot of money?"

"Millions."

"Does he get it all?"

"Sure does. He told me it was a spur of the moment trip, but I know he reserved the boat the day before. He said he originally thought he might use it himself, to go fishing, but then on Saturday his wife decided to go, so they both went. I'm not buying that. I think he had something in mind and it didn't have nothin' to do with the fish in that lake'."

"Any kids?"

"None. And they had been married less than two years. It just doesn't fit for me."

"Was there an autopsy performed?"

"Yes. She had a mark on her forehead. Of course, we can't prove how it got there, but it's still a factor a jury could consider."

"How did he meet her, on line?"

"No. He met her at church. I asked him if he had been back to church since she died. He told me he had, but I talked to the minister and some of the people that go there on a regular basis. They say they can't remember him coming back since she died."

"Do any of them know anything about the case?"

"They don't seem to."

"Has the guy always lived here? What is his background?"

"You know, I'm about to find out. Talking this through with you has confirmed my conclusion that I need to take this further—I can't just let it sit here without a little further research."

"You're welcome. Anytime. You know, I live just to talk these cases through with you. Let me know if there's anything else…."

Sam had phone in hand as he punched in the numbers. He looked at Terry and said, "Shut the hell up."

"Art, Sam Harvey. How are you?"

"Good, good Sam. How is everything in Nashville?"

"Good. What about Denver? You got snow out there yet?"

"Not yet, but funny you should ask. It's on the way. What's going on in Nashville?"

"You got a second?"

"I do."

"I got a guy down here whose wife just died. She drowned, and I'm a little concerned she may have drowned with a little help from him. He told me he came from around Denver. He hasn't lived here long, and I'm just wondering if you guys have anything on him. Can you do a little looking for me? He's been here about two years. Can you run your records on the guy—you know, do a little research for me and see what might pop up?"

"Did you try the computer…Google him, and all that crap?"

"I did that. I couldn't find anything. I thought maybe you could ask around and see if the guys might remember his name or something. I'm specifically wondering if this is the first wife he's lost in this manner. He says he ended his prior marriage in a divorce, but I'm just not so sure."

"Absolutely. What's his name?"

"Edward Hall."

"There might be a few people with that name out here. You got a middle for him?"

"Let me look."

Sam sorted through paperwork until he came to the information provided him by the investigating officer. "Yeah, his middle initial is B—for Bennett."

"I'll get back to you as soon as I can. Great to hear from you, Sam."

A week past, and he never gave it much thought—he had more important issues to work through rather than what was most likely just a routine drowning anyway.

His phone rang. It was Art.

"Hey. How's everything in Denver?"

"Good, Sam. I just wanted to let you know we were able to find a few things on this guy you were interested in."

Sam picked up a pen, and said, "Great. What did you find out?"

"Well, the first thing we did was check marriage records starting a couple of years ago and working back. We assumed there were no name changes. If there was, we obviously wouldn't have a chance of locating him. We found where a guy by the name of Edward B. Hall married a Jacqueline a few years back."

"Sounds about right."

"Good thing we had a middle name. We figured it could be the right guy. So, we checked divorce records after the date of the marriage and nothing showed up. So, if he told you the truth and he moved to Nashville from here, he didn't divorce her."

Sam laid his pen down, sat back in his chair and said, "Sounds like the son-of-a-bitch lied to me."

"There's more. Then, since we had both of their names, we started doing research concerning both of them, and low and behold we find a brief obituary in the Denver paper showing where a local citizen had died from a fall off a cliff near Estes Park while hiking with her husband. It went on to say she was survived by a loving husband, but the article never mentioned his name. She had no children or other heirs mentioned in the obituary. But we thought it was strange the obituary didn't name him. That's unusual. I'm assuming they were asked not to print his name. That's why there's nothing on the net about him. He's making sure his name doesn't appear anywhere."

"I don't suppose you have any of those reports from the sheriff of the county Estes Park is located in, do you?"

"No, I don't Sam, but I could probably get them for you."

"No, don't bother. I think it's time to make a trip to your neck of the woods, Art. I'll be up there within the next week. I'll stop in to see you first thing when I get to town. Thanks for all your work. I owe you one."

As he terminated the call, Terry said, "What's going on?"

"It sounds to me like we may have a black widower on our hands. Hall's previous wife died in Colorado. He wasn't divorced, she fell off a cliff. Now, I wonder if there may have been more."

"What are you going to do from here on?"

"I think I'll head to the lovely state of Colorado, slick."

"Great. When do we leave?"

Sam laughed. "You idiot. You really think you are going? You got work to do here. You aren't going anywhere. I'm sure as hell not going on no trip with you."

"Whatever, you old bastard. When are you leaving?"

"As soon as I can."

"Okay. If anything comes up concerning Oliver, I'll take care of it."

Sam leaned forward in his chair, pointed his finger at Terry and said, "Don't you do a god damn thing concerning Dean Oliver until you at least call me. And I mean *nothing.*"

Terry smiled and said, "You're not taking me with you, so I will just have to take care of whatever comes up, including anything involving Oliver. Now, get your old ugly ass out of here. I'll take care of business here while you're gone. Who knows—I may even arrest that Oliver guy myself. Never know."

Sam never even looked up. It was obvious his partner was upset he wasn't going to Denver, but now wasn't the time to spar with him. He was busy locating phone numbers for the airlines. He needed a reservation on the first plane to Denver—the sooner the better.

Chapter 25

Although unusual for this time of year, the ground was covered in a thin layer of white, wet snow. Very seldom did anyone use the words 'snow' and 'Nashville' in the same sentence during *any* month of the year, including December. But nonetheless, it was an issue all early morning drivers had to contend with while on their way to work this morning.

Ruth felt fortunate she was able to take a bus and not fight that thin layer of snow, along with the stupidity of so many Nashville drivers as they ventured out into that great unknown—out into that incredible danger associated with driving in snow. It amounted to only a short inch and would most likely disappear by 9:00 a.m.

This morning, rather than going to her office, she would meet Paul in Harold's office and they would discuss the will contest. It was time to determine trial strategy and discuss exactly what their position might be at the time of trial.

She had to smile as she continued to watch people drive by the bus, their hands glued to the steering wheel, as if letting go would somehow result in a swift, painful removal of their body and soul to a different dimension.

Upon arriving at Harold's office, Paul was already there. They proceeded to a conference room, where Harold had a large coffeemaker and a box of pastries waiting for them while they planned.

Paul said, "I really think the first thing we should discuss is whether we are going to try to settle with her kids or just move forward—forget any attempt at negotiating."

Both looked at Ruth.

"I'm not interested in settling. That's been my position from the day I learned about the contents of the will, and I'm not changing my mind. She didn't like her children for good reason. They get what they deserve, which is zero."

Paul smiled and said, "Well then, okay. I guess that part of the discussion has quickly been put to rest. Let's talk about discovery and trial. Harold, you already filed an answer to their petition, correct?"

"Yes. I just basically denied everything. I have no doubt they are going to want to take depositions of the two of you. Paul, are you going to testify?"

"I am if you need me."

"I think it's important that you testify as to Martha's thoughts involving leaving everything to her kids. She discussed that with you, didn't she?"

"Oh, yes. She made it certain on more than one occasion that she did *not* want to leave anything to them. I talked her out of that approach many times, and left them in the will, but it wasn't what she wanted."

"Great. I also want you to testify as to her demeanor—that it appeared to you she was lucid and competent each time you saw her. I'm sure they will object to you testifying using any type of medical phraseology because you're not a doctor, and of course, are not able to testify concerning any type of medical conclusion. I might have her doctor testify to that. While competency is not really an issue, I still want to make sure it remains a nonfactor throughout the trial. Her doctor can settle that issue. I've already talked to him. He told me she was as competent as anyone he ever knew, right up until the end."

"Are you going to call any of the neighbors?"

"Yes. I have talked to a couple of them, and they are willing to testify she was her old self right up until she died. They will also testify she hated her kids. The neighbors of course, don't know much about Martha's feelings concerning Ruth. They really never discussed her."

Paul said, "Harold, assuming you are going to testify, you can't do both—testify *and* be the attorney of record. Who's going to try it?"

Harold looked at Ruth, then at Paul as he said, "You, if you'll do it. Do you have a problem with trying it? We certainly both have faith in your abilities."

He hesitated for a moment, took a deep breath, and said, "Okay, if that's what you both want. Do you want me to just go ahead then and respond to their petition?"

"Yes. Deny everything in our response and go ahead and file it."

Paul said, "Do you know the opposing attorney yet?"

"Yes. George Grisham."

"I know him well. Pompous prick, but a good attorney. We go back a few years. He will work hard for his client, but he tends sometimes to lose sight of the prize at the end of the journey. He can really get wrapped up in issues that aren't that important. He is extremely meticulous, to a fault and really a bore, but he's a good attorney. We will have our hands full."

"What about a trial date?"

"George told me they wanted a date as soon as possible. We need to get depositions out of the way, but with both sides wanting a speedy conclusion, I can see us in court by mid-March."

"Ruth, do you have any issues concerning testifying?"

"No. I know what she told me about her kids, and when the issue of leaving her money to me came up, I called Harold. I was done with her from that day on. That's exactly what happened and that's what I'm prepared to testify to."

As Ruth reconsidered her answer, she mentally concluded that wasn't exactly truthful, in that Martha never really said she wanted to leave everything outright to her. But no one would ever know the rest of the answer, of that she was certain. She looked at Harold and said, "Have you reviewed the video? Are we okay with it?"

Paul said, "What video?"

"Oh, I thought we discussed that. Maybe not. Harold has a video, done by an independent firm, that shows Martha answering questions about leaving her money to me and not her children. I've seen it. It's pretty convincing to say the least. What are you thinking, Harold? Have they seen it yet?"

"No and when they do, it *could*, and I emphasize *could*, make a difference in whether they proceed any further."

Paul said, "Is it that damaging to their case?"

"I think it is."

Ruth said, "I do too. In the video, she is as firm as she always was with all three of us, concerning not wanting to leave her children anything. I'm assuming we will have no trouble getting it into evidence."

Harold said, "No, I don't think that will be a problem at all. Of course, George will do all he can to keep it out, but I don't think that will be a problem either."

"If they lose this trial, Harold, do you have a feel as to whether they're going to want to appeal the decision?"

"You know, I'm not sure. Neither child is wealthy, which was why they continued to come to Martha for money—they have none. So, unless something happens at trial which weakens our case, I don't really think they will appeal, assuming, that is, we win and they must then make a decision in that respect."

"Who do you think the trial judge might be?"

"I'm really not sure at this point."

Paul said, "I know most of the judges, so as soon as we know who it is, maybe I can shed some light on how they might approach the case."

Harold grinned and said, "Okay, thanks Paul. Good to know you are so familiar with all the judges. I'll remember that not only for this hearing, but for any other hearing in the future where you and I might be on opposite sides of the table."

Paul laughed and said, "I probably should have kept that bit of information to myself."

After discussing a few additional fine points of the trial, Harold stood and said, "Okay guys, I think we have gone about as far today as we can. I need to be in court in an hour, and I've a few items I still need to review. Let's plan on meeting prior to depos to review everything one more time."

Both Ruth and Paul stood to leave. Harold looked at Paul and said, "Well, you've now had a chance, at least superficially, to listen to all the evidence and consider the witnesses we have to present. What are your thoughts concerning our chance of winning?"

"Based on what I've heard today, I'm not sure we can lose. Obviously better factual situations then we have involving other cases have ended up in the shitter, but it appears to me, they will have a hard time winning. I think we have an excellent case."

Ruth never said a word, but she could feel the beating of her own heart as she considered a winning result, realizing she would be, in that instant, worth more money than she figured she would ever earn in a lifetime.

Chapter 26

Sam was able to catch a flight to Denver later that afternoon. He checked into a downtown hotel and had just started to review all his notes one last time before he met with Art Sands the next morning at the precinct located near his hotel.

Just as he was ready to shut out the light and get some sleep, his phone rang. "Hey, you old fart, what's going on? Have you met with the cops in Denver yet?"

"What do you want? I thought you went home at night and shut your phone off. Isn't that what most you young cops do now days?"

"Only when they have a partner like you."

"I'm tired. Now, what the hell do you want?"

"There was another murder tonight. Jacki Thompson went down. She was shot twice in the back of the head."

"Did you talk to Oliver?"

"Yup. That was the first place I went. Of course, he had an alibi, so there wasn't much I could do, but I just wanted you to know he asked about you."

Sam sat up. "What did he say?"

"He wanted to know where the hell you were. He said he was going to file a complaint against you for harassment. He said you were behind blaming him for every murder in Nashville. He got pretty upset. I told him to back off, but he was pretty agitated."

"Good. That's when they make their mistakes—when they get plenty pissed off. Don't bother him until I get home. We can both go see him again then. Just leave him be until I get there."

"Okay. I just thought you should know. I still think you should remove yourself from anything involving him."

"I need to go. See you when I get home. Don't forget to go to work in the morning."

"Real funny, you jerk."

At precisely 9:00 a.m. he walked through the precinct door, where Art was waiting for him. He escorted Sam to a conference room, where they could talk privately. Art handed a file to him and said, "I made a copy of what we found here in Denver. It's not much, but we did no investigating concerning the fall since it didn't happen here. The only items in there are a copy of the marriage license and a copy of the obituary."

"Did you run a criminal history on the guy?"

"Yeah. He has nothing on his record. It's as bare as a baby's bottom."

"You said there is no mention in the obituary about her having any heirs?"

"Nope."

"Well, if he killed her, it was the perfect murder."

"Correct."

"Could you do me a favor? Do you know anyone involved with law enforcement in Estes Park? Could you call them and see if they have any records concerning the fall?"

"Sure. I know most of those guys. Our family goes to the Estes Park area frequently during the summers. Normally, I stop in just to say hi. I'll call Jack Dillard and see what he says. Wait here."

A short while later, Art walked back in the room. "They got a file. Jack actually investigated the case. I told him I thought you were going to drive up and talk to him. He said he would be waiting. He is in all day."

Right after he had finished an abbreviated lunch in Loveland, Colorado, he drove up the Big Thompson Canyon and into Estes Park. He located the police station where Jack was waiting for him.

As they sat down at one of their conference tables, Jack said, "I remember the case well. They were hiking alone, late summer, and she fell."

"Any witnesses?"

"Nope."

"Anything out of the ordinary?"

"Nothing at all. We wrapped things up quickly because there was just nothing about the situation that indicated there was any foul play."

"Can I take a look at your notes?"

"Sure."

"Did the guy happen to mention where he lived prior to moving to

Denver?"

"No. I doubt anyone ever asked him. No need."

Jack made a copy of all the paperwork. After a cursory review by Sam, he thanked the department and drove back to Denver.

When he arrived, Art was preparing to leave for the day.

"Art, let me ask you one last question. During your short investigation for me, did you ever see anything that might indicate where this guy came from? I'm thinking he wasn't from here. I just got a gut feeling we are dealing with a black widower here, and I'd really like to know where he lived before he moved here."

"No, I never saw anything that indicated where he was from."

Sam quickly looked at the obituary. "I see they list their home address in here. Do you think the post office might have a prior address for this guy when he moved here?"

"They might."

"Would you drive down there with me and check it out before you go home? I'd like someone local with me when I visit with them."

"Sure."

Upon reaching the post office serving the location for the address, they talked to the post master who checked his records. In their forwarding information, he quickly determined Ed Hall *did* show a prior street, city and state. He had moved to Denver from Sacramento, California.

That night, Sam called Terry and told him he would be a few more days. He needed to follow up on one more lead. He then called and booked a flight for Sacramento, leaving first thing in the morning.

Upon arriving in Sacramento, he took a cab to the local downtown precinct and met with the chief. After a discussion concerning the reason he was there, he sent an officer with Sam to the courthouse to review death records.

They asked the clerk to review death records starting approximately four years ago and go back in time from there, looking for anyone by the name of Edward Bennett Hall. He returned shortly, indicating a woman by the name of Dorothy Hall had fallen and died in her home about four years ago. He further indicated the name of her husband was Edward B. Hall.

Sam had the clerk make a copy of the record, then returned to the precinct. There had been a file made concerning the death, but the file indicated there was absolutely no indication of wrongdoing. No charges were filed and the investigation was closed shortly after it was opened.

Once again there were no children—no one to complain about the facts or circumstances surrounding the incident.

Sam flew home from Sacramento later that day. The next morning, he was in the office by 7:00 a.m. already reviewing the notes and messages on his desk which were placed there while he was gone.

Terry walked in an hour later, and said, "How was the trip?"

Sam said nothing. Terry started to look over his own files, making notes as he did. About an hour later, Terry said, "How was the trip?"

Sam looked at him over the top of his glasses and said, "When did you get here?"

"I've been here for at least three hours. How was the trip?"

"My ass—you haven't been here that long."

"How was the goddamn trip?"

"Good." He leaned back in his chair and folded his hands over his stomach. "I was able to go back two wives. He killed them both, one in Denver and one in Sacramento. I don't know what happened prior to that, but I don't guess I need to. I *do* know what he did in both those cities. The guy lied to me. He's murdered at least two prior women and got off without an investigation of any kind. He is a black widower and he's gone as far as he gonna go."

"Sounds like you got him. But, why was he never charged in either of those two cities?"

"Absolutely no evidence. This guy's good, believe me, he's really good."

"By the way, have you documented the trip? I mean like made notes on your computer—or maybe made copies of your notes for me, so I can refresh my memory from time to time about the case *we* are working on?"

"Not yet. I will. I'm going to get him in here and give him one last chance to come clean before I book him. What about Oliver? Anything new?"

"No. they haven't charged anyone for her murder yet. I don't have any doubt he did it, but no one's been booked. When are you going to get this guy Hall in here? I would like to sit in on the interview if you don't mind."

"I don't know. I'll contact him and set up a time. If you are around,

I'll let you know."

Terry started to look over some new paperwork, as he said, "You know I've heard that same thing from you a thousand times before. I really don't know why I even waste my time. I should ask for a new partner. You aren't going to let me know. You have no intention of letting me know. You will do it alone like you do most everything around here, even though I am your partner, you jerk."

Sam smiled, but never looked up.

Chapter 27

Outside, it was a cold winter's day, but inside those precinct walls, Sam Harvey was warming up, preparing to put a suspect on the hot seat. He had called Ed Hall and asked him to either come to his precinct office or he would come to his house, which ever was acceptable. Sam told him he had some additional questions which needed to be answered before he could close out his investigation. Ed said he would meet with him at the precinct, and they arranged a convenient time.

Once he arrived, Sam wasted no time. "I just have a couple of questions about each death if you have a few moments. But, first of all, have you hired an attorney like you said you were going to?"

"No. I wanna make damn sure I need one before I lay out the fee for a retainer. Do I need one? What do you mean 'each death'?"

"First things first. I can't tell you whether you need an attorney or not. Do you want one? If you do, we can stop and you can call him."

Ed thought for a moment, and finally said, "No, let's go ahead for now. I assume I can stop whenever I want and get one, can't I?"

"Absolutely."

"Then let's proceed for now. What do you mean by 'each death'?"

"Let me just get started and it will become clear. First, I have a question about how you met Janice here in Nashville. How did you first meet her?"

"Like I told you before, through the church, why?"

"You just started going to that church out of the blue and met her there?'

"Yes."

"She just happened to be rich, no children, single and you just happened to meet her by chance?"

"Yes."

Sam jotted down a few notes, then said, "And again, why did you rent that boat on Friday when you said the boat ride with her on

Saturday was spur of the moment?"

"I changed that. I told you it wasn't. I had considered going out by myself late Saturday afternoon and fishing which is why I reserved it on Friday. Saturday, she decided she wanted to go." Ed looked around nervously. "Do you think I need a lawyer?"

"That is all up to you. I haven't charged you with anything. I am still trying to get the facts straight. But if you want to get a lawyer it's up to you."

Ed thought for it for a moment, then said, "What else do you want to know?"

"Did someone introduce you to Janice?"

"Not that I recall, no. We just met by ourselves in church."

"Okay. I think that's all I have for Janice. Now let's talk about Colorado."

"What about Colorado?"

"Didn't you say you lived there before you came here?"

"Yes. What about it?"

"Did you tell me your marriage there ended in divorce?"

He hesitated. "I don't recall. Why do you ask?"

"How *did* your marriage end there, Mr. Hall?"

"What difference does it make?"

"Probably none. How did it end?"

Again, a slight hesitation, before he said, "She passed away."

"I thought you told me it ended in divorce."

"No, I don't think so."

"How did she pass away?"

"What difference does it make? She's gone and that's that."

"What was her name?"

"Why?"

"Okay, let me ask you this. Was her name Jacqueline, and did she die in a fall?"

"I'm not sure I should answer any more questions today."

"This information is all a matter of public record, Mr. Hall. You can either tell me or I will just look it up. The more you cooperate with me the easier this is going to be to finish up."

Again, Ed nervously cleared his throat, but finally said, "True, true. Yes, that was her name, and yes, she died in a fall off a cliff."

"Did she have a family?"

"No children, no."

"Did you inherit what she had?"

"What she had I got, yes. It wasn't a lot, but I got what she had."

"How did you meet her?"

"Oh, I don't remember when I first met her…maybe a singles club or something."

"Were you introduced?"

"No."

"And it was after her death, you moved to Nashville?"

"Yes."

"Okay, let me just take a moment and get that all down. This information should be what I need to finish up."

Ed sat patiently, while Sam made notes. Once completed, Sam said, "Now, where did you live prior to Denver, Ed?"

"Do you really need that information to finish your investigation concerning my wife's death here?"

"I really do. My captain said to get it—I am just following his instructions. I'm really almost done here, Mr. Hall. Just bear with me another minute or two."

After scribbling his notes down on a small pad, Sam said, "Sacramento, California—were you married there too?"

"I was."

"How did you meet her, Mr. Hall?"

"That was a long time ago. I honestly don't remember."

"I assume someone introduced you?"

"Might have, I just don't recall."

"What happened to her?"

"Again, why is that relevant to what happened here?"

"It probably isn't, but did you divorce her?"

"Yes."

"Hmm, okay. Did she have any children?"

"A few, but we weren't close."

"She didn't have a fall and die while you were married?"

"Nope, divorced her. Nice woman but we couldn't live together."

"And again, Ed, all this money you have accumulated, you say you made in real estate deals and the markets, is that correct?"

"Yes, that's correct."

"Were you seeing another woman at the time Janice died?"

"Certainly not."

"Where did you come from when you moved to Sacramento?"

Ed crossed his legs, hesitated, but finally said, "Canada. I lived in Canada for quite a while before I moved to Sacramento."

"Where about?"

"All over. I never lived in one place very long."

"Were you married in Canada?"

"Nope."

Prior marriages or prior addresses were of no concern to Sam anyway. He had most of the information he needed already. But he wanted a response to that question, just to observe his demeanor and hear what he had to say.

Sam closed the folder, smiled and said, "You know, I think that's all I need for today. You're not planning on leaving the area are you, Ed? I mean, you mentioned you were listing the house. Has that been done?"

"Yes, but we haven't had any lookers yet. I imagine it will be a while before it is sold and closed."

"Ed, who's the 'we'? I thought the house was yours and yours alone."

"Oh, sorry, it is. I was just used to it belonging to the both of us, my wife and I. Sorry."

"If you do plan on leaving town, just let me know."

Ed got up to leave and as he did, he said, "Oh, I will. Thanks."

Sam rose, they shook hands and Ed walked out the precinct door. He was just finishing up his notes, when Terry walked in.

"I just finished interviewing Ed Hall."

Terry sat, and as he did, he said, "I thought you were going to include me in the interview. At least that's what you told me the last time we talked about the case. Of course, I don't expect you to remember. I know memory, at your age, is the first to go, right after your ability to get it up. So, what happened?"

"He said what I expected him to say. I knew he was lying concerning some of his answers, and I'm assuming he lied on others. But I didn't call him on those answers because I just wasn't sure."

"Did you arrest him?"

"Nope."

"Why not?"

"You know, I got a feeling he's not working alone."

"Why?"

"I just do."

“I mean why do you *feel* that way? Was it something he said, or are you just guessing based on your experience?”

“It just seems to perfect. He just *happens* to find the right women in every city he moves to? That’s too much of a coincidence to me. Now, maybe that’s just what happened, but I don’t think so.”

“I cut him loose, but I got enough to charge him today, right now. I want you to tap his phone and put a tail on him starting today. I have no doubt he won’t leave town until he sells that house. He loves the almighty dollar too much to leave town without getting the money from the sale. He’s pretty cocksure of himself. He doesn’t think we have enough to charge him. He’s not going to leave that much money, the money he would net out of that house, here, and run off somewhere else. We have a little time, and I want to try to catch whoever’s setting him up with these women before he, or she, most likely she, gets away.”

“You want me to take care of that right now, or can I finish up with some desk work first?”

“No, go ahead, finish your office work, then go home, milk the cows and feed the chickens. Hell yes, I want you to do it now—*right now.”*

Terry just looked at him, motionless and silent. Finally, he said, “Okay, old man whatever you want. One thing about it,” he said as he got up to leave. “At least I’m still young enough and got enough left in me to do those things—I can still milk a cow or two, and I can sure as hell feed…the…chickens. You, on the other hand, can’t handle either, you old fart.”

Sam never looked up as he continued to finish his notes. Instead, he was considering the next step in his continuing efforts to tie down all the loose ends, and put this killer, this Edward Bennett Hall, along with whoever his partner might be, away for good.

Chapter 28

Ed drove home deep in thought. The criminal investigation had progressed much further than he had ever expected. He really thought maybe he was free and clear before today's meeting with the cop. What made the death of Janice so different from the others? What had he said, what had he done, to change the flow of a simple question and answer session, into a full investigation? He did not want to hire an attorney. He didn't trust them, any of them. But now, after today's meeting, he knew it was time to at least visit with one.

He needed to talk to Patricia, but he needed to be absolutely certain the contact with her would not, in any way, implicate her. A phone call using the burner phone hidden under the seat of his car, would need to suffice. At this point in time, they simply couldn't take a chance and meet anywhere. Now, there was a distinct possibility he was being followed. Pat could never handle a meeting with a cop like the one he had just been through.

"Where have you been? You haven't called for a week. Are we still okay?"

He pulled the shades while he prepared to respond. As he did, he noticed a black and white police cruiser drive by. That was unusual in that he hadn't seen one in the neighborhood since he moved in with Janice. Obviously, they were watching. Not a good thing, but at least it was good to know.

He walked to the bar and poured a half glass of bourbon, as he said, "Yes, we are fine, Patricia. But we do seem to have a problem or two."

"Where have you been?"

"You mean today, or the last two weeks?"

"Take your choice."

"Well, today I was doing what I could to keep us out of jail."

He waited for her response. She finally said, "Well, go on. What the hell is the problem? Do they *not* believe you? What is so different this time from the other times we have done this?"

"I have tried to figure out that very issue since I came back from being grilled by him. I think it's *this* cop. He seems to be the difference. He just apparently feels something is wrong, and he's carrying the investigation to the extreme. I found that out today."

"Can we meet—discuss this over coffee, or a stiff drink, or naked in bed? Any of those options available?"

"Absolutely not. I think I got a cop watching the house as we speak. At least I saw one drive by as I was closing the drapes. It's the first one I have seen in this neighborhood since I moved in."

"So, what is he stuck on? What's his major issue?"

"Well, for one thing he keeps harping on why I rented the boat on Friday. I thought I took care of that problem, because he quit bringing it up. But I guess that wasn't the case. That is apparently one problem."

"Go on."

"He has been to Denver and apparently Sacramento, the best I can gather."

"How did he even know where you were from in the first place?"

"The original officer I talked to asked me, and I just rattled it off. I had no reason to believe anything would come of it. To me it was a routine drowning, and in the past, we have just never had problems of this nature. I guess I was too comfortable with it all. It just seemed so routine. I'm sorry… but what's done is done."

"Yeah, that was pretty stupid. Certainly not one of your better moments."

"But what if they would have investigated and determined I wasn't truthful—that I wasn't from where I said I was from, and had lied about my prior residence. I thought about that later. If they caught me lying about something so simple, could it then lead to bigger issues? I think now, that I did the right thing. It just came back to bite me."

"So, what do they have on you from Denver and Sacramento?"

"They know about the deaths of both women. That's a problem."

"You know, it might have helped if you had changed your name. I told you that at the time."

"Oh sure, easy for you to say. I couldn't go through the court process of changing my name every time we killed a woman. I didn't know an attorney in each city we were in, and it would have taken a hell of a lot of time. Then I would have had to change all my documents everywhere we went. To be perfectly honest, it has worked just fine up until now. You and I discussed this very issue and agreed we didn't need to go through that process—*remember*?"

She remained silent.

"There's also one additional problem."

"What is it?"

"I think they have an idea I'm not in this by myself."

"Why would they think that?"

"Because he kept asking me if I just happened to meet all those women on my own. I just got the feeling he was trying to figure out if I acted alone or with someone else. He asked me if I was seeing another woman when Janice died. I really think he believes someone else is involved. I figure that's why they let me loose and are tailing me. I wouldn't be surprised if they are going to tap my phone too. We really have to be careful so you don't get pulled into this."

"What about just getting out of here."

"I can't. There's no doubt in my mind they are following me. I make a move they will throw my ass in jail. Besides that, do you want to leave all the money this house is worth, just sitting here? I don't. I think we wait this out for a while and see what happens."

"Do they have anything else on you?"

"Well, the autopsy showed Janice had a mark on her face. They can't prove what happened, but I'm sure he thinks I hit her, then pushed her in the lake. They can't prove it, but they can certainly use it against me as a possibility."

"Is that it?"

"He asked me where I got all my money. I told him I made it in the markets, land and things of that nature. He hasn't asked for proof of that yet, but I sure as hell bet he will. And of course, I got *nothing* to show him'."

"You know what this sounds like to me?"

"What?"

"It sounds like to me they got a pretty good case—that's what it sounds like to me."

He could hear her start to cry.

Ed quit pacing and took a seat. "Don't cry, Patricia. Please don't cry. It will all work out. We've made it through a hell of a lot these past few years, and we will get through this. It's just going to take a little longer this time. Are you going to fly down to the Caribbean?"

"I'm not going anywhere without you. I'll stay here until something happens one way or the other."

"I am thinking he is probably going to charge me. I might be wrong, but I'm thinking he's going to file the charge, and I will have to go through the process of getting an attorney and fighting this."

"How can they use those two deaths in Colorado and California against you if neither death was ever established as a murder?"

"I don't know, but I suppose I better find out. I am going to see that attorney I told you about. I'll call her office tomorrow and make an appointment as soon as I can get in to see her."

"What do you want me to do? Is there some way I can help? I feel so helpless. How can I help get you out of this?"

"Liston to me. This is really important. I don't want you to get caught. No matter what happens I do not want you to get caught up in all this. You are free, you have a lot of money, and looking at a worst-case scenario here, there is just no sense in both of us ending up in prison."

"But I don't want to go on without you. You're my life. You have been for years. All our plans, the future together, days on the beach, nights under the stars in the Caribbean—Ed I don't know..."

She continued to cry...softly, but he could still hear her.

"I'll tell you what. Let's figure out what we're going to do if we *really do* end up with a problem. I'll go visit with the attorney. As soon as I know anything, I'll call you. Don't worry now, Patricia. We have made it through a lot in the past few years. I don't have much doubt we'll get through this. Just keep thinking about our life together and how much fun we will have when this is all sorted out and behind us."

"Okay," she said softly.

"I love you. Never forget how much I love you."

"I love you. Let me know as soon as you've talked to the attorney."

Ed terminated the call. He would set up an appointment to see this Ruth Andrews as quickly as he could get in. He tried not to convey all his concern to Patricia, but he was definitely worried this time—this time was different. He wondered—if he was convicted of anything and he gave up the name of his co-conspirator, would they cut him a break. It certainly wasn't an option he wanted to use, but he would keep it in the back of his mind as a possibility. All his life, number one had *always* come first. This situation, in that respect, was certainly no different than any other.

Chapter 29

So far, the most important decision Ruth needed to make today was whether it would be appropriate to purchase her boss a Christmas present—and if so, what? They hadn't known each other that long. But after all he had done for her, she wanted to show her appreciation for not only hiring her in the first place, but for being such an incredible mentor and putting up with her on a daily basis.

As she sat in her office while having that first cup of coffee and starting the day in a relatively slow fashion, she glanced down at her scheduled appointments for the day. The first, was with someone she wasn't familiar with—Edward Hall. Apparently, he had criminal issues. At least that was the minutia of information Mr. Hall provided Hanna. He was her first appointment of the day and was to walk through her office door at 9:00 a.m.

Shortly, before eight-thirty, Hanna informed her Edward had arrived early and was waiting to visit with her now, if possible. She told Hanna to send him on back.

He walked through her office door. Ruth stood, but had trouble remembering what to do next—he was so good looking, so put together. She walked around her desk, extended her hand and said, "Hi, my name…"

She took hold of Ed's hand as he waited for her to finish the sentence.

When she didn't, he said, "Okay, so is mine."

She never responded, continuing to hold his hand. Finally, she said, "What?"

He smiled as he said, "Just messing with you. You said your name was something, but I guess I never caught it. Actually, mine is Ed Hall. Are you hard of hearing? Nice to meet you…"

"Ruth…Ruth…Ruth….is my name and no I can hear." She continued shaking his hand until he stopped the motion.

"I hope it was okay for you to see me a little early today."

Ruth remained speechless, attempting to shake free of her fixation, while she moved behind her desk, never taking her eyes off him.

"Should we both sit now?"

"Yes, sure, it's good for you to sit. We all have to sit. And there you are…standing when you should be sitting. And me…look at me…I'm not sitting, but I'm going to, just right now."

As he sat down, she stopped talking, finally taking a deep breath. She suddenly realized she had made a complete fool of herself. "I am so, so, sorry. I don't know what got into me. Where were we? Probably nowhere. Let's start over. My name is Ruth, Ruth Andrews, and you, you are Ed Hall, correct?"

He smiled. "Correct."

Again, that smile, and again that awkward pause, as she continued to regain the simultaneous use of both brain and mouth. Finally, she said, "What… can I…do…to you...I mean, *for you*, Mr. Hall?"

"Well, it seems I'm in a bit of trouble. Can I discuss it with you? You do handle criminal cases, don't you?"

Now, finally living in the moment, she sat back and said, "I'm sorry. I really don't know what is wrong with me. Forgive me. Would you like a cup of coffee while we talk?"

"Not really. I just need some advice and your thoughts about what to do."

She smiled. "Okay, why don't you tell me a little about yourself."

"Well, I moved here about two years ago. I married a local woman. I have no children. My wife drowned here, on Piercy Priest Lake. Now they want to charge me with murder. They think I murdered her."

Ruth's face turned from interest to concern. "Have you been charged?"

"No, but I have a feeling it's not far away. Can you help me?"

Ruth leaned forward in her chair. "Well yes, we do handle criminal matters. I specifically handle and try criminal cases. But, why would they think you murdered her?"

"Because it happened during the evening, there were no witnesses, and I inherited about two mil from her."

"Well, those are all pretty good reasons, I guess. Just between you and me, did you kill her?"

"No! No, absolutely not. All our money was comingled. If I had died, she would have inherited mine. I didn't kill her."

"Who is handling the investigation?"

"Some cop by the name of Harvey something or other. I can't remember his first name."

She smiled. "Are you talking about Sam Harvey?"

"Yes, that's him. Do you know him?"

"Not personally, but I have heard of him. He's a weirdo, but he is good at his job. So, how did she die?"

"We stopped in a small cove. As we started to leave, I told her to sit down. I hit the throttle. When I turned around, she was gone. End of story. They found her a few days later."

"Did they perform an autopsy?"

"Yes. They said they found a mark on her face, as if something hit her, I guess. It wasn't me. I have no idea what it was, but that's it. That's all they have."

"And they are charging you with murder based solely on that evidence? Okay, that doesn't make much sense."

"She has this relative that keeps putting the heat on this Harvey character. The relative was previously named in her will, but now, as a result of a change my wife made, she doesn't get anything. She is the one pushing it."

"That makes sense. I've seen that happen before. There were no witnesses, nor other facts to support the charge?"

"No." He cleared his throat, and crossed his legs. "Now I must tell you I've lost two prior wives in accidents before this one—one in Colorado and one in California—but they have nothing to do with this case. Mr. Harvey knows about both of those. I think that's another factor as concerns why I'm being charged."

Ruth looked at him a moment, leaned back in her chair and said, "You lost two prior wives, both as a result of accidents?"

"Yes. I was never charged in either case, and I shouldn't have been. One fell down some steps and one fell off a cliff."

"You got to be kidding me. You were never charged in either?"

"Absolutely not. I didn't do anything wrong."

"Well, that may be, Mr. Hall, but the fact there were two prior unnatural deaths would tend to shed some light on why he is charging you in this one."

"No, actually it doesn't. I did nothing wrong."

"Did you inherit from the other two?"

"Yes. Before we go any further, I'm assuming nothing we say goes any further, is that correct?"

"No matter what comes of this conference today, nothing ever leaves this room. Were there any other spousal deaths prior to these three?"

"No. This Sam whatshisname also thinks that I have an accomplice. He's had a tail on me all week and I have no doubt he's tapped my phone. I think that's why he hasn't charged me yet. He is trying to figure out who my accomplice is."

"Do you have one?"

"No. I have no one else in my life. Janice was my life here in Nashville, and now that she is gone, I have no one." He looked down, and said nothing.

"You have no other woman you're seeing now or that you were involved with while married to Janice?"

"No, absolutely not."

"You know, Mr. Hall, no matter what the situation might be, whether I represent you for the next month or the next 100 months, I can't represent you adequately if you lie to me. Now, let me ask you again. *Are there any other women involved?"*

"Absolutely not."

Ruth started taking notes. "So, these other women that died while married to you—never any charges filed concerning either of them, is that correct?"

"Yes. Can their deaths be used against me here?"

"There is a possibility, yes. Once we determine whether you want us to represent you, I'll need the specifics concerning each of the other two cases. In this case, we would probably want to file a pretrial motion asking that any testimony concerning their deaths be kept out of this trial. That would take care of that problem, assuming we were successful."

Neither said anything, until he said, "Can you help me?"

Ruth sat forward in her chair, and said, "Yes, I think we can. We will need to talk about the fees, but I believe we may be able to help. It depends somewhat upon the rest of whatever evidence they might have. Tell me, Ed, have you ever been in trouble before?"

"Never. Not even a speeding ticket."

"Were all your conversations with law enforcement recorded? Could I get a copy of those interviews?"

"I don't think anything was recorded. They took place mostly at the dock, on the lake and at my home. Nothing was ever said about anyone recording me at any time."

"Well then, nothing should have been recorded. That's good. Now, how much did you inherit from these other women? Was it significant?"

"No, not really. Probably a total of over four million or so."

"Whoa, that's certainly not *insignificant.* At least you should have no problem paying us a retainer."

"I guess it depends a little on how much it is."

"Well as concerns the charges, there's not much we can do until you are actually charged. Are you planning on leaving town?"

"No. He told me not to, and besides that, I'm in the process of selling the house, so no I'm not leaving anytime soon."

Ruth leaned back, smiled and said, "Good. Now let's forget about the criminal case. Why don't you just tell me a little more about yourself? Where did you live before, where is your home here, what's your occupation—you know personal stuff—before we talk fees. You tell me a little about yourself, and I'll tell you a little about myself."

Their discussion lasted well into the afternoon. A couple of additional clients waited past the time of their appointment before they were able to see Ruth. At the conclusion of his appointment, after they had come to an agreement concerning fees, Ruth was sure of two things. First, if any evidence concerning the two prior deaths of his spouses was allowed into evidence, he was in one hell of a lot of trouble. Second, no matter what happened concerning the evidence, she actually hoped before everything was all said and done, she was avoiding her own troubles resulting from having a sexual relationship with *this* client. He was one hunk of a man. She was in love before he ever sat down.

Chapter 30

Ed Hall had been waiting almost two weeks for a cop to arrest him. It had been a week and a half since he had met Ruth. She was an interesting woman. Good looking and clearly intelligent, he had found in her the combination he was looking for—the combination that would work best. for *him.* The fact that she appeared to be interested in him *personally*, certainly did not go unnoticed. That issue alone might work to his advantage along the way.

It was near midnight. All the lights in his house were out. He had been sitting near the front window for over an hour, watching that cop car a block away. They had to know he knew they were there, yet they remained in the same spot day after day—ever since his last visit with Sam Harvey.

He stood and walked into the garage without turning on a light. He opened his car door, then pulled out the burner phone he used for only one purpose.

As he walked back through a darkened kitchen, he took his seat while continuing to watch the cop car, then dialed her number.

"Hi. How are you?"

"I'm good. What's wrong? Why are you calling this late at night?"

"Did I wake you?"

"No. You know I never go to sleep until about three anyway. What's going on?"

"Oh, not much. I'm just sitting here watching the cop. I'm thinking it's about time for them to make a move. They probably know by now I am never going to divulge who my co-conspirator might be. I'm thinking in the next few days they will arrest me and charge me."

"Is your attorney ready to jump in if that happens?"

"Yes. She knows it's inevitable."

"What about my contact with you?"

"That will be difficult. I will find a way, but it'll be difficult. Are you leaving town—heading south, anytime soon?"

"No. At least that's not in my plans within the near future."

"Oh, by the way, this will be the last call I make on this phone. I can't let them find it here, and I imagine when they arrest me, they will have a search warrant. They will find nothing, but this phone has to be destroyed. That's going to happen right after we finish this conversation."

"How will we remain in contact?"

"I will probably buy another. I don't think following me is going to last long after I'm arrested and released on bail. All these police departments are short-handed. Once I am absolutely certain they have determined I am *not* going to give you up, they'll lay off. When they do, I'll buy another phone and call you then."

They visited for only a few more moments, at which time he terminated the call, walked to the basement and crushed the phone in a work bench vise. The fragments that remained, he took to his back yard, spreading it out over a quarter acre of grass.

It was near 8:00 a.m. when he heard a loud knock on the door and the words, "Police, open the door." He jumped up, threw on a robe, and walked to the front door, but not before they had again screamed the word, "Police."

As he opened the door, he said, "Good God, I hear you, I hear you. By the way, so does half of Nashville. What do you want?"

Sam Harvey walked out from behind three officers as he said, "I'm arresting you for the murder of your wife, Janice. These officers have a warrant to search your house. Move out of the way, so they can accomplish that."

Ed stepped aside, as the officers walked in, each moving to a different section of the house.

Sam read him his Maranda rights. Once completed, he again asked him if he could afford an attorney and if he had one representing him. Ed told him he did, and he wanted her with him at each and every stage of the proceedings. Sam then told him to put his clothes on while they were searching the house. As soon as he finished dressing, Sam took him straight to the station, where he immediately called Ruth.

They placed him in a holding cell. A half-hour after he was booked, Ruth walked up to his jailcell and said, "How they treating you?"

"Good God, I'm glad you're here. What happens next?"

Two hours later they were seated in Ruth's office with the door shut and a cup of coffee in front of them.

"Okay, what the hell just happened? I have no idea what I just went through. Thank God, you were with me. I have no idea how I would have ever made it through that without you by my side."

She smiled, winked at him and said, "That's my job Ed, that's what I do, that's who I am. I'm just here to help, to lead, to guide—that's what I live for."

His quick smile just as quickly disappeared when he said, "Under other circumstances, that whole verbal stream of consciousness thing you did right there would have been pretty funny. But I'm sorry, I've just been charged with murder. I'm not in much of a jovial mood."

"You're right. You are absolutely right. This process is not to be taken lightly. I have just been through it so many times it's become old hat to me, I guess. The process is always the same. I shouldn't take it so lightly. I'm not the one being charged."

"How did I stay out of jail? I just figured they would keep me."

"Well, you did have to make a slight concession, as I'm sure you remember. They were going to keep you, until I told them you were a homeowner, you lived here, the charges were at best, questionable, and you had absolutely no criminal record. You were going to be held without bail, but after the judge set bail at a million, and you wrote the check, they let you go, pending further proceedings. I think personally, you would have had a difficult time remaining in jail until trial. You strike me as a lover not a fighter, and inside, you would have come in contact with a lot more fighters than lovers. You probably would have had to fight both types off though. So, you're out, and that's exactly where I wanted you—out. We need to get ready for trial. I have no doubt the grand jury will indict you."

"Okay, so being out on bond means what? What can and can't I do?"

"Do not leave town. Don't do anything that appears the least suspicious. Hang around the house until this is over. If you really want to go out and eat, call me. I'll go with you, *and* we can eat, *and* prepare for trial."

Ed sat back, looked at her for a moment, smiled and said, "Are you hitting on me? Is that what I'm getting here?"

"No, no of course not. I can't date clients. But I could eat with one while discussing his case."

"What about this damn ankle bracelet? Do I have to keep this on until the trial, or is there a way to buy myself out of it too?"

"You are stuck with that, I'm afraid. They want to make sure where you are and when you are there. That is not going to change until after the trial. By the way, I'll be talking to the attorney generals attorney's office later this week about a number of other cases. Do you want me to try to bargain this out? Would you be willing to plead to something in exchange for them dropping the murder charge?"

Ed thought for a moment and finally said, "Well, I guess so. I haven't thought much about it. Maybe littering or slightly polluting the lake, something like that?"

Ruth laughed and said, "That probably won't work. Let me talk to them, and get a feel for what they might offer. We can discuss it then. I can tell you that one of the pivotal issues in your case will be keeping any evidence or testimony concerning those other two wives and their deaths, out of this case. That will be absolutely crucial. In that respect, I'll file a motion long before trial. We will know how the trial judge feels about it before the first witness is ever sworn."

"I suppose at that time we will have a good idea how the trial itself might proceed, is that correct?"

"Yes. Without that evidence, they will really be hard pressed to get a conviction. On the other hand, if it *is* allowed into evidence, we may have trouble winning the case. I hate to say this Ed, but it's pretty damning."

"I understand. When will we know what the grand jury is going to do? I don't suppose we can do much until they indict me."

"That is correct. They are in session next week. We should know by the end of the week. I'll let you know as soon as I know."

"Should I be worried?"

"You've just been charged with murder. Yes, you should be worried. This is serious business, Ed. You could go to prison for a long, long, time, even if the jury convicts you of a lesser included offense. Let me ask you this. Do you want to move this along quickly, or does it matter?"

"It matters. I want you to have time to do your job, and get ready, but if I could have this all wrapped up by the end of the week, that's what I would prefer."

"Well, that's not going to happen, but I understand what you are saying, and I will do the best I can to keep it moving along. First things first. Let's wait until you're indicted, see what the grand jury indicts you for and go from there."

"Okay. You did a great job for me today. I'm just glad to be out and walking around—not in some jail cell with Big Tommy and his friends looking at me as their next girlfriend."

Ruth laughed, then said, "Why don't I give you a call when I get the results of the grand jury's deliberations, and maybe we can meet then?"

"Over supper?"

Ruth smiled. "If you wish, but only if you buy."

Ed smiled as he thought to himself how easy she would have been, if she had only been a victim instead of his attorney. But those days were over. Yes sir, those days were over.

Chapter 31

There remained only a couple of weeks before the beginning of the trial which would determine Ruth's wealth or lack thereof. It was time to review each and every detail of the case—make sure they were completely prepared.

Harold and Ruth had spent most of the morning discussing witnesses and exhibits. Before they separated for the day, Harold felt it necessary to summarize and if necessary, to discuss their position one final time.

"Ruth, do you know anything about the judge?"

"No, but Paul does. He will fill us in on how the judge handles his courtroom the next time we meet. Paul has been briefly filling me in on cases tried in his courtroom—what he allows, what he doesn't allow. It really doesn't sound atypical from any of the other judges we practice in front of."

"You have the doctor lined up, right?"

"Yes. There is no reason to believe he will testify any differently than he did during his depo. Certainly, that is a positive for us."

"By the way, you nailed that depo. Great job, Ruth."

"Thanks. I just told the truth." She smiled, "Mostly anyway."

"They have copies of the video. The witnesses are all subpoenaed, and I've talked to each one. Once Grisham watched the video, they waived any foundational issues, which helps. Now, they have no problem with me handling representation since I'm not really a witness, and I have nothing to gain or lose as concerns the outcome. The disc will speak for itself, and Martha's will just reflect what's said in the video."

"What about this Grisham? What is his take on all this? Is he ready to go?"

"Yes. He has received all the discovery he requested. He basically understands what he is up against here. What Martha wanted is clear and consistent throughout most of the evidence. He has acknowledged that, but the kids want their day in court, so he has no choice and neither do we."

Ruth said, "In going through their depos, it sounds to me like the kids are having trouble scraping together the money to pursue this. If that's the case, an appeal, if they lose, doesn't seem likely. Do you concur?"

"Yes. I think this is it for them. They either win or they are done."

They visited for only a few more minutes before Ruth returned to her own office. She had a number of items to finish up and needed to visit with Paul before he left for the day.

She walked in his office door as she said, "Do you have a few minutes? I would like to discuss the VanArsdayle trial, if you do."

"Sure. Have a seat."

As she sat down, she said, "I met with Harold all morning and part of this afternoon. I think we are ready to go. All the witnesses are lined up and subpoenaed. Either Harold or I have talked to each of them. He has also had a number of visits with Grisham. It appears to me we are ready to try this and move on. Are you ready? Do you need anything from either of us? You'll be handling their witnesses and Harold, of course, will handle ours."

"No, I'm ready. I will be glad to get it all over with for the sake of the office as much as anything. Obviously, I'll get paid for my time by the estate, but the office gets nothing from your time while you are involved in this. Your number of billable hours has shrunk considerably since this all started. I'll be glad when you get back to working full time, because you are certainly not doing that now."

"No, and I'm sorry for that. But it will all change once this case is tried and done with, one way or the other. I did pick up a good retainer the other day. That new client, Edward Hall, should be a pretty good client for us, and he's rich, so they will be no problem with him paying us after the retainer has been used up. Hopefully, we can produce the desired result. I'll discuss his case with you as it moves along. So, back to Martha. Will you be ready to proceed in a couple of weeks?"

"Yes, as ready as I'll ever be."

After briefly discussing a few other issues involving the VanArsdayle case, Ruth returned to her office. She noticed she had received a call from Ed. She closed her door before she punched in his number. It wasn't necessary that Paul listen to *every* conversation she had in her office. She was surely entitled to a little privacy.

"Hi, Ed, I noticed you called."

"Yes, I did. Have you heard anything else about my case? Where are we at?"

"I've heard nothing since your arraignment. Of course, you already know the grand jury charged you with first degree murder. Your bond continues and we have entered a plea of not guilty. I'll provide you with copies of the depos as soon as I have reviewed them. After you have reviewed those, we will get together and discuss what each individual said."

"What about the trial? Still no date?"

"No. I'll discuss that with the Attorney Generals office next week. They do know I want an early trial date. I think they will accommodate us on that. I'm sure they are getting tired of all the calls from her niece concerning disposition of the case."

"Okay, I will just wait to hear from you, I guess. I tried calling earlier in the day. I left no message. Your secretary said you would be back before the day ended."

"Unfortunately, I've been out all day. I have been getting ready for my own trial in a couple of weeks."

"Really? Hmm, I wonder. Do I really want an attorney that's completely wrapped up in her own crimes and who must deal with her own substantial issues as well as mine? I wonder."

"No, no it's not like that at all. I represented an older lady. When she drew her will, she left her money to me. The kids are upset, and they are trying to set her will aside. That all comes up for trial in a couple of weeks."

"Oh, oh I see. So, nothing to do with criminal law—it is a civil matter, correct?"

"Yes."

"Well, if you don't mind me prying a little, how does the case look?"

"Good. Our evidence is substantial and includes a video of her in which she's very specific as to what she wanted done with her money. Once she told me what she wanted to do, I quit representing her, and had another attorney step in. I think it will turn out fine."

"If you don't mind me asking, is it a large sum of money?"

"No, I don't mind. It's already a matter of public record in the clerk's office anyway. It amounts to a little over two million, and she also has some real estate which is worth quite a sum. So, I am thinking it might total around three million before it's all said and done."

He hesitated before he responded. "You will be a rich young lady."

Ruth laughed. "I just hope it all turns out the way she wanted it to. She didn't want her kids to get anything. She made that very clear. Hopefully, it turns out that way."

"Can we meet and discuss my case over dinner some evening?"

"I don't see why not, as long as the main purpose is business and not pleasure."

He laughed. "I cannot assure you there won't be a little pleasure involved, but business will definitely be discussed. Let me check a couple of things I had planned later this week and get back to you with a time and place."

"I'll wait to hear from you."

Ruth terminated the call. There was something about this guy that was different than most. He was extremely charming, but there was just something about him. If and when they had dinner together, she hoped when the meal ended, he didn't suggest a continuation of their evening together at some hotel close to where they ate. Because, if he did, she would most likely go with him.

She had little doubt that if the evening continued on after the meal, their relationship would then most likely change radically, involving much less *verbal* interaction, and one hell of a lot more *physical i*nteraction.

Chapter 32

Paul Thomas sat alone, with a cup of hot coffee, watching as the sun slowly rose above the horizon. He hadn't realized, when he first walked out on his deck, how cold it really was. Now as he sat motionless, he noticed a chill in the air, even though the deck was enclosed. He watched a few early-morning walkers in the distance. He could see their breath as they exhaled. Even as far south as Nashville was, on occasion it was cold in late February, and today happened to be one of those occasions.

He hadn't dressed yet. He was fully aware of the volume of work that awaited him at the office, but today it would just need to wait. He was tired, he still had his robe on and hadn't even begun to prepare for his drive to the office. It had been a long night. Paul's mind wasn't on what he would wear the rest of the day, nor on what might happen at the office.

He thought of the number of times they would sit here, at this table, at this hour of the morning. They would discuss their day's activities before leaving the house, then each would enter into their own world, there to remain until they once again returned home later that day.

She was gone. She had left this world during the night and journeyed on without him for the first time since their marriage. He had checked on her as he always did about 3:00 a.m., and she had passed. He sat by the bed and cried until he knew it was time to call them to come get her. Paul knew she was dying. He knew she didn't have long, but it didn't make her death any easier. He always knew when it finally happened it would be unbearable. But the incredible sense of finality, of loss, of despair, was even worse than he had imagined it would be.

He had thought of nothing but their life together since she died. Work seemed completely meaningless. His clients, their problems, his responsibilities, meant nothing.

Neither of them was spiritual. Neither of them believed in the Bible from cover to cover. But they both believed in something greater than what this world had to offer. They both believed in a form of life after death and the possibility of life beyond human form. This morning that was what he would focus upon—that somewhere, somehow, they would someday be together again. That would be the positive factor he would carry with him while he tried to process her death.

A few minutes later, he decided it was time. He needed to call everyone and tell them she had passed. He needed to schedule and prepare for the funeral. He needed to remove everything from his calendar at the office until he had given her life on this earth, the focus it so clearly deserved. Until that was over, all of his office responsibilities would remain unfinished. He owed this woman a least that much. Until those tasks had been completed, he would accomplish little else.

He finally arrived at the office near ten-thirty. Hanna watched as he walked through the door, and said, "Hey, you're a little late today."

He continued to walk, offering no response of any kind. Once in his office, Ruth, through her open door, yelled, "Paul, do you have a minute to discuss a couple of issues?"

He never responded, instead simply closing his door as he walked in. He dreaded making the calls, but it was time. One by one, he called all of her close friends and her family. They all responded as he knew they would. First, they expressed sorrow, then they told him how much better off she was—that she wasn't going to get any better and that she was in a better place—all bullshit clichés, all predictable, but all humbly accepted by him.

Halfway through the last call, there was a knock on his door. He said, "Come in" and quickly ended the call. Everything that could have been said, had already been said anyway.

Both Hanna and Ruth were standing at his open door. Hanna said, "Is everything okay, Paul?"

As he started to cry, he stood, walked to the door, put his arms around both of them and whispered, "No, she's gone."

They both embraced him, then all three stood in the doorway and cried.

As the phone started ringing and people started walking through the door, he wiped away the tears as he said, "Hanna, go take care of whoever walked in. Either set up an appointment, or tell them to go away and come back later—frankly, either way is fine with me. Ruth, sit down. Let's figure out the rest of the week."

Both did as instructed. A few minutes later he noticed the phone lines both reflected they were off the hook. He then heard Hanna lock the front door. When she walked back in his office, she said, "I took the phone off the hook and put a sign on the door that we were closed the rest of the day because of a death."

"Okay, good. As for the office, the funeral is Friday. I'll be out the rest of the week. Just tell people what happened and hold them off."

Ruth said, "What about next week? Do you want to put Martha's trial off for a week or two? I'm sure they would all understand if you did."

"No, no absolutely not. After I do all those things that need to be done this week, I think working will be best for me. Let's just keep everything off the schedule for this week and start fresh next week."

The remainder of the week would be a blur consisting of family, work related issues, caskets and old friends. He found himself making many major decisions—the type of decisions both Anna and he would have made together—by himself for the first time in many, many years.

The funeral was well attended. Most of Anna's family went home immediately after it was over.

That night he walked into an empty house, poured himself a bourbon, and sat out on an empty deck as he watched the sun sink below the horizon.

She was all he had ever known. They met at a young age. There was never anyone else for either of them. Even when Anna reached the point where she was unable to communicate, to respond, he still told her his troubles. Even when she couldn't communicate verbally, she could still listen and understand his problems.

If only it had been him instead of her. While dying in that manner was such a horrible death, now that she was gone, there was no doubt he would have preferred it had been him. Without taking a moment to even consider, he would have changed places with her in the blink of an eye.

He never left his chair for well over an hour, except to refill his empty glass. He sat in silence as he watched the sun disappear. When he finally went to bed, he was drunk to the point he forgot she was gone. He woke up and remembered he hadn't told her good night. Her empty bed refreshed his memory.

He cried as he walked in his bedroom. Paul never even undressed, lying there until finally his eyes were simply too tired to remain open another moment. He passed into a restless sleep, dreaming only of Anna and remembering how incredible their life had been together.

Chapter 33

Paul looked back over the past week, and while he had somewhat of a general idea what had occurred, he hoped no one asked him to chronicle exactly where he went, who he saw, or what he did. Most of it was simply a blur. He got through it somehow, but as to his hour-by-hour activities on a day-by-day basis, he knew there were many things he would simply never remember.

The trial concerning the will of Martha VanArsdayle was to commence in only a matter of days. He had tried to concentrate, to prepare for the witnesses he knew he had to handle, but it had been difficult. In reviewing what his role would be, he concluded all the witnesses that would be called to testify would be important, but none as important as Ruth. She needed to be convincing. She needed to convince Grisham, Martha's children, and most importantly the judge, that she had done nothing wrong—that she had simply tried to comply with what Martha wanted. Even when it became clear Martha wanted to leave all her money to Ruth, she would still need to convince the judge she was only acting in Martha's best interest when she sent her to Harold.

"Paul, John Stone is on one. You want to talk to him?"

"I better. I can't ignore the chairman of the ethics committee."

He knew what this conversation would involve and while, now that Anna was gone, the issue of finances as concerned her care, was a nonfactor, he was still deeply in debt, and needed the income that an open, thriving law office would provide. There was never an opportune time for disbarment, but for it to happen now, considering his financial issues, the result would be a total disaster.

"Morning, John."

"Good morning, Paul. First of all, let me express my condolences concerning the death of your wife. I know how close you were. I know how long you took care of her and how much she meant to you. I'm truly sorry for what you have had to endure during the past number of years, and, of course, now with her death."

"Thank you, John. That really means a lot to me."

"I wish that was the only reason for this visit. But, as you are aware, the committee is looking closely at that case involving your associate and Martha VanArsdayle. I very seldom make these kinds of calls, but I did want to generally discuss the situation with you. I've been informed the trial is scheduled for next week. Is it still a go?"

"Yes, it is."

"Paul, you and I have known each other for quite some time. While our contact has not always been under the best of circumstances, I've always considered you a friend and an excellent attorney—your issues with the bar association while your wife was ill, notwithstanding."

"Thanks, John. That's kind of you. I have exactly the same sentiments about you, but I have a feeling that isn't all you have to say."

"No, you're correct. Unfortunately, I wasn't finished. The committee is looking at this situation very closely. I am afraid if you, or Ruth, or both of you, end up before us, it might get a little ugly. Your prior appearances before the committee won't help your situation with the committee members, that's for sure."

"So, are they looking at what Ruth did, or at what I did, or at both of us—what are they concerned about?"

"Well, first of all, I can say for a fact that the decision in court will affect our position. The legal issue of undue influence would be the issue we consider. What that means is if the judge rules favorably, we won't carry our inquiry any further—it will be dispositive of all the issues before the committee. But if the judge rules in favor of the children, you are most definitely going to hear from our board."

"But *who* is going to hear from you? Since Ruth was the one involved in all this, will she be the one who's actions are reviewed by the board, or will the actions of both of us be reviewed, even though I wasn't involved with the will?"

"You will both hear from us. You will both have to support your own respective positions. The board will sort it out from there, but the actions of both of you would then be scrutinized."

Paul took a deep breath.

"I know, I know what you're thinking. You don't understand why your actions should be reviewed in this particular factual situation. But, Paul, you are the boss. You're the one responsible for the office.

Now, while you may not have actually been physically involved in the preparation of the will or whether you actually masterminded the whole situation, will be for the committee to determine after they ascertain all the facts. I'm not sure, even if the decision doesn't go your way, they would look at punishing you if you weren't specifically involved in all this. But I *know* they're going to want to talk to you, to get your side of the facts, your thoughts about how this all happened. Sorry, but I'm quite sure, in visiting with all of them informally, that's the approach they'll want to take."

"I understand. I'm just hoping the court's decision turns out in our favor, and no one needs to determine who did what to whom. I wasn't involved in any of this, but we will let the trial court judge sort everything out. Thanks for calling, John. It means a lot to me, not only as concerns your sentiments involving Anna and I, but filling me in on what to expect once the trial has concluded."

After terminating the call, he sat alone, considering John's remarks. He heard Ruth walk through the front office door and as she walked down the hallway, he said, "Ruth when you have a moment, could we visit about Martha's trial?"

She poked her head in the door and said, "Sure. Let me put these files down and pick up the trial file. I won't be a moment."

When she returned, as she sat down, Paul said, "I just heard from the bar association."

She scooted toward the front of her chair, her eyes wide open, and said, "That can't have been good. The trial hasn't even started yet. What did they want?"

"John Stone, their chairman, just wanted to forewarn me that if this comes out bad, both of us are going to hear from them. Conversely, he said if it comes out good, most likely neither of us will hear from him." Paul leaned back in his chair, and said, "I guess it's all or nothing, when it comes to Martha. We win, we win all the way around, we lose, we lose all the way around. I hope you are ready for this, because there's a hell of a lot on the line here."

She said nothing, obviously contemplating his comments before her response. Finally, she said, "I don't know what else to do, Paul. I didn't cause this problem. She did what she did because she wanted to do it, and that's just the way it is. I hope you are not blaming me for any of this. I've told you repeatedly this was all her idea. As soon as I was sure she wasn't going to take no for an answer, I got out of it."

Paul said, "And yet here we are. Are all our witnesses lined up, everyone subpoenaed, everyone prepped as to their testimony?"

"Yes."

"Are you ready, or do you want to review your testimony again?"

"One more time."

He opened the file and rummaged through his notes until he found the general outline of issues both he and Harold wanted her to testify to. She never moved and never said a word while he found what he was looking for.

"Are you nervous?"

"What the hell do you think, Paul? Shit yes, I'm nervous. Now, on top of everyone looking at me, blaming me for what I did to those poor kids of Martha's, I have the additional burden of possibly getting both of us disbarred. Yes—I'm scared to death."

Paul smiled. "Look, you have nothing to hide. You are probably over prepared. You know the facts better than anyone else, Ruth. Just tell it like it is, and everything will turn out fine."

She said, "That is easy for you to say. Now let's do this."

For the next couple of hours, they reviewed and continued to revise Ruth's testimony. When they finished and Ruth, along with Hanna had left for the evening, he thought about the future of the office after Martha's case. He would need to reassess whether he wanted to keep Ruth, even if they won the case.

She was a gifted attorney, of that there could be no doubt. But there had been two or three other instances, beyond Martha's situation, in which he felt if he hadn't been monitoring the case, she might have made a decision that wasn't exactly ethical—nothing big, but just enough to make him feel uneasy.

He didn't need someone like that in the office. He already had enough issues with the bar association. He would wait until the trial was over, then assess whether or not he wanted to keep a bit of a loose cannon in an office where there was unfortunately already one loose cannon—the one that hired her.

Chapter 34

"So, should I be more worried about *my* trial then you appear to be about *yours*?"

"Don't be silly. I am extremely worried, Ed. I just don't show it like you do. By the way, can you take a position on your chair and *hold it*, if only for a few seconds? Would that be too much to ask?"

Ruth was trying to explain what she would expect from him at the time of his trial, which was now but a short eight weeks away.

"What? What? I don't do anything. I don't move around…I don't…well, maybe I do a little. Okay, I do a lot. I'll stop. I will at least work on it."

"You are like a frog on a hot stove. Now slow down. If you do that when you're on that stand, I will tie you to the chair."

"Let's change the discussion for a minute. We have been doing this long enough. Let's change the subject for a moment and talk about *your* trial tomorrow. If you win that, you are going to be one rich girl, girl, *one rich girl*," he said with a twinkle in his eye.

She leaned back in her chair, and said, "You know, I don't really care about that. I just want to make sure Martha gets to do what she wanted with her money. I don't want that changed. I want her wishes to be honored and respected."

Ed said nothing for a moment, then leaned forward in his chair and whispered, "You don't honestly think I believe that shit, do you? I mean come on now. I don't know you all that well, but I know you well enough to know you are trying to out bullshit a bullshitter. But, my friend, you need to know you are up against the biggest and the best bullshitter ever lived. You got no chance."

She moved forward and started to say something, thought better of what she was about to say, and just smiled. Finally, she said, "Well, the money would be nice, but really I want her wishes carried out."

"Now, don't tell me…."

"Enough about my trial. Let's move on."

"Okay, just one more question. How long do you think your trial will last?"

"Oh, I don't know, probably three or four days I would say."

"Can anyone sit in on it while it is going on?"

"Yes, why?"

"Oh, I don't know, I just might show up. Would that make you nervous? I mean, if I were to say show up and watch you testify, would that bother you?"

"No, not really. In fact, it would probably do just the opposite. Support from the grandstands never hurts."

"When do you think you might testify?"

"I'm guessing maybe the day after tomorrow."

"I think I'll stop in and just see how good you are under fire."

"Okay, okay, let's move on. Let's talk a little more about your case. I have a lot to do before we reach the day we pick the jury that will determine *your* fate. Now let's go through potential witnesses for you."

"What kind of witnesses do you need? I haven't lived here long, as you know. Not many people really know me. I could have some of the people from the church testify for me. They could explain how I was always there—at least while Janice was alive—and that we had a great relationship."

"That would help. I need names and phone numbers. I will give all of them a call. Now, was there ever more than one cop asking you questions at any one time?"

"No, not that I remember."

"So, when Sam Harvey says you told him you were divorced from your Colorado wife, you can say you never told him that and it would just be our word against his, correct?"

"Yes. I never told him that."

"And your statement that you reserved the boat the day before so *you* could go fishing…no one else could refute that, correct?"

"No."

"How long before she died did you commingle your money?"

"Maybe six months or so. I'm not sure, but I can find out."

"Yes, I need that. And get me copies of any records which show the actual date of the commingling."

"Sounds like, to me, this cop is the key to everything."

"He is. He's vital to their case. By the way, the guy's integrity is beyond reproach. He has been an officer a long time, and he's well known within the department. His word is gold. I know that doesn't help, but those are the facts. In addition, the guy is really difficult to break on cross-examination. He is just very good at what he does. His conviction rate is astronomical."

"Thanks for that bit of positive information. Maybe I should just plead guilty now and get it over with."

"Oh, don't be so dramatic. We will be fine, but I wish you had a few more witnesses to call on your behalf. Obviously, it is going to come down to you and the cop going head-to-head. That doesn't always work out the best because people do tend to believe the cop rather than the defendant. But that has changed a little lately with all the issues there have been around the country with cops. Of course, you only hear the bad, never the good, but when it comes down to this type of trial, the fact the prospective jurors have heard about only the bad cops on social media, is a good thing for us."

"I am assuming I'm going to have to testify. I don't suppose I can just skip that part, right?"

"That's correct, you can't. I don't take many cases where I believe it's not necessary for the defendant to testify. I really want them to get up there, with no fear, no reservation, and say 'I did not do this.' I think that's important for the jury to hear. The defendant has the right *not* to testify, and the jury can't use that against him. Unfortunately, I believe in many cases they *do* use it against them, even though they are not supposed to. Don't worry about testifying. You will be well prepared before you ever take the stand."

"You mentioned something about this motion you were considering filing. What's that all about?"

"It's called a motion to suppress, and it's filed to keep certain evidence out of the trial because its content really isn't relevant, or it's misleading or it could tend to taint the jury panel against the defendant for an inappropriate reason. I plan on filing it next week. Its purpose will be to keep any evidence out of the record as pertains to those two prior wives. There was absolutely not a shred of evidence indicating any foul play in either case, and I want that all kept out of the trial. If it's allowed in, we're going to need to reassess our position, because that evidence could really hurt us, even though you were never charged or convicted of a crime in either case."

"If they exclude it, will we still need to go to court?"

"If that happens, then *they* will need to reconsider their position, but I imagine they won't stop until the case has been finally decided one way or other. We'll just have to wait and see."

"When will we know the ruling on the motion?"

"Probably a couple of weeks before trial. If it's adverse to our position, we may ask for a continuance. We will figure that out then."

"Why would we want it continued?'

"I may want to make a trip to Colorado and California—maybe talk to the officers that originally investigated both those cases. I might have them testify there was absolutely no evidence of any wrongdoing. We will figure that out if we lose the motion. Is there *anyone* that could testify the two of you had anything other than a great relationship?"

"Absolutely not. No one. I think I could get you ten people that would say we had a great one, though. You just let me know how many you need."

"Do you have idea how she got that bump on her head?"

"None."

"No one can testify you were seeing another woman at the time you were married to her?"

"No, no one."

"How did you initially meet her?"

"I just walked up to her and introduced myself as I did with others that I didn't know, and over a period of time I knew everyone in the church."

"You know, I just think if this motion works, and it should, if we can keep that evidence out, we may be home free."

"That's good news, for sure. Did I just hear someone lock the front office door?"

Ruth looked at her watch. "You did. How about catching a bite to eat. There's a sandwich joint down the street. Not much to it, but I'm willing to chance it if you are."

"Sure. I'll buy, since as of yet, you are not rich. After your trial though, you can do the buying with all the loot you will have."

"I'll tell you what. After it's all over, if I win, I will buy—steak, potatoes, the whole nine yards."

He smiled as he said, "I'll hold you to that, Ruth. I'll just hold you to that."

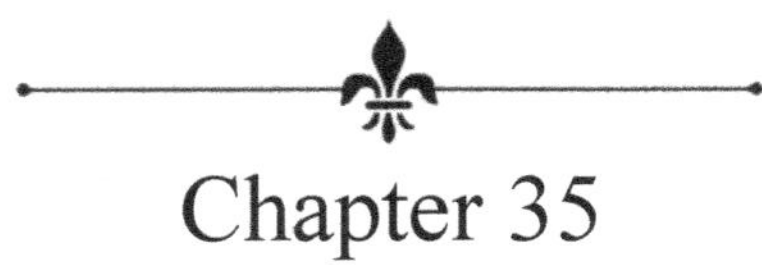

Chapter 35

Davidson County Courthouse
Martha VanArsdayle Estate Trial, Day two

It was not his turn. He would get his turn in time, but for now, it was up to George Grisham to question the witnesses. They were his witnesses. But Paul would get his chance at them, and it shouldn't be long. Although if George had his way, if he could handle direct examination the way he wished, they would all just remain glued to their seats while George talked and talked and talked his way into the thirty-first century.

Paul had known George and known *of* George since he first started practicing. George was old then—he was *way* old now. He had handled cases with him before. Mr. Grisham was the consummate southern gentleman. He could charm you to death, with his slow deliberate, southern drawl. However, he was now finally starting to show his age. He wasn't quite as quick to 'get it' nor were his arguments as much on point as they once were. But George in his subprime, was still better than most attorneys in their prime.

They had been battling for two days. George had presented a considerable amount of evidence establishing the character and characteristics of Martha VanArsdayle. He had paraded a number of witnesses before the court all of whom said the same thing—that Martha was strong willed, but her opinions, as she grew older could be altered. She could be swayed. Her mind could be changed if you presented what might appear, at first glance, to be a viable option and that option sounded as though it made more sense than the option she had previously approved.

But Paul noticed that no one had testified Martha changed her mind easily, without considering all options. In addition, no one had testified that, as she grew older, she seemed to lose her ability to reason or to process all available options. No one had testified that she tended to accept other opinions rather than figuring out the solution to the problem she was considering by herself. They hadn't presented any evidence whatsoever concerning these factors because evidence in that respect did not exist.

At the moment, George had just finished completing foundational testimony with what apparently would be his last witness—Rhonda Collins, Martha's only daughter.

George had made it clear that Steven, Rhonda's son, would not testify, although he was in the courtroom listening to the evidence.

Direct examination of Rhonda, even as concerned foundational issues, had taken much longer than other attorneys would have taken. He was hoping George just got tired and ran out of energy, perhaps shortening Rhonda's remaining testimony concerning the most important elements of the case.

George followed his notes word by word which he had previously prepared as his guide for examining Ms. Collins. He would figure out his next question, then look over the top of his rimless glasses and slowly deliver each word, as if it were the most important word everyone in the courtroom would hear the rest of the week. Slow and deliberate was his way, and would remain his way until he finished. All others seated in the courtroom would need to accept his way of doing things, until he finally finished, which Paul hoped would be sometime today.

"Now, Ms. Rhonda, how many kids do you have?"

"Two."

"How long you have been married to that husband of yours, Greg."

"Thirty-one years."

"You ever been married to any other man?"

"No."

"What do you do, Ms. Rhonda? Do you work?"

"No. I haven't worked in years."

"What does your husband do?"

"He is a car salesman."

"What was the relationship between yourself and your mother?"

"It was wonderful. I loved her as much as she loved me."

"What about the kids and your husband, Greg? What type of relationship did they have with her?"

"It couldn't have been better. She loved each of them and they loved her."

"I'll just bet they did. Did you ever talk to your mother about her money?"

"Yes, on occasion."

"Specifically, what did you discuss."

"We would discuss how much she had, where it was invested, and how she wanted it divided amongst family members when she died."

"Did that type of conversation abruptly stop?"

"Yes."

"When?"

"Not long after Ruth Andrews became her attorney."

"Did you continue to try to discuss monetary issues with her after that?"

"Yes."

"What was the result of those attempts?"

"After Ms. Andrews became her attorney, she never wanted to discuss money issues with me again."

"Did she discuss them with Steven, if you know?"

"No. She never discussed money issues with any member of the family after Ruth became her attorney."

"Did you notice any other changes in your mother after Ruth became involved with her?"

"Yes. I never heard from her. It was seldom she would call, and when *I* called, she didn't have time to talk. It was a marked departure from what our relationship had been before."

"Did she talk about Ruth?"

"Oh god, yes. It got so old. It was Ruth this and Ruth that. When I was finally able to talk to her, all she talked about was the nights Ruth would eat supper at her house, or Ruth had taken her out to eat, or her visit with Ruth at Ruth's office. It was sickening."

"Were you surprised when the will was read?"

"At first, yes, I cried for a week. But then as I started to think back, I was able to figure out what this Ruth character had done. She had poisoned our relationship with our mother and influenced her to the point she gave her everything. It was so obvious that was what she had done. And it was too late to do anything about it…to discuss it with mother and point it all out. She was gone. So, we filed this suit to make things right again."

"What do you think should be done here, Ms. Rhonda, to make things right, to fix the wrong that's been perpetrated upon you…upon you *and* your lovely family?"

"The will needs to be set aside and the money and property allowed to pass on to her children the way it was supposed to, and would have if that woman, that attorney, hadn't poisoned her against us."

"Your Honor, I don't believe I have any more questions for this witness."

"Mr. Thomas, cross?"

"Yes, Your Honor."

Paul stood, and said, "Your Honor, may I approach?"

"Of course."

Paul walked toward the witness as he said, "You indicate your relationship with your mother was close. How often did you see her the last full year of her life?"

"Once."

"Any reason?"

"It was Christmas."

"No, no ma'am, any reason you visited her so *seldom*?"

"No, I guess not."

"Is that about the same number of times your children saw her?"

"Yes."

"Did you ever ask her for money?"

She hesitated before saying, "Well, on occasion. Yes, there were times when we needed extra money, and I would ask her for it."

"How often would you say that happened during the last year of her life—and remember now, you are under oath."

"I don't know for sure."

"Guess for me."

"Oh, I don't know, maybe six or seven. I just don't know."

"You have had money issues in the past few years, haven't you?"

"A few, yes."

"And when those issues would come up, you would use your mother as your own personal banker wouldn't you?"

"I guess so, yes. She would help us if we needed help."

"What did you get her for Christmas last year, Ms. Collins?"

Slowly, George stood, and muttered. "Objection. Relevance."

"Overruled. The witness may answer."

"Well, nothing. She said she didn't want anything, so I got her nothing."

"What about the year before?"

"Probably nothing then either."

As Paul returned to his chair he said, "Was this always a one-way relationship—she did the giving; you did the taking?"

"Objection."

"Sustained. Move on."

Paul knew he had made his point, even though the objection was sustained.

"So apparently you knew this Ruth person, was involved in your mother's life for quite some time before she died, correct?"

"Yes, I did."

"What effort did you make to determine exactly who she was and what effect she might be having upon your mother?"

"Well, I asked mom about her and I looked her name up in the phone book a few times."

"Did you ever call her?"

"No."

"Did you ever observe them when they were together?"

"No."

"Did you ever do *one* thing to try to tie down what was going on with Ruth and Martha?"

She looked down and said, "Nothing other than what I just described, no."

"Did you ever offer to help your mother with her finances?"

"No, I guess not. I just figured she knew what she was doing."

"Did you ever check into perhaps an assisted living facility for her? She was at the age where that might have helped her."

"No. I just figured she would tell me when she was ready for that, I guess."

"Did you ever check with her doctor, to see if there might be dementia issues, or loss of memory issues?"

"I did once, yes."

"What did he tell you?"

"He said she knew what she was doing."

"He is going to testify at this hearing. He, in fact, told you on the day you talked to him, she had never been sharper, didn't he?"

"Objection."

"Overruled. The witness may answer."

"Yes, that's what he said."

"You knew Ruth was spending a lot of time with your mother,

didn't you?"

"Yes. I knew what she was doing. She wasn't kidding me."

"Then why, in god's name, didn't you do something about it? If that's what you really thought, why didn't you do something about it?"

She said nothing.

Paul's voice became elevated, as he said, "The fact of the matter is Ms. Collins, you had little, if any, relationship with your mother, did you? Ruth took the role of a daughter she never had in the first place, didn't she? She cared about Martha, and Martha cared for her. Ruth became the daughter she never had. That's the truth now isn't it, Ms. Collins, that's the god's truth, isn't it?"

"Objection!"

"No, that's not the truth, Mr. Thomas. You believe whatever the hell you want to believe, but no…"

"Hold on here, hold on." The judge rapped his gavel on the sounding block a couple of times and said, "We have an objection here. Let's all just calm down. The objection is overruled. She answered the question, now Mr. Thomas, move on."

Paul took his seat and said, "That's all, Your Honor. We have nothing more."

Harold leaned over and whispered, "That certainly went well."

Paul smiled and said, "It was easy. She is an idiot. They had no relationship at all. I think they are out of witnesses. I hope so, because what they have provided so far doesn't appear to me to be enough to win the case. If Ruth comes through, I think we are home free."

Harold nodded, as the judge, said, "Next witness."

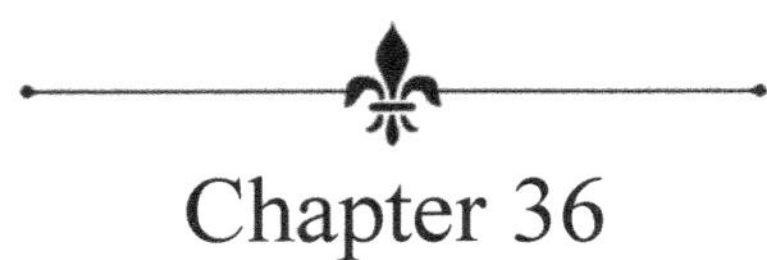

Chapter 36

Davidson County Courthouse
Martha VanArsdayle Estate Trial, Day 4

They had been in court three full days and would wrap everything up on this, the fourth day, unless there was rebuttal evidence on behalf of the plaintiffs. Paul doubted that would happen.

Everything the plaintiffs had to say had been said. The Rules of Evidence provide there could be no *new* evidence that could be introduced during rebuttal. Only testimony to rebut what was originally testified to by Ruth and her witnesses could now be introduced. He just didn't figure Grisham would take the court's time to simply deny all the evidence their witnesses had offered.

Once Grisham rested, the estate had a number of Martha's friends that hadn't already testified, provide their opinion as to her competency. All of them explained to the court that, in their opinion, Martha was competent right up until the end. They also informed the court that nobody, absolutely nobody, told her what to do. She was strong in will and mind right up until the day she died.

The estate had introduced the video into evidence. Everyone sat quietly while Martha detailed her reasons for leaving her money and other assets to Ruth, rather than her family. Harold had been crafty in selecting his questions, and the resulting answers made Martha's final conclusions appear thoroughly considered and rational. There was never a word spoken about Ruth's responsibility to distribute money to family and friends.

At the conclusion of the children's presentation of evidence the estate had filed a motion to dismiss the children's case, which the court overruled. The ruling was no surprise. It was clear to everyone the plaintiffs had not presented enough evidence to win the case, but the judge wanted to hear everything before he ruled, which included evidence from the plaintiffs *and* from the estate.

"The estate would now call Ruth Andrews to the stand."

Paul would watch her testify and do nothing more. Harold would handle this witness. Ruth would most likely make or break the case. Even though the preponderance of evidence was clearly with the estate, her testimony offered in an appropriate manner, was crucial.

Once the necessary foundational requirements were dispensed with, Harold said, "Now Ruth, how long did you know the deceased, Martha VanArsdayle before she died?"

"Almost two years I guess."

Ruth had dressed conservatively. Paul smiled as he compared her choice of apparel to Hanna's attire which Paul had observed in the office before he left for the courthouse. Ruth appeared poised and professional, yet approachable and somewhat vulnerable—perfect for her role today as a witness, rather than as an attorney.

"How well did you get to know her?"

She looked down for a moment, before she said, "Very well. We spent a considerable amount of time together before she passed."

"What did you do when you were with her?"

Ruth smiled. "Whatever she wanted to do. Some days we would just talk about issues around the city. Some days she would want to discuss her family. Some days she would want me to take her on a ride around the city. We did what she wanted to do. There were many, many days I never even charged her, even though our relationship grew out of the practice. I just enjoyed her company, her wit, her wisdom. I couldn't charge her for those things and I didn't. She was a wonderful woman and I miss her every day—even now…"

"You say she discussed her family?"

"Yes."

"What did she say to you about them?"

"She didn't understand why they didn't come see her more often. I had no answer—I had no idea—so I wouldn't respond. But she grew bitter about it near the end. She said the money was all that was important to them."

"Did she tell you what she was going to do with that money, with her property?"

"Yes, she did."

"What was your response?"

"I just told her I would rather not discuss that issue."

"What happened then?"

"She would bring it up at least once a week. I finally said I do *not* want to discuss that subject. If you are really interested in leaving something to me, you need to see a different attorney, because I can't draw up a will leaving *anything* to me."

"What was her response?"

Ruth grinned and said, "She said, 'Then by god go hire another attorney for me because that's what I'm a gonna do.' I lined one up for her, and he handled that issue from there on."

"Was it ever discussed with you again?"

"She tried to bring it up one other time, and I just told her I couldn't discuss it. I never did after I lined her up with you."

"Were you there when she was asked questions on the video?"

"No. I didn't even know you did it until a couple of weeks later, and she was the one that told me."

"Was there ever a time you requested or suggested she leave what she had to you?"

"Never. As every witness has testified, she was a woman who did what she wanted to do when she wanted to do it. Nobody told her what to do or how to do it. She was the most independent woman I ever knew." She looked down and whispered, "I was proud to call her my friend."

"Nothing further."

"Mr. Grisham, cross?"

"Yes, Your Honor, just a few questions. Now, ma'am, how often would you meet with Ms. Martha?"

"Oh, I guess probably once a week."

"And you never discussed her money, or how it would pass in her will?"

"At first, we did, because she wanted me to handle it. She changed her will about every other week. It was discussed around the office. She literally changed it every other week and always for some silly, petty reason. But, once she told me she wanted money to come to me, we never discussed it again—never."

"Now, Mr. Vorhies and you were classmates weren't you—at Vanderbilt?"

"Yes."

"Why did you send her to him?"

"I have known him for years. I trusted him. I wanted to send her to someone I trusted and who I felt would do her a good job. That was Harold. She told me later how well she had gotten along with him, so I figured they had been a good fit."

"You have some kind a deal with him, did you?"

"What do you mean, 'deal'?"

"He made the changes you wanted…Martha wanted… in return for a kickback at some point in time. That's what I mean."

Harold stood and said, "Objection! That's way out of line, Your Honor. I realize it's cross, but that's out of line."

"Overruled. Answer the question."

Ruth looked directly at Grisham, and said, "We neither *had* nor do we *have* a deal, Mr. Grisham. Harold did what Ms. Martha wanted him to do and that is the end of the story."

"You ever buy her things, Ms. Andrews? When the two of you went out to eat, did you ever buy her supper, or any little thing or two for her house?"

"Never. She always paid for the food, and I never, ever purchased anything for her. She had enough stuff in her house for two houses anyway. She never indicated she ever wanted any more than she already had."

"Did you ever make any effort to contact her family, to tell them that Martha missed them and wanted to see them more frequently than she did? Did you ever make any effort to ease the pain that seemed to be causing her?"

"No. At first, everything she told me was confidential—I was her attorney. But later, when it became clear someone else needed to handle the will issue, she just asked me to keep all these family issues to myself. That is exactly what I did."

Grisham looked at his papers scattered across the council table, trying to make a determination as to whether he had covered everything he wanted to. As he did, Paul looked around the courtroom, trying to find anyone he might recognize, that might testify on rebuttal. But, the only person in the courtroom other than Martha's family, was that Ed whatshisname that Ruth had taken on as a client. He was seated near the back, by himself. Other than that, the courtroom was empty.

"Your Honor, I believe that's all."

"Mr. Vorhies, any redirect?"

Harold leaned over and whispered to Paul, "I don't think we need to go any further with her, do you?"

"No. She has done a good job. I agree. Let's not press it."

Harold stood and said, "We have no redirect, Your Honor. In addition, we have no more evidence to offer on behalf of the estate. We rest."

The judge looked down at Ruth and said, "You may step down, Ms. Andrews. Any rebuttal, Mr. Grisham?"

Grisham leaned over to whisper a few words to Rhonda, then turned toward the judge and said, "No, Your Honor. We have nothing further."

"Thank you, Mr. Grisham. Closing statements by either attorney or do you waive?"

Harold stood and said, "Your Honor, there's no jury here. You heard the evidence as well as we did. We will just let it speak for itself."

Grisham stood, and said, "We concur, Your Honor. No sense in wasting your time and ours in repeating evidence you've already heard."

The judge nodded his approval, then started to gather up all the paperwork on his desktop. He looked down at the court reporter and said, "Make sure we have all the exhibits and bring them back when you have a moment. You attorneys can provide briefs in support of your position if you wish. I will give you 14 days to do that and not rule until I have had a chance to review them. Thank you, everyone. Court is adjourned."

Ruth stood and walked toward the council table. Once there she said, "Paul, I have someone I need to visit with—a client actually, Ed Hall. I'll just see you back at the office. Thanks, Harold."

Paul watched her as she walked to the back of the courtroom where Ed stood as she approached. He wondered about the body language of both. He was concerned there might be more to the relationship than attorney/client. But, at least for now, that wasn't any of his business.

What *was* his business, was the ruling in *this* case. The trial had ended. He would help Harold put a brief together, and they would submit it within the two-week deadline. Then they would wait. They would all wait for a decision which would affect everyone's life that participated—and affect it in a permanent, substantial manner.

Chapter 37

Sam Harvey was not having the best of days. He had caught a cold, he was having an argument with his wife and later this morning, he had to meet with an assistant attorney general he did not like. As he sat at his desk, in the early hours of the morning, he tried to work through those issues he had some ability to control. But as he considered each problem, he realized he probably had no control over *any* of them.

First of all, he couldn't *stop* getting sick—he had absolutely no control over that. Secondly, his wife would need to get over the fact he worked so many hours—that just wasn't going to change. Third, the only assistant attorney general he didn't like, had been assigned to prosecute Edward Hall. He couldn't change that either—he had to deal with whoever was assigned to the case, but that didn't mean he had to like it. The prosecutor was soft. He wanted more than his share of easy wins and to hell with anything that might provide a challenge. He hadn't had a chance to visit with him about this case, but nothing good had come out of the cases he had prosecuted with Sam in the past—he didn't figure the Hall case would alter their history.

"Morning, boss. How was your night?"

Sam stared at him and finally said, "What the hell do you care?"

His partner smiled and said, "Oh my, what a great start to *our* day. I think I will let you go off by yourself today. I've got plenty of office work to do at my desk that will keep me busy most of the day. Clearly you need time to yourself. Oh boy, *do* you need time to yourself."

"You didn't happen to hear from our guy inside Oliver's group, did you? I haven't heard from him in a while, and I'm starting to worry."

"Not a word."

"I am going to ask around. I hate to do that. I don't want to compromise his cover, but I'm starting to worry about whether he is even alive."

"He will show up."

A couple of hours later, Sam walked into the office of Jack Hopkins, assistant attorney general for Davidson County. His secretary ushered Sam directly into his office, where the prosecutor was waiting.

Jack stood and said, "Morning, Sam. How are you this fine day?"

Jack stood about five feet seven, but his girth was what caught your attention, coming close to exceeding his height.

Sam shook his hand, and said, "Oh, I'm fine, Jack, how about yourself?"

Both men sat, as Jack said, "Oh, I am just peachy. It's been a while since I've seen you." He laughed and said, "I wasn't sure whether you had retired, quit or got shot."

Sam wondered what the hell Jack had for breakfast. His breath smelled like he had just eaten road kill. There was nothing about this man he liked.

"Oh, I've been around, Jack. I guess I just haven't drawn you on any of my cases, but I work most every day, just like I am sure you do."

His comment was true right up to the 'just like I am sure you do.' He really figured the guy never worked a full day in his life.

"So, Jack what do we need to discuss? What are the issues with the Hall case we need to talk about?"

"Well, I thought maybe we just needed to discuss it in general for now. You know, his trial isn't far away. In a month or so, we will be trying this before a jury so I thought we should just touch base. What are your thoughts about a plea bargain? You want me to try to bargain this out?"

He had assumed that would be the first issue they would discuss. He figured Hopkins would first look at a way to make it easy.

"Hell, no. This guy has murdered at least three women that I know of. I haven't had much luck going back any further, but I don't have much doubt there have been others. He's a rich man because of each one of those murders. No, I think we should push this all the way to the end."

"You understand that the best evidence we have, is the death of those prior wives, don't you? I mean, sure, we have the evidence from this case—renting the boat early, the wound on her head, all the money. But to be honest, I don't know that that, in and of itself, is going to get us a conviction."

"But, in my opinion, you haven't even adequately considered the strongest part of our case. We have the information concerning those other wives. That should cinch a conviction."

"Well, that's one of the reasons I wanted to visit with you. The defense attorney has filed a motion to suppress any evidence involving those prior deaths and if it's sustained, any information concerning the deaths will be unavailable for use in our case."

Sam slid forward in his chair. "You got to be kidding me. Why would the judge even consider keeping that information out of evidence?"

"Because there was never even an investigation concerning either of those cases in those other two states. Law enforcement simply took statements and ended it right there. But, if that is introduced as evidence in this case, even though there wasn't a shred of evidence indicating that those other two cases were crimes, the jury could find him guilty even though there is a serious lack of evidence in *this* case. The judge has the right to keep it out and make us get a conviction based solely on the facts, the evidence, in *this* case."

"But the three situations are all connected."

"That's *your* opinion. It is not well supported by the facts, because neither law enforcement agency found any evidence of wrongdoing in either of those first two cases."

"That is just pure bullshit to me. What are our chances here?"

"No idea. They filled the motion, and I resisted it. If it is sustained, you and I will really need to look for any additional facts we can come up with to further support our case, because that ruling could definitely hurt us. I don't think the grand jury would have even indicted him if we hadn't been able to present evidence concerning those other two cases. I am sure you are aware we can use about anything we have to get an indictment, but the rules are much more restrictive when we are actually trying the case."

"So, if the motion is sustained, are you throwing in the towel?"

"No, no, not at all. I have every intention of pursuing it even without those other deaths." He stood. "But certainly, you and I will need to discuss it," he smiled, "and together, decide what to do." He extended his hand, "Hey, thanks a lot for coming in today. Good seeing you."

Sam stood and without shaking his hand, turned and walked out the door. He already knew what the bastard was going to do without evidence concerning the other two cases.

A couple of hours later as he sat at his desk, his partner walked in the door and toward his own desk.

Sam said, "Where you been?"

"Out to lunch. You know, like a normal person, I eat at noon. You should try it. Maybe you wouldn't be so damn mean the rest of the day."

"Screw you, you prick."

Terry laughed and as he sat, he said, "You know, you look awful. Not that you ever look good, but today you have really, really taken a turn for the worse. Are you sick?"

"I just finished talking to that prosecutor Hopkins. He was telling me we may have a problem with the Hall case. I hate that jerk. Always have. He has no drive. He takes easy convictions and never, ever wants to work for the hard ones."

"So, are they going to toss it?"

"Not yet. They're waiting on the results of a motion the defense filed and then they will move on from there. Who knows what this son-of-a-bitch will do. You heard any more from our snitch with Oliver?"

"Not a word. I'm not hearing much of anything from that whole group. They are really quiet, which bothers me more than when they are active."

Sam stood and put on his suit coat.

"Where you going?"

"I'm going to go nose around a little concerning our guy inside. I got a few people I can see that might tell me something about what is going on."

"Want me to go with you?"

"No. I'm going alone. You told me how much office work you had to do anyway. So do it."

Sam walked towards the door and, as he did, he blew his nose. His cold was getting worse, he had this idiot prosecutor to deal with, he had lost his snitch with the Oliver gang, and his wife hated him. On top of it all, he now needed to go talk to a couple of hoodlums about a subject they would *not* want to discuss.

It was time to consider retirement. Time to put his feet up and relax. Time to…Oh, who the hell was he kidding—because it sure as hell wasn't himself. He would leave this job kicking and screaming, hopefully when he was 90 years old. But he had to admit today had been just a little over the top, even for him.

Chapter 38

It had been a couple of weeks since the conclusion of the hearing involving Martha's will. Both parties submitted briefs outlining their legal position prior to the two-week deadline. Now everyone waited for a ruling.

Ruth tried to move on. It was difficult to say the least. There was an underlying tension within the office. The three of them knew how much was at stake. No one discussed it.

She immersed herself in her work—particularly as concerned the Hall case. Trial was but a few weeks away, and she needed to find people that would testify on his behalf, especially as concerned Ed's relationship with his wife. She felt that was a crucial element of evidence for their case, and she had already lined up three women that would testify favorably for the defense. She was still waiting for a ruling on her motion to suppress. The judge had taken it under advisement and was researching all the issues the motion presented. She knew it wasn't a simple legal issue to decide and the ruling, whichever way it was decided, would substantially affect the case.

She had met with Ed a number of times, both in her office and over supper. He had never expressed any personal feelings concerning her, but she felt, in her heart, there was much more between them than attorney/client. She was doing what she could to suppress the feelings she had about him, but she wasn't sure she could or would do that much longer.

She walked out her office door, stopping to stand in the door frame of Paul's office, as she said, "How are you doing, Paul?"

"Professionally or personally?"

"Personally. How you getting along without her?"

"Fine, I guess. It's tough. I just muddle through the day, and try to make sense of everything. The worst part of it is going home to that empty house." He looked down and cleared his throat before he proceeded. "Even though she was sick, she was still there. I could talk to her, explain the problems I had—just verbalize it all. Even though she couldn't respond, it was a positive for me. Now, the house is so damn empty…and cold. I've considered moving. There are just too many memories."

"I'm so sorry, Paul. I'm so sorry you have to go through this."

"Thanks. I appreciate that." He hesitated for a moment before he said, "Now…let's… move on. What's going on in your professional life?"

"I am getting ready to try the Hall case. I know you haven't been much involved in it so far, but do you want to second chair me on that or would you rather not?"

"Hey, Ruth, tell him the clerk's office is on line one," Hanna yelled down the hallway.

"Interesting intercom system we have here, Paul. The clerk's office is on line one."

Paul picked up, and while he visited with the clerk of court, Ruth continued to assess their position concerning the Hall trial.

Paul finished his conference with the clerk, and hung up. "We have a decision. The judge filed a written ruling this morning. She's going to fax it over."

Ruth thought she was going to be sick. There was so much riding on one decision. She watched as it came through the fax machine. She watched as Hanna stood and started down the hallway. Everything moved in slow motion. Nothing mattered but the paperwork in her hands. Nothing existed, but the words on those sheets of faxed paper.

Hanna laid it on Paul's desk and stood with Ruth while Paul read the decision.

Ruth couldn't read him. He read with no emotion—not a line on his face moved as he went from page to page to page. Finally, he set it down, looked at Ruth, smiled and said, "Break out the booze, Ruth. You are one rich woman."

Ruth whispered, "We won?"

"Absolutely. Not only that, but all costs, including all professional fees for the people we had testify, have been assessed to the plaintiffs. We won alright! Get the bourbon out. I don't give a shit what time it is. This is a monster decision. We're going to celebrate, at least for a moment."

Hanna locked the front door. Ruth grabbed the bourbon and three glasses. For the next hour, they dissected the decision word by word. It was a well-considered decision, supported by legal precedent throughout. The judge's ruling would be very difficult to overturn, even if it was appealed. It touched upon every legal issue presented by the plaintiffs, and in ruling against each of their points of law, he had included both factual support and legal precedent. There would be little chance of overruling his decision, assuming they appealed.

An hour later, as the quickly organized party just as quickly disbanded, Ruth walked into her own office, shut her door, and called Harold.

"Hey, Ruth. I figured I would hear from you this morning. We came out pretty well, didn't we?"

"It concluded as it should have, Harold. I just want to thank you for all you did."

"We work pretty well together. Maybe we should form our own partnership. What do you think?"

Ruth leaned back in her chair and laughed. "I think I like it where I am. Besides, how are we going to do this again if we are both in the same office. I don't want to have to be fighting you as we each try to take over the others clients. I think I like it just like it is."

"But we should do this again sometime, don't you think?"

"Sure. If the right situation comes up, I'm all for it. I better wait a while before I pay you. I think we should wait for the appeal time to run, regardless of whether or not they plan on appealing."

"George just called. They aren't going to appeal. The cost is more than they can handle and he feels the odds of overturning the decision were very, very small. I don't think we need to worry about that."

"I still think we need to wait. It's only 30 days anyway. After the time for an appeal has run, we can transfer all the money to me, then figure out how to pay you without leaving any trail of the payment. Does that work for you?"

"Yes. Do you need any help in investing the money? I've helped quite a few people get a pretty good rate of return if you need some help."

"That would be great. I will discuss it with you at the appropriate time. Thanks again, Harold."

She hung up and as she did, she felt euphoric! She needed to discuss, to celebrate, to enjoy this moment with someone…someone other than her coworkers.

"Hey, Ed, what's going on?"

"Oh, I'm just sitting here wondering how long they are going to lock me up. I'm just starting to pack a few things. You know, just contemplating my immediate, fricking future, that's all. And you? What are you doing? I suppose you're thinking about meaningful, significant issues too…like wondering which dress you might wear to work tomorrow?"

"Now, come on. You need a change in attitude. After all, you just *might* be as lucky with your decision as I just was with mine."

He hesitated. "Did you win? Did you win your case?"

"I did. I just got the decision. What are you doing tonight? How about supper—maybe this time without all the discussion concerning witnesses and legal issues. What do you think?"

"I'm in. And I think you said something about paying if you won? Does my memory serve me correctly? Isn't this the meal *you* buy?"

She laughed. "It is. So, let's go somewhere that's not so costly. What about Burger King."

"What about Husk? I'll make reservations."

"Whoa. You been there? That's pretty expensive."

"It's also one of the best in Nashville. I'll meet you there 'bout seven."

As she terminated the call, she thought about him—and his money. She was literally shaking. She was rich. No, was *very* rich.

But there was more to it than that. The sense of accomplishment, of total victory, of successfully deceiving so many people and ending up with such a reward for doing it, was almost more than she could stand.

She would need to figure out what to do with the money. She would most likely invest it, conservatively for now and became slightly more adventuresome as she started to learn the investment game.

But more importantly than that, she needed to move on. She had only just begun. This was way too exciting to stop with only one major victory.

Of course, now there was Ed to consider…and on so many levels. He was rich, but that didn't seem quite as important as the fact that she was attracted to him romantically. He was tall, good looking, great personality…*and* rich. She might need to do some sole searching. What would take priority when it came to Edward Hall—romance, or money? Maybe she could work on a little of both. Maybe she could swing this deal to work both ways. She would sure as hell sleep with him whenever he was ready, *but certainly a girl could always use a few million more.*

Chapter 39

Ruth had at least a dozen issues that needed to be resolved and resolved today. As she continued to prepare for the Hall trial, there were litigation issues involving other cases that needed to be either settled or put off.

As she continued to check her calendar and contact clients, Hanna informed her Jack Hopkins was on line one. She knew this call would involve Hall—she also knew Hopkins was an ass.

"Morning, Jack. How are you?"

"Fine."

"How can I help you?"

"I just wanted to touch base with you concerning this Hall matter. Do you have any thoughts about a resolution?"

"Sure, just dismiss it."

He hesitated. "Obviously, I can't do that. What about pleading to something? How about manslaughter? I've got my bosses permission to reduce it to manslaughter. That at least gives him the benefit of the crime being a spur of the moment decision, rather than her death being preplanned. How's that?"

"Oh, I really doubt, since he had nothing to do with her death, he would agree to plead to anything of that nature. What about some type of charge associated with driving the boat in a reckless manner? I haven't looked yet, but I'm sure there's a code section which would fit that situation."

He laughed. "Are you kidding? You're joking, right?"

"No, not really. He never intended to hurt her in any respect. That's why it will be hard to get him to plead to anything involving injuring or killing her. He never intended for any of this to happen."

"I suppose that was the case in Colorado and California too? *Those* women just happened to die of unnatural causes *too*? Give me a break. We need to resolve this prior to Judge Dimmler's ruling on your motion. Once he rules that the evidence concerning the other wives' deaths can come in, all negotiations are off. I have some leverage with my boss *right now*, in that if the motion is sustained, it might be more difficult getting a conviction. After his ruling, if the motion is overruled, which I expect, I'll have no leeway whatsoever. Now, what do you want to do?"

"At this time, I'm not really sure—I would need to discuss this conversation at length with him. But I do know one thing—I *can't* plead him to manslaughter."

"Okay, why don't you go ahead and discuss it with *him*, then contact me."

He hesitated for a moment, then said, "You are not going to get this guy off, whether *that* evidence comes in or not, I can tell you that. He is done. He's murdered at least three women, and he's going to pay. That you can take that to the bank."

It took everything she had to contain herself. She bit her lip, she thought of all the money she just inherited, she thought of pretty little kittens—she tried to consider everything good in this world. Finally, after a deep breath, she said, "Let me visit with him. I'll get back to you."

"Just so you know, this is the last time we are going to discuss a bargain. You either work this out with him and plead to something realistic before the judge's ruling or we are done."

He terminated the call. She looked at her quiet phone considering how he had just ended the call. As she continued to smolder, she just hoped the motion was sustained and all that evidence was kept out, not so much for Ed's sake, but just so she could rub the ruling in that bastard's face.

She had just started another project when, again, Hanna buzzed her. "Ruth, John Stone is on line 1."

"He wants to talk to *me*?"

"That's what he said. What do you want to do?"

"I guess I better take it."

She took a deep breath, griped the phone tightly just before she spoke, as if it might jump out of her hand, and said, "Good day, Mr. Stone. How are you?"

"I'm fine, just fine and you?"

"I guess I'll let you know at the end of the call."

He laughed, and said, "This is a good call, not the kind I normally make. I just wanted to let you know that you, your office, your boss, are all off the hook as far as our committee is concerned. The ruling in the VanArsdayle matter was very clear in vindicating you and your actions. It was short and to the point, clearly establishing that not only did you do nothing wrong, you in fact took affirmative action to make sure you did everything right. I, along with the members of the committee, were impressed with how you handled yourself."

She took a deep breath, leaned back in her chair, and said, "Thank you, sir. That means a lot coming from you. I'll pass our conversation on to Paul. I'm sure he too, will be happy to hear that."

"Carry on."

She terminated the call and walked to the doorway of Paul's office where he was reviewing a transcription of a deposition he had finished a couple of weeks ago.

"I just got a call from John Stone."

His head snapped up as he said, "What for? What did he want to talk to you for.?"

"He was very complimentary. He just said we, you and I, the office, were off the hook concerning any issues involving Martha's will. He mentioned he thought I had done a good job in averting a problem and there would be no further investigation concerning the estate or us. Good news for sure."

Paul sat back in his chair, started to smile, and said, "Why don't you come in for a moment. Let's talk."

Ruth hesitated, then said, "Okay. What's this all about?'

As she took a seat in front of Paul's desk, he said, "I was a little concerned when all this came out about Martha and the will. I was concerned about whether I had made the correct choice in hiring you, especially in the beginning, when it all came out and the suit was filed."

"Okay, so where are we at now?"

"Of course, Anna died too, so my whole frame of mind was somewhat distorted. I really wondered if you were a good fit here." He hesitated for a moment, then said, "What do you think, Ruth? Are you a good fit here?"

She considered all her options in the blink of an eye. "Yes, I think I'm a great fit here." She thought for a moment. "So, what's going on here...are you getting ready to fire me? That's not what I want. I love working here." She started to tear up. "I love working with you, with crazy Hanna. I don't want to go anywhere else."

Paul smiled and said, "I don't…."

She interrupted him. "I love working with you." She dabbed at her eyes. "I don't think I did anything wrong. I really, really don't want to find another place to work."

Paul leaned forward in his chair and said, "That was the same…"

"I think we make a great team. I don't want to give that…"

"Stop! Stop, Ruth. That's why I called you in. I have come to the same conclusion you have. We are a pretty good team, and even under the most difficult of situations—the death of my wife, the lawsuit involving Martha—we were able to work it through and come out just fine. Not only do I want you to stay, I'm going to increase your pay."

"Oh my god, really." She stood. "Can I just kiss you? Just on the cheek. I could kiss you right now, you know. That's how happy I am. Thank you, thank you, thank you."

She started to come around the end of his desk, when he stood, and extended his hand. "How 'bout just a handshake?"

She shook his hand, and said, "And just a little hug."

She embraced him, as he embraced her.

"Have a seat. What are you going to do with all your money?"

As she sat back down, she said, "I don't know. It has already been transferred to me before the time has run for the appeal. Not what I wanted, but on the other hand, they have made it clear they aren't going to appeal so I guess it's all right. I think I'll just spread it out between five or six Nashville banks, and put it in CD's for now. I'll figure it out as I go along."

"What about Hall? Have you got that one figured out yet?"

"No. I just got a call from that prick Jack Hopkins this morning. He wants to bargain it out, but of course only on his terms. I need to talk to Ed about that, but I'm sure he won't plead to anything that's acceptable to Jack."

"So, what's the plan?"

"I'm just going to wait and see how Judge Dimmler rules on the motion. If he would happen to sustain it, I really think the State's in trouble. I think that's why he called—he believes they will have a problem getting a conviction without the evidence concerning the death of the other two wives. I'm gambling a little here because I'm not going to recommend Ed plead to anything. I really think the motion will be sustained, and the State will have a hell of a job getting a conviction. I'm willing to roll the dice, I guess. So, what do you think?'

"You know the case a lot better than I do. I probably need to review the file. The trial comes up in a few weeks, doesn't it?"

"Yes. I wish to hell the judge would rule. It's going to make a huge difference concerning trial strategy. Hopefully, we will get his ruling in the next few days."

"You know, just to cover yourself, you might want to discuss that plea bargain matter in depth with Ed. Maybe have him sign off on rejecting any and all plea bargains so you have it for the file. You don't want to get into a 'he said/she said' situation if they convict him."

She stood. "I had already planned on that. I will have the paperwork ready for him the next time I see him. Thanks for your vote of confidence. I won't let you down, I promise."

She turned to leave his office and into hers. As she did, she thought it best to discuss the matter of the plea bargain soon—maybe discuss both the plea bargain and his finances over dinner. She would be subtle, but while they would certainly discuss business, she was also interested in knowing how he invested his money…and where.

Chapter 40

Ed Hall sat alone, with a half cup of cold coffee, in his robe, watching a dark TV screen. He had turned it off ten minutes ago. He understood he was in Nashville, but he figured if he had to watch another rerun of *Heehaw*, he might lose his mind.

His situation the past few months had turned into a life of slow motion. Janice was dead, so he lacked his normal day-to-day contact with her. Of course, he had elected to live that way once he decided to kill her, but the fact still remained his days had become somewhat protracted without intermittent conversation with someone.

They made him wear an ankle bracelet which restricted where he could go and what he could do. While he didn't think they were continuing to watch him, he still didn't feel comfortable meeting up with Patricia. The bracelet told them where he was—he didn't want to meet with her while they unknowingly watched.

He had gone fishing a time or two, but even that had become old. It had been so much more exciting when he was fishing *and* planning her murder.

Even though he couldn't see her in person, Ed still needed to visit with Patricia. That was the plan for this evening. Tonight, he would call her and plan for the future while breaking up the boredom of the evening. Punching in her number, would be however, somewhat difficult for him. He knew she would want to know when they would again be together, and she would whine about it all through the conversation. It wasn't as if he didn't love her, because he did. But she could be such a load. She wasn't a strong person. She relied on him for literally everything.

He couldn't help but compare her to Ruth. They were such opposites. Ruth was strong-willed. She clearly knew what she wanted and went after it. She never showed any sign of compromise or fear when it came to the litigation issues involving the VanArsdayle estate. He liked that. But, in addition, he *loved* the amount of money she had inherited. It was difficult to determine which was more important, the fact he really cared for her, or the fact she could possibly be another one of his victims—each possibility appealed to him.

He punched in Patricia's number.

"Hey. Where have you been?"

"Hi, Patricia. Great to talk to you, too. As you know, I have been a little busy lately. What have you been up to?"

"Say the words, before we go any further."

"I'm sorry?"

"You know what I mean. You know what I'm talking about. Don't play stupid with me."

Ed hesitated, thought for a moment, then said, "Oh, ok. I love you."

"Thanks. I needed to hear that. I just wanted to make sure I heard it sooner, not later. What's going on?"

"Oh, you know, I'm just sitting here in my tux, getting ready to go to the ball with my princess. Not much else. How 'bout you?"

"I get it, I get it. I know you're not doing anything, but neither am I. You are not alone, Ed. My days are as empty as yours are. It's just too bad we can't go through this together. By the way, how are you calling me now?"

"Well, I crushed that other burner. They took my old phone and went over it with a fine-tooth comb, but of course found nothing. After I was arraigned, they quit following me. I went in to buy some supplies the other day and bought a new burner. That's the one I'm using now."

"How much longer?"

"We still have another week before the trial begins. Are you getting along okay?"

"I'm fine."

"That's it, just fine? Are you doing anything, or just sitting in your apartment?"

"Just sitting here mostly. I'm a regular viewer of those stupid daytime TV shows."

"Maybe you could learn to fish—that would take up some of your time."

She said, "Yeah, that's just pretty funny. I would have gone south by now, but I thought I would hang around until the case was tried, and then we could come to a decision concerning our next move. What's your attorney—what's her name—Donna, or something like that, think about your chances of winning?"

"Her name is Ruth and she thinks we have a good chance, but we are all concerned about a ruling on a motion she filed. If we win it, we have a good chance of winning the case."

"When is it to be ruled on?"

"Sometime before the trial. We don't know, but we're thinking within the next couple of days."

She hesitated, then said, "How well are you getting to know this lawyer? Are you and her becoming close? Is she married?"

Ed laughed. "You know, I don't really know if she's married—that's how close we are. She's my fricken attorney, Patricia, no more, no less. Although, I must tell you, she did just come into quite a sum of money recently. That certainly interests me."

"I thought we were done, Ed. I thought we had enough money."

"We are, we do, but I mean she's got at least a couple of million now, and she would be *so* easy. I thought about the possibility of maybe one more job before we leave the country. Just a passing thought, but it did cross my mind."

"That is what it needs to remain—just a passing thought. You told me we were through. That's one of the reasons I stuck around waiting for you. That and the fact that I love the hell out of you. We need to stick to the plan, Ed. We just need to get this silly case out of the way and hit the road."

He was quiet.

"Do you not agree? Have you changed your mind now? If something has changed, at least have enough decency to tell me the truth. What's going on?"

"No, no, nothing has changed, Patricia. We are still on the same page. I was just thinking she would be such an easy mark and would add to our funds by at least a million or so."

"How much longer would we need to stay here?"

"Forget it. Forget I said anything. We are going to stick to the original plan. I better go. Why don't I plan on calling you sometime this weekend? Will that work?"

"Yes. I miss you. I *cannot wait* until this bullshit is all over, and we can move on. Do you think I should fly on down and find us a place?"

"No. Just wait. It shouldn't be much longer and we will have some idea what's going to happen. I know how frustrated you are, as am I. I can't wait either. Hopefully it's not far away. I love you."

Ed terminated the call. She was always so negative—and weak. He had provided *all* the strength throughout the relationship.

One more call, before he quit for the evening.

"Ruth, Ed. Did I call at a bad time?"

"No, not at all. I'm just finishing up supper… for one."

"I wish I would have known. We could have turned two suppers for two singles, into one supper for a couple."

She hesitated. "Well, maybe we can do that. Aren't you coming in tomorrow morning?"

"Yes"

"Why don't you come in about four instead. We can discuss your case and then go out for supper. Will that work for you?"

"Sure. I will have to cancel six or seven other social events I already had on my calendar, but I'll make that work. By the way, any news concerning our motion?'

"Not really. Paul did talk to Judge Dimmler informally the other day. He just happened to mention a ruling in the case was close. He said he had decided what to do, but needed to have it typed up and copied. He wouldn't tell Paul how he had ruled, but Paul was able to get that much out of him."

"Do you have anyone you are seeing on a regular basis?"

"Whoa, that's a change in direction. Why do you ask?"

"Just interested. You've never talked about anyone else in your life. I just wondered if you had someone you were currently involved with."

"No, not at the moment. Do you?"

"You know better than that. You've been down that road with me through all those questions you asked while preparing for trial. No, I'm seeing no one."

"Probably not a good idea to become involved with your lawyer, your doctor, your financial advisor—you know, those types of people that find their way into your life. Oh, I suppose there are exceptions, but I would think as a general rule, it's a good one to follow."

"I've never been much good at following the rules."

"I concluded that long ago. Of course, it's unethical for me to become involved with a client anyway. That's a pretty important rule for me to observe."

"I don't figure you for one that is much good at following the rules either, Ruth."

She laughed. "Maybe we have a lot more in common than I thought we did. Why don't I make reservation s for us somewhere tomorrow evening? Maybe we can discuss all those rules and how many ways there are to break them without getting caught."

"That sounds great to me. See you tomorrow afternoon."

"I'll look forward to it."

Chapter 41

It had been a long day, to say the least. Ruth waited patiently for the clock to slow wind itself into late afternoon, when she knew he would arrive for his appointment. She loved being with this guy, this Edward Hall, and today was no exception. He would be early—he always was.

Finally, when he hadn't arrived by three-thirty she started to punch in his phone number when Hanna let her know he had arrived.

She quickly pulled out a small mirror and looked herself over before she told Hanna to send him in.

Ruth walked around the desk before he entered her door. When he walked in, she met him halfway between the chair and door, smiled and give him a gentle hug, as she said, "Good to see you, Edward. How are you today?"

As he took a chair in front of her desk, he said, "Not bad. I had to clean up the kitchen, and do some wash. You know—insignificant but necessary jobs. Other than that, I've done very little. Have you heard anything yet?"

She leaned back in her chair, and said, "You know, I did hear a bit of news today. The judge called. He has set up a hearing Monday morning, He wants the attorneys to appear personally, and he wants the attorney general's office to provide all additional information they might have concerning those deaths in California and Colorado, that hasn't previously been provided to him. He also wants oral arguments concerning the introduction of that evidence into the record."

"Okay, what the hell did you just say? I didn't understand any of that crap. Explain."

"We're not sure what it all means either, but we are guessing it means that the judge is not satisfied with the state's response to our motion. He wants more information from them concerning the fact that the other two deaths involved some type of criminal activity. We think he believes they haven't supplied enough information to prevail, and he just wants to make sure they have nothing else before he rules. So, he's scheduled this hearing to make them put up or shut up. We feel it's a positive for us."

"Great. Do I need to be there?"

"Yes. It shouldn't take too long, but you are required to be at every hearing involving your case unless you waive your presence. So, be at the courthouse, near the front door, Monday about eight forty-five. I'll meet you there and take you to the room where the hearing will be held."

"If we win our motion, is it all over?"

"Nope. If they wish they can still prosecute it to its conclusion, but their case will become decidedly more difficult."

For the next hour, talk centered around the upcoming trial. Witnesses and their testimony were discussed at length, until Ruth stood, and said, "Look at the time. We need to go. I made reservations for five-thirty and it's almost that now."

"Why so early?"

"I always eat early. Allows my food time to kind of digest before I go to bed."

"What time do you go to bed anyway?"

She stared down at him, smiled and said, "Depends upon whom I'm with. Now, come on Mr. Hall, let's go. I'm hungry."

Ed stood and together they left her office, each taking their own vehicle and arriving about fifteen minutes after the time set for their reservation.

About halfway through the main course, she thought for a moment and said, "Okay, now it's just you and me, buddy. Tell me the truth. Did you murder those other two women?"

He put his fork down, leaned on his elbows while folding his hands, and said, "What do you think?"

"Hell, I don't know. I know what you have told me. I have no reason to disbelieve you, but it does seem like a huge coincidence. You have been married at least three times and all three are dead."

"You disappoint me, Ruth. I really thought you were a better judge of character than that. Now you make me wonder if I should get a different attorney."

In spite of the question, he returned to enjoying his slightly rare steak, before it got cold, and as he did, she said, "Don't get so defensive. I'm not accusing you of anything. I have looked at all the evidence there is. Nothing indicates to me it's anything except a hell of lot of bad luck. But I wanted to see your reaction when I mentioned it. You know, you are going to get a lot worse than that when I put you on the stand. They are going to do everything they can to nail you to the wall."

"Can I assume from that you don't think I killed *any* of them?"

"This fish is incredible." She smiled and said, "No. If I thought that was you, that you were really like that, I would have given up on your case long ago. I just wanted to catch your reaction when I said it. Sorry. I didn't mean to make you second guess whether we were a good fit as attorney/client. I believe in you. I like you. I enjoy being with you. I was very much looking forward to tonight. Now, is that enough for you, or should I go on?"

He smiled and said, "Thanks. I was concerned I had lost you somewhere along the way. I'm about done here. Would you like to split a desert?"

"My desert is already sitting in front of me."

"Sorry?"

"I took a few minutes this afternoon and called next door—you know the hotel that stands next to this restaurant. I have a room if you wanna use it—if you wanna be my desert, so to speak."

"You know that's just pretty corny. You know that don't you?"

She closed her eyes, and whispered, "I know, I know, I knew it the second it left my mouth. Let's start over. Would you like to walk next door with me, Mr. Hall? I believe you'll enjoy yourself at the end of the journey. Now, is that better?"

He stood. "Works for me, let's go." He waived for the waiter, and gave him his credit card to process, while she waited in the lobby for him to join her.

She unlocked and opened the door to their eighth-floor room. The lamp on the bedside table was turned to dim, and the curtains were opened, revealing the lights of Nashville spreading out almost as far as the eye could see.

He shut the door behind them. She continued walking forward, towards the bed, and when she reached the nightstand, she turned the lamp off. The only remaining light in the room was the soft glow from the city, and that only provided enough to make out forms, nothing more.

She moved toward him, tossing her shoes along the way while

unbuttoning her blouse. She pushed him back against the door and unbuttoned his shirt while kissing him.

She looked down to unbuckle his belt as he said, "Whoa, you get right down to business, don't you?"

She stopped, took a deep breath, and said, "Been awhile."

As she worked on pulling his boxers off, he said, "I can tell."

"Want me to stop?"

As he took a deep breath, he whispered, "Are you insane? I didn't say I didn't like it. I simply was… just…somewhat amazed… at your speed."

"Shut up."

She awoke with a start. He was sleeping beside her. She looked at the clock which indicated she had about an hour to get to work. The curtains had been drawn, apparently by him, and the room remained dark.

She jumped out of bed, turned on the light, and began darting around the room grabbing clothes and dressing.

He awoke, just as she had pulled her shoes on. "What are you doing? You can't leave yet. We haven't finished."

"We have for now, Mr. Hall. I need to get to work. But first I need to go home and put makeup on. I hadn't intended on staying all night."

"Hold on. Will I see you this weekend? When will I see you again?"

As she backed out the door she said, "I'll see you Monday morning at the hearing. Call me."

She ran to the elevator, looking for the keys to her car. As she started the quick drive home, she thought briefly about their time together. She worried she had embarrassed herself. Was she too aggressive? Should she have…taken a slower approach? Was it good for him? It had been a while…*Hold on! What the shit was she thinking? She had a good time—she hoped he had a good time—that was the end of the story, plain and simple.*

Chapter 42

Ed hadn't seen Ruth since early yesterday morning. All he had seen then was her back as she rushed out their hotel room door. He tried to call her during the day, but Hanna told him she was with a client and would be with clients the rest of the day. Hanna said she would leave a note, but doubted Ruth would have time to return the call. He hadn't tried to reach her last night nor yet today.

Ed had promised Patricia, he would call her within the next few days. Today he would get it over with. He wanted it out of the way. He didn't want to think about it—leave it hanging—so he figured the best way to resolve that issue was to get it out of the way now and talk to her this morning.

That was his thought process two hours ago, but he still hadn't punched in her number. It wasn't that he didn't want to talk to her, but he had nothing to tell her, nothing of any significance to pass on. The conversation would drag, and he would once again be obligated to listen to her whine about why this isn't all over—why they can't be together *now*. In addition, if he was going to talk to someone, he would rather talk to Ruth, a conclusion he had quickly reached yesterday.

His house phone, the one he figured the cops had tapped, rang and he noticed it was her—it was Ruth.

"Good morning. Good to hear from you. Apparently, you were just too busy to return my call yesterday?"

"Hi. Oh my god, I was so busy…"

"I'm tied up. Can I call you back shortly?"

She hesitated, then said, "Sure. I'll be around."

He terminated the call, picked up his burner phone and punched in Ruth's personal number.

"Sorry about that, Ruth. I think they have that phone tapped. I'm on a burner. This is really the only phone I feel I can use with any degree of privacy."

"I miss you. Sorry I couldn't call yesterday. The office was crazy. I saw where you called, but I just couldn't get to you."

"Where are you now?"

"At the office. I have a couple of appointments this morning."

"Do you work on Saturday?"

"Of course. I work every day, in some way or another. Even on Sundays, I have office work I take home to review, or I come in here. I work every day of the week. Why do you ask?"

"I thought I might meet you for coffee."

"You know, I'd love that, but I thought about you and I a lot last night. I just think maybe we better keep a low profile until your case has been tried. I may have pushed the limit a little the other night. I didn't see anyone I knew, but I'm not supposed to have this type of relationship with a client, as you know. If Paul found out, he would probably fire me. Let's hold off until the case is over, and then we'll see where this takes us."

"You make it sound like you and I having a relationship even after the trial is over, might be unusual? Isn't that just sort of normal? I mean, is it unusual for you to want to have this type of relationship with a client? Please don't take that wrong, because I am truly asking the question out of an abundance of complete ignorance. But I kind of figured it might happen all the time with clients and attorneys."

"No, it doesn't. At least not with *this* attorney. Never with me. It probably shouldn't have happened this time. But it has, and I know I don't want anyone to know before the trial is over. We must keep it quiet, under wraps, until then."

"Okay. I understand. I don't like it. I really don't want to do it that way, but if you think that's the right way to handle this, then I will abide by your wishes. I assume if we shut your office door, I could get a short kiss, or hug or whatever…correct?"

"Of course. By the way, I had a great time the other night. I didn't get to tell you that. We will work out something to have a little time together before the trial is concluded, but it's just a little touchy, and we need to be careful."

"That sounds great. By the way, you are a little crazy in bed. Have you been told that before? You're what I would term an aggressive lover to say the least."

"I *told* you it had been a while."

"So that means if we did that on a regular basis, you would be more subdued, more laid back so to speak?"

"I didn't say that. I told you it had been a while." She hesitated. "We need to continue this line of conversation some other time. I need to go. Talk to you later."

"Hold on. If I don't talk to you tomorrow, are you still planning on meeting me Monday morning at the courthouse?"

"Yes. Nothing has changed. The hearing is still on, and I will meet you as planned."

"Okay. You have this number now, so use it the next time you call."

"Okay."

He smiled as he concluded the call. She was so different from the one he was about to call. She was upbeat, positive and exciting to be with. In addition, she had all that money.

"Morning, Patricia."

"Ed, have you heard any more about the trial?"

"As a matter of fact, I have. Ruth told me we have a hearing scheduled for this Monday concerning the motion. It could decide one of the major issues in the case, so I am glad at least that portion of it is about to be decided. She thinks we have a good chance of prevailing. I'm hoping she's correct. She appears to me to be competent and well respected in her field, so I have confidence in her, and in her assessment of the case. Ruth ..."

"Okay, just stop right there. You mentioned her name enough times in the short time we have been talking. You did the same thing the last time we talked. Do you have feelings for her? I'm getting some bad vibes here, Ed. What's going on between you two?"

"I'm just telling it to you like she told it to me. She is the one in charge. I am just passing on what she told me, that's all. I could use 'whatshername' rather than her own name, I guess. Would that help?"

"Don't placate me, Ed. It just seems to me you two are getting pretty close. Are you? Just tell me. I'll be glad to leave, to get out of your life forever, if that's what you want."

"Oh, for god's sake, don't be silly. We are in this together. We have been for a long time. I intend on spending the rest of my life with you. I don't know how else to tell you what's going on without using her name."

She hesitated. "It's not the fact you're using it, it's how you come *across* when you talk about her. I understand your life is in her hands, that you respect her, that you need her, but just remember what we have been through. Just remember who's always been there for you.

Just remember who loves you Ed, and always will."

"I do, I do, and I'm sorry we have to go through this. But, neither of us have a choice. I hate this. I figured by now we would be long gone. But that's not the hand that's been dealt, and we need to deal with it. You know very well that if I had a choice, you and I would be swimming naked in the ocean off some beach in Aruba. But that's not where we are. We are here dealing with this problem which I am hoping will end favorably."

She was quiet. He could hear her start to cry. "I'm sorry, Ed. I can only imagine what you must be going through. It has just been so long without you. I miss you so much."

"Maybe it *is* time you flew down and found us a place to live. At least look around and check out the area. What do you think?"

"Let's wait until this hearing is over on Monday. Maybe then, we will have at least some idea where this is all going."

"Okay. You know, as concerns Ruth, I keep telling you she is rich. She's got a nice chunk of change you and I could use. Keep that in mind, because I think she would be easy."

"Don't go there again, Ed. I'm done. No more of this for me. We had decided Janice was it, and now you are looking at your attorney as our next victim. This needs to end. I can't go through this again with you. We end it now, or I'm out of here—and without you."

"Okay, okay, I agree. I'm sorry. I shouldn't have even brought it up. I will call you after the hearing on Monday."

"I'll be waiting. I love you."

"Love you too."

He terminated the call. What a fine line he walked. If he upset Patricia, or left her, he knew her well enough to know she would most likely turn him in. She would then find a way for them to grant her immunity and testify against him. So, he needed to be careful.

But the idea of one more job, one more victim, did excite him, almost as much as Ruth, the potential victim, had excited him the other night. He was walking a fine line with both women. If he alienated either one, the results could be a total disaster—maybe not for them, but most certainly for the one walking that fine line.

Chapter 43

Ruth escorted Ed to the conference room where she had been waiting, and where she had left paperwork on the table so no one else would use the room. She had arrived early to insure she found one still vacant. As soon as she closed the door, and turned around she was in his arms. He kissed her once, leaned back, smiled and kissed her again. She pulled away.

"You know Paul is going to be here for this hearing too, right? I would hate to have him catch us. That would *not* be good."

"Sorry. I just needed to hold you. I just needed one kiss, that's all...just one to tide me over until we are together again. I won't do...that...again—unless, of course, you approve in advance."

She smiled. "You don't have to make it sound like it needs to be part of an agenda or routine. That's not the case at all. I just get a little nervous when I think we are in a situation where Paul might find out about us."

Ed walked to the door and inspected the door knob. "What are you doing?" she asked, as she followed his every move.

He turned and said, "Looking for a lock."

She smiled and put her arms around his neck. "One more and that's it."

She kissed him and walked away. "He will be here any minute."

"Have you heard anything else about our motion?"

"You know, this is really the judge's party. We've filed everything we had. It is going to be up to him to lead the way, not us. And to answer your question, no, neither of us has heard anything."

Paul arrived shortly thereafter. Precisely at 10:00 a.m. they walked through the courtroom door and took their seats. Jack Hopkins was already seated, giving them a disingenuous wave of the hand as they took their seats.

Judge Dimmler walked in and took his place behind the bench, taking his time starting the hearing, as he continued to review his paperwork. Eventually, he looked up and said, "Good Morning, everyone. Y'all ready to proceed?"

Both parties answered in the affirmative.

"Well, folks, let me explain why we are here. This trial is set to commence Wednesday. One of the important elements is the issue of two other women who died while married to the defendant. The question of whether or not to allow evidence concerning their deaths is one which really concerns me. I have read everything both sides have submitted. But I wanted to find out if there is anything in addition to what has already been submitted, for me to review. In addition, I wanted to give each side a chance to argue their position. So first off, I would ask the assistant attorney general whether or not he has any additional evidence or information concerning those two out-of-state deaths that he wants to present to the court. Mr. Hopkins, anything else?"

Jack stood as he said, "I guess not, Your Honor. We provided you with the information we have, and, of course, we feel that information is more than adequate to allow everything into the record concerning their deaths."

"I understand. Be seated. Ms. Andrews, do you have any evidence you wish to present or that you might plan on presenting at the time of trial in an effort to keep information concerning these two deaths out of the record?"

Ruth stood and said, "No, Your Honor. What we presented in our brief sets out our position."

"Thank you. Be seated."

"Here's the problem, folks. I have concluded, based on what has been submitted to me, that I just can't justify allowing evidence concerning the other deaths into the record. I have nothing to indicate a crime was committed. I have nothing to show it was anything but just a run of bad luck. Now, maybe that wasn't the case here in Tennessee. If that is true then the state can prove it with the evidence they acquired here as concerns this crime."

He hesitated, and cleared his throat. "But from what I can see, the state is attempting to use those two deaths, both of which were determined *not* to be crimes in the eyes of those that investigated, as proof that he murdered his wife in Tennessee. And I'm afraid if I do allow it into the record, it's going to influence this jury based upon two situations that were not even crimes. I believe the evidence of the other two situations could be extremely prejudicial. They could substantially influence the jury concerning whether or not he committed a crime here as concerns Janice, and I'm just not about to let that happen."

Jack stood and said, "But, Your Honor, have you considered the similarity of the three cases. It is always the same. First, dead wives, then the defendant inherits. It's all part of a pattern, a routine and this defendant is responsible for it all."

"I understand, Mr. Hopkins, but I'm just not going to allow it in. You know, I may very well be wrong. I have been before and I will be again. But I would rather be wrong protecting the rights of the defendant than in allowing evidence into the record that shouldn't have been allowed in and which results in a conviction."

"Your Honor, what if we come up with additional evidence—a co-conspirator, or anything that might help tie all these events together? Will we be allowed to resubmit?"

"Well, that's one of the reasons y'all are here. Trial is in two days. How are you going to acquire anything in two days? Won't you need additional time?"

Ruth stood and said, "Your Honor, we are prepared to start this trial in two days. We will *not* agree to a continuance of any kind at this late date."

"I didn't figure you would. But in good conscience, I took a long time with this issue, trying to figure it out. I really feel I owe the state some additional time now that they understand the courts thoughts. What about a few additional days for you to work on the problem, Mr. Hopkins?"

"That would help, Your Honor. I'm afraid you already have all we have, but I'll put the boys back to work and we will see what we can come up with."

"I am going to continue this trial for two weeks. I'm sustaining the Defendant's motion to suppress at this time, and am not going to allow any evidence whatsoever as concerns the death of the defendant's two prior spouses. That ruling is, however, subject to the submission of additional evidence same to be presented to this court at least five days prior to trial. If the state comes up with any additional evidence, please, Mr. Hopkins, provide it to the defense, and I'll set a time for hearing on the motion as soon as it is received. Other questions or thoughts?"

Both parties answered in the negative.

"Okay, then this hearing is concluded. Thank you, everyone."

Jack continued to remain seated as if he were stunned—stunned and unable to move in any direction.

Ruth waited until the judge had left the room. Paul along with Ed were walking out the back door of the courtroom before she walked over to the table where Jack remained.

She leaned over the table, looked at him and said, "What are you going to do now…*Jack.* Still as cocksure of a conviction as you were a couple of weeks ago?"

He looked at her, smiled and said, "We will get him." He stood and said, "I'll beat your butt before it's all over with. This is not over. Not yet."

She turned to walk away as she said, "Yeah it is. It's *completely* over."

She walked through the door of the conference room where both Paul and Ed were seated around the conference table.

"Where did you go?"

"Oh, I had to shove that ruling down Hopkins's throat, the piece of shit. He's a real deal that guy is."

Paul said, "I've never heard you talk about another lawyer like that. Do you two have issues? Should I be the one trying this case?"

"Over my dead body. It's my case, I'll handle it. That guy just pisses me off, that's all. Now, let's move on. What are we discussing?"

Ed smiled and said, "It sounded to me like we had a minor victory today. I know nothing about what was said in there, but I assume if the assistant attorney general didn't like it, it must have been good for us."

"It was," Ruth said. "I wasn't happy about the continuance, but winning that little battle in there today, was a major stride in winning the overall war. Now we just have to wait and see what they come up with. If they can't use that information from the other two deaths, I think they're in trouble. What do you think, Paul?"

"I agree. We just need to wait and see what happens. Are you prepared to try the case, Ruth?"

"Yes."

"Then I think we probably just need to set back and wait…see what they come up with, if anything." He stood. "I need to run. Ed, take care. Ruth, I'll see you back at the office."

As the door closed, Ed stood. He walked to the doorway, standing with his back against it to insure it remained closed.

He extended his arms, and said, "Come here."

She stood and walked into his arms. He put both arms around her, kissed her and said, "Thanks."

"For what?"

"For successfully getting me through today. It sounds like we are home free."

Her eyes flashed as she said, "I'd feel a hell of lot better if we didn't have that prick on the other side. He's not..."

"Hey, hey, stop, relax, breathe in, breathe out. You are way tense. Calm down. It's over for now, and you did good. I was proud to say you were on my side."

She kissed him then walked away. "If they fail to come up with anything else, I think we are going to win this thing."

"I hope so. I don't know much about the law, but you rocked in there today lady, you rocked."

She said nothing. She only hoped there was nothing more for them to uncover. Because if there wasn't, this case, in a couple of weeks, was most likely one for the dead files and this guy she was falling in love with, would most likely be set free, *which was right where she wanted him—for more reasons than one.*

Chapter 44

Sam Harvey was a strong believer in the old wives' tale suggesting that negative events happen in threes. As he looked back through the years, there were many times in his life when major problems occurred in a series of threes. Of course, there were also times they occurred in fours and fives, and even once or twice, in twos, but the most common were threes.

So, today his wife was mad at him, again, which was the first of the three. His allergy problem was the second. The budding flowers, weeds, and grasses, all contributed to that issue. He was constantly sniffing and blowing his nose. He had tried all those over-the-counter cures, but they made him tired or cantankerous, at least according to his wife. Even when he did take them, they never seemed to quite do the job. He still sneezed most of the day.

The third in the series hadn't happened yet. He was still waiting, but it was early. Terry was just walking through the door, so there was plenty of time left in the day for that third and final event to occur.

"Hey, old man, what's up? How was your weekend?"

Sam said nothing, but he did blow his nose.

"Oops, got the allergies again today, huh? You know, there are clinics now that can actually take care of that problem. I assume you are a home-remedy type of guy though, aren't you? Probably a little horseradish, combined with some shoe polish and maybe a little ant shit thrown in will cure you, right?"

"Could you shut the hell up? Leave me alone. I'm miserable enough as it is without your incessant line of bullshit."

Terry laughed. "Just trying to help, old man, just trying to help. What do you have going on today? We need to go out and do something together for once. Or are you going out on your own—again?"

Sam said nothing.

"Hey. Wake up over there. I have to plan a schedule here too, you know. You're not the only one in this partnership. Now, what are we doing today?"

Sam finally acknowledged him, looking up over the top of his glasses, as he said, "I need to go see that dick, Jack Hopkins. Apparently, there's some issues in the Hall case he wants to discuss. Of course, the ass wouldn't discuss anything with me on the phone. I need to be at his office at precisely eight-thirty so we can discuss those issues together, the prick."

"He wouldn't provide you with any specifics?"

"No. I do know the trial date has been moved, but I don't know why."

"You want me to go with you? I got some time if you want me to go too"

"Do you *want* to go with me? Do you *really want* to go see this jerk? No, you don't, and I can't blame you. I'll handle him then be back here to discuss what he wanted. Do we have any more news on Oliver? Once again, I haven't heard from that kid we got inside his organization. When I finally got to talk to him the last time, he disappeared. He said he would stay in touch better than before, but that hasn't happened."

"No, I haven't heard one word. Let me check around a little. I will try to have something for you when you get back."

An hour later, Sam was waiting, as patiently as he was capable, for Jack to make his appearance. It was now eight-forty-five, and he hadn't seen nor heard from him since he sat down.

Finally, the office door opened and in walked Jack Hopkins, now, some fifteen minutes late.

"Where you been?"

"Sorry. Unavoidably delayed. Come on in."

"Sure, you were. You tell me not to be late, then *you're* late. What am I here for? You didn't even tell me that. I got work to do. Now, what's going on?"

Sam followed Jack through his open office door. He took a seat as Jack sat down and pulled a file out from under a pile of files setting on the corner of his desk.

"I don't know if you've heard yet, but we got a bad ruling from a judge the other day in the Hall matter. He ruled we couldn't introduce any information from those cases in California and Colorado unless somehow we could provide additional information that they were actually crimes."

"What! Are you kidding me? Those two other murders were a big part of our case. Why did he rule that way? *How* could he rule that way? I don't understand."

"His ruling was based on the fact that there were never any charges filed in either case. As a result, introducing information from two situations that didn't appear to be criminal in nature could unfairly sway the jury. He said he needed more information to establish there was a crime committed. Then he would let the evidence in. He also suggested we work a little harder and find a co-conspirator." He smiled as he said, "So… what additional information do you have for me?"

Sam moved forward in his chair, and his voice became elevated as he said, "Do you honestly believe I would give you only part of the evidence I had uncovered and withhold the rest? Are you nuts? I gave you everything I had before he was indicted. I don't *have* anything else."

"Okay, okay, calm down, I understand. But without more evidence indicating that those two incidents were criminal in nature, we can't introduce anything into the record about them."

Sam stared at him for a long minute, slid back in his chair, now well in control, and said, "We have nothing else. It is just that simple. We have nothing else. So, what happens now—you going to dismiss?"

Jack laughed and said, "No, no Sam, we aren't dismissing. I will just rely on you to handle it. You can testify as to what you found out yourself, and we'll hope it's enough. Knowing you as I do, if we don't pursue this guy to the bitter end, you will scream all the way to the attorney general's office."

"You're right about that. Regardless of the judge's ruling, I want it pursued. This guy is a cold-blooded, murdering son-of-a-bitch, and win or lose, I think we should pursue the case to the end. Maybe it will at least stop it from happening again."

Jack stood and extended his hand as he said, "I agree. I'll let opposing council know we have nothing more and tell them we will just see them in court with what we have."

Sam looked up at Jack and said, "I guess that means we're done here. Do you have time to talk about Dean Oliver? He's another one that needs to be stopped. Can we talk about him for a minute?"

"Oh, no. Can't today. Maybe, tomorrow." Again, he gave Sam that sickly smile as he continued to offer his hand as a symbol of this meetings termination.

Sam lowered his head, stood, turned and left the room. He never shook his hand. He didn't make a habit of shaking the hand of any worthless prick he didn't respect, and he wasn't going to start today.

Shortly after noon, Sam was again seated at his desk. He watched as Terry walked through the precinct door and toward him.

"Hey, old-timer. How did the meeting go?"

"You don't wanna know."

Terry took a seat behind his desk, as he said, "The hell I don't. What happened?"

"They aren't going to allow anything into evidence concerning those murders in Colorado and California, unless they have information they were crimes. So, unless I can come up with additional evidence that they were in fact crimes, we can't say anything about them, that's what happened."

"You are kidding me. So, are they going to dismiss? Because you know as well as I there is no more evidence than you already gave them."

"No, they're not dismissing. I have to testify and just give them all I have. Hopefully it will be enough. I wonder if I'll even get what I *know* into the record. If the other side objects, I doubt I even get *it* in."

"When is the trial?"

"Hell, I don't know. Couple of weeks, I guess. He never even told me, the prick. Pisses me off. What about Oliver—anything on him or our snitch?"

"No. I made some calls. No one knows where he is. No one can find him. I guess there was another murder last night, too. They used the same method—she took two to the back of the head. Not much doubt who did it."

"You know we got to stop this guy. We just got to find a way to stop him. This can't continue."

"You can't do it all by yourself. Give it some time. We'll come up with something and nail him."

Sam stood, put his hands on his hips and said, "Maybe it's time we *made* something happen. Maybe it's time to stop waiting and just push the guy into doing something stupid."

"I don't understand. What do you have in mind? What could you possibly do to entice the guy into making a mistake? He's not stupid.

He couldn't have gotten away with as much as he has and been stupid."

Sam started to pick up files off the top of his desk, and as he did, he said, "I am going to *find* our snitch. I'll figure it out from there."

Terry stood. "I'll go with you."

"I am going alone. I'll probably be gone most of the afternoon. I'll just drive home later today instead of stopping here first."

As he grabbed the Oliver file, he also picked up a larger, thicker file and started to walk toward the door with both files in hand.

"What other file have you got there? Are you going to work on *two* of our cases without me?"

Without ever turning around, he said, "I'm taking Hall home too. I'll see you tomorrow."

"Whatever. Let me know when I can be your partner again, old man."

As Sam got in his car, he once again mentally reviewed his conversation with Jack Hopkins. He was the third and last of the bad-event scenario. He was glad it was over. Now he would proceed through the rest of the day, without waiting for the final shoe to drop. Hopefully doing what he had in mind concerning Oliver, would not backfire on him and start the trilogy process all over again later in the day. He wasn't sure he could survive going through three bad events twice in the same day.

Chapter 45

It had now been over a week since Ruth's hearing involving her motion to suppress. Neither she nor Paul had heard anything from Jack or anyone else involved with the attorney general's office. She had no doubt the ruling had greatly affected their approach concerning the trial.

Assessing the prosecutor's position, there now existed an insurmountable deficiency in proof which could not be overcome by any evidence they currently had in their possession. Ruth felt, as did Paul, that without that crucial piece of the puzzle, without being able to even mention the other two deaths, they would eventually fail in presenting a case that would survive a motion for judgement of acquittal submitted at the conclusion of their case. Paul felt if the investigator *did* testify as to the results of his investigation, including the two out of state deaths, that *could* be enough evidence to result in a conviction. But it was clear to both Ruth and Paul, without information concerning those two deaths, an acquittal seemed imminent.

"Do you have a minute, Ruth?"

"Yes. Why?"

"Come in."

Paul stood in his doorway as she walked down the hallway to her office.

It was early. Hanna hadn't arrived yet, but both attorneys had walked through the office door long before the start of the bedlam that best described most days in the office.

She followed him in and took a chair before she even turned the lights on in her own office. "What happened? Did I do something wrong? What's going on?"

Paul laughed. "No, no. Quit thinking so negatively. You did nothing wrong. In fact, that is why you are in here. I just want you to know how much I appreciate your good work. Your work ethic is incredible and you have really developed into a great co-worker. I just wanted you to know that if this continues as it has, we are going to be partners before long. It's only fair. You certainly deserve it."

Ruth looked down, obviously affected by his comments. When she looked up at him, she had tears in her eyes, as she said, "You have no idea how much I appreciate what you just said."

She hesitated as tears started to stream down her cheeks.

"Paul, even though you are not all that much older than I, you have become a father figure to me. As you know, my father and I are estranged. We cannot seem to see eye to eye on anything. My mother dares not think on her own, so she follows his every move. As a result, I never hear from either of them. I am an only child. My grandparents that are still alive, live across the country. I have no spouse. You have taken the place of all of them, along with being my teacher. I love working with you, seeing you on a daily basis, being in court with you. Thank you. Thanks for all you've become to me—for becoming such an important part of my life."

By then, Paul had tears in his eyes, which he wiped away with his coat sleeve. "Whoa, that was something I never expected. Thank you."

Ruth stood, and said, "I need to go to work. Enough of this. Thanks again for all you have done for me and for those kind comments, Paul."

She turned and walked across the hall to her own office, where she quickly grabbed a tissue to wipe away the rest of her tears.

An hour later, after Hanna had arrived, she said, "Ruth, you have a call on line one. It's your buddy, Jack Hopkins."

"Yeah, sure. Thanks a lot." She picked up. "Hi, Jack. Dig up a little more evidence, did you?"

"I wish. No, as a matter of fact I have some pretty good news for you. It's not the best news for the rest of us, but pretty good news for you."

She moved forward in her chair. "What's going on?"

"Well, you know that detective that handled the Hall case—Sam Harvey?"

"Sure. What about him?"

"He is missing."

"Oh no. How long has he been gone?"

"It's been almost four days. His wife has no idea where he is. His partner hasn't heard from him. They tried to track his cell, but it was apparently turned off and didn't show any activity much beyond a half mile from the station four days ago. They can't find any trace of him, or his vehicle."

"I'm so sorry, Jack. Did you say he's married? What about children?"

"Yes, he's married, but they have no children. She is about crazy. From what I understand, she really relied on him."

"Do you need to continue Hall? Maybe you can find another officer that might testify. I would think the judge would continue the case while you bring someone else up to date."

"We, here at the office, have discussed that, but the consensus is just to dismiss—maybe wait a day or two and see what happens, then dismiss. The judge really hurt us with that ruling a week ago, and now, without Sam, we don't have much left."

"I assume you at least have his own records as to whom he talked to and what they said. Won't that help someone else take over and maybe testify? I'm not trying to help you make your case, but I just feel bad it has to end in this manner. My client certainly won't mind, but it's just sad it has to end this way."

"Sam was known for his hatred of the computer. He was terrible at keeping records on one. He had a habit of inputting a very small amount of information concerning each case, to his computer. But most of his notes were in the file he took with him when he left the office that day. None of that has been found either. So, we have none of the evidence from Colorado or California, we no longer have our chief investigator, and his records are missing. We have an idea who's behind it, but we can't touch him until we have more evidence. One of the files he took with him, concerned a man Sam has been after for years. The guy apparently even threatened him. But we have nothing yet to indicate he was involved."

She sat back in her chair. "I understand now why you want to dismiss. You really do have a problem."

"Unless you hear from me tomorrow morning, I will go ahead and dismiss, probably late morning. I'll have the clerk email you a copy of the dismissal. If he turns up tonight, I'll let you know, but I am afraid Sam is not going to turn up—ever."

"Okay. I will say nothing to my client until noon tomorrow. Sorry it had to end this way."

By noon of the following day, she had heard nothing. Ruth waited patiently for the call—the call from Jack that Sam had been found, and all was well. But it never came. Finally, the email she had been waiting for, came through. The case had been dismissed.

She printed the dismissal and walked into Paul's office just as he was prepared to leave for the noon hour. She laid it down on his desk. He looked at it, then at her. "What's going on?"

"Apparently the lead investigator has disappeared and with him all the files on this case." She smiled. "You don't know anything about that do you?"

He quickly looked up from the document, then realized she was joking. "First hand? Not hardly. Is that true? Did he disappear? Is the case really dismissed?"

"Yes."

"Well, congratulations. I am sure that will please Ed."

"I really do hope the officer is all right, but regardless of the circumstances, I'm sure Ed will be pleased. I think I will give him a call and have him come in this afternoon."

Paul left for lunch as Ruth punched in Ed's number. She simply told him to stop in, the sooner the better. He said he would be right there.

He arrived a short time later. Hanna never took her daily noon break—too much to do. She ushered him into Ruth's office as soon as he arrived. Ruth asked Hanna to shut her door on the way out.

"So, what is so important that you had to see me today? Aren't we already prepared to try the case?"

She leaned back in her chair. "I have some good news for you."

He smiled and said, "Oh yeah, what? Are we going out for supper and getting a room tonight? That's about the best news you could possibly have for me. Now, tell me—what's the good news?"

She shoved the dismissal across her desk. "Read this."

He picked up the single sheet of paper and read it. He furrowed his brow as he continued to read. He read it again. Finally, he put it down on the desk. "I don't get it. Is this some kind of joke? What's going on?"

She stood, walked around the end of her desk and stood next to his chair. "Stand up, Mr. Hall."

"No. Come on now, this isn't funny. What is going on?"

"Stand, Mr. Hall."

"Okay, okay fine." He stood. She wrapped her arms around him and kissed him. "It is no joke. You are *one free man*. The case has been dismissed. It is all over."

He pushed her away, while still keeping his hands on her hips. "Explain this please. Don't tease me like this. What happened?"

"Well, it seems the chief investigator has disappeared, along with all your files. When that happened, coupled with the judge's ruling on our motion, the state just decided it wasn't worth it and dismissed. It's all over Ed. You are a free man."

"Oh… my…God, are you kidding me? This is no joke, right?"

"No, Ed. It's no joke."

She kissed him again, then returned to the chair behind her desk.

"So, what's it going to be now, Ed? What are you going to do now that you are a free man?"

As he sat back down, he said, "Hell, I don't know. I never thought about it. I just figured this trial was going to take a while, and when concluded, I would figure out what I was going to do then based on how it all turned out."

"Well, that is all out of the way. Now it's time to figure out the rest of your life, buddy."

He smiled. "You are exactly right. Do you want to help me do that?"

He had no way of knowing she had devoted most every waking minute to that very issue since early yesterday morning.

"Absolutely! There's nothing I would rather do."

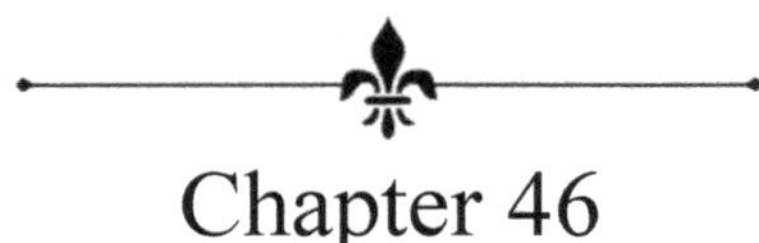

Chapter 46

Ruth sat quietly in the living room of her small, yet comfortable home in East Nashville, waiting for Ed to pick her up. They had decided, after their major victory yesterday, to have supper together tonight and enjoy the fruits of their endeavor.

She was currently in the process of sorting out her convoluted, confused feelings about Ed. There was an element of love associated with her relationship with him, but the *stronger* feeling, and the one which tended to prevail the majority of the time, was how she could remove some of that pile of money he had, yet maintain their relationship. It was workable. There was no doubt it was workable. She just needed to figure it out, which she started doing as soon as his case was dismissed.

Ruth knew she was most likely playing with fire, but that just seemed to increase the excitement. She would keep her eyes open and watch him like a hawk. No matter how long and hard she tried to justify the stability of his prior relationships, in her mind, she had little doubt he played all three of those women. Now, whether he actually intended on killing them was another story—there was little proof that he had actually murdered any one of the three.

For Ed, this time around would be a little different. This time, *he* was the one that would get played. But she would not do it without knowing all about him, a luxury none of the other three women had enjoyed. She did love him, there was no doubt about that. But, more importantly, he was a potential victim, and that issue continually seemed to trump the fact that she loved him.

He knocked on the door. As soon as she opened it, he walked in and said, "Hi. You ready to go?"

Once inside, she shut the door behind him. She started to remove his shirt.

He said, "I thought we were coming back here and doing this after we eat."

"I don't want to wait."

Later that evening they sat together in a small, but well-considered restaurant located not far from her home in East Nashville.

"So, Mr. Hall, the case is over, our sexual issues have been resolved and your whole life stretches out before you. What is your next move?"

The waitress had already brought a couple of glasses of wine, and an hors d'oeuvres. Both glasses were now empty and the hors d'oeuvres consumed, as he said, "I'll have the strip, she'll have the pork loin."

He had started ordering her food for her. She quickly decided that was another control issue which he would need to stop. She was old enough to talk herself; she was old enough to order herself.

"I am not sure yet, I guess. I have a couple of lookers at the house, both of which appear promising. I'll know more about that within the next week. Both have given me time to move if they buy, so if that happens, I'll have to figure out where I'm going. Beyond that I'm just not sure. What about you? Do you intend on staying here in Nashville, in your current employment, or are you going to move on?"

"I like it where I am. Paul is a good guy, a good boss. Oh, by the way, I guess I haven't had a chance to tell you—he's thinking of making me his partner. He seems happy with the work I have done. He mentioned the other day it shouldn't be long and we would be partners. That means a big increase in pay, along with an equal say in what happens around the office. I was humbled by his comments, I can tell you that."

"Great! How much of a pay increase?"

"I'm not sure, but it should be substantial. The practice is really thriving right now. I know there is plenty of income coming through that front door."

"What is the situation with your family, Ruth? You don't talk of them much. What is your current relationship with your parents?"

"Not good. I haven't talked to either of them for well over a year. I don't expect that to change. It has been difficult, but we just don't see eye to eye, and none of us are about to alter our positions. I am an only child so that just pretty much leaves me out there by myself. What about you? Do you have family that's close? You never discuss them."

"Not really. I, too, was an only child. Both my parents are

deceased." He smiled as he said, "And as you know, all my wives are gone too."

She smiled, and said, "So, we are both pretty much in the same situation—neither of us have family around. Just you and I against the world so to speak."

"At least you have a few friends to keep you company. I just haven't ever made much of an effort to develop many friendships."

"Paul is probably the best friend I have. I have always been kind of a loner. I've always worked pretty much by myself."

They continued to discuss their past, their present, and of course their future, while patrons, waiters and waitresses swirled around them, ultimately bringing a plate holding a New York Strip, and another, holding a generous piece of pork loin for her.

Conversation was nonstop—nonstop until Ed made an off-the-cuff remark about having no place to live if his house sold—about perhaps moving in with her until he figured out exactly what he was going to do.

She was quiet, as she continued to consume her supper. Finally, she said, "Is that really what you want? Let me ask you Ed, do you love me? I mean, are you *in* love with me? I know sometimes when clients get to working closely with their attorney, they may respect them, they may like them, and some may even *think* they're *in love.* What about you, Ed? Are you in love with me?"

He hesitated just long enough to swallow. He looked at her, smiled and said, "Yes, Ruth, I am. I have been for quite some time."

She remained silent.

Finally, he said, "How do you feel about me? Is it mutual? Do you feel the same way, or am I just a toy, just a pawn in this silly little game you play?"

She looked up. He was smiling, clearly playing his own game.

He said, "No, I mean it. Regardless of that silly little comment I just made, I do love you. I hope you feel the same."

She said nothing.

He took her hand. "I understand if you don't feel the same way. I'm a big boy. I can handle it."

"No, Ed the problem is not that I *don't* feel that way, the problem is that I *do*. I've loved you from the day you first walked through my office door. Now the issue is, what do we do about it, if anything?"

"You know, between the two of us, we have enough money to travel all over the world, do exactly as we wish, live wherever we want. Obviously, we have already figured out we enjoy each other's company immensely."

"No question about that. Should we get…married? Do you think we should do that? I've never been married; you have been three times. What do you think?"

He smiled. "You know, that sounds perfect to me. Maybe this one for me will last. I'll protect you the best I can."

She smiled. "I just have to remember that we can only buy a house without a staircase, not to climb up any mountains with you and never stand up in the back of the boat. That should cover it."

He smiled and said, "It seems all three of my wives died because of a lack of balance—just don't lose yours."

"Let's finish and go back to my place. Can you go again?"

"Waiter, bring me the bill."

He turned toward her, smiled and said, "Hell yes, I can go again. Let's get out of here."

Chapter 47

Paul sat quietly, waiting for the time he would leave his office and meet Judge Dimmler at a small bar in the 5 Points area of Nashville. Both Hanna and Ruth left for the day, and he was alone with his thoughts—again. For all intents and purposes, he was alone all the time. At least that was how it felt to him. Even in a room full of friends, he found himself alone.

He was clearly living a life in stark contrast to how Ruth was living hers. She was beside herself with happiness. She was getting married in a few weeks. They both seemed happy…just as he and Anna had been when they were about to marry. Love was the operative word around the office. Even Hanna had found a new boyfriend she enjoyed being with. He didn't feel the least bit sorry for himself. It was more a feeling of overwhelming sadness.

It was early summer. The weather in Nashville was just short of spectacular. This was the season she did love. Spring, and its segway into summer, was the time of year for which she waited. It had been almost half a year since her death, since he had been without her, but the feeling of despair and loneliness continued to overwhelm him.

Those feelings were at their most intense when he walked in the front door of their home each night. She dominated his time when he was home. While she was healthy, they were together a considerable amount of time. Even when she was sick, every waking hour away from the office was centered around her, whether it was talking with doctors or simply holding her hand.

Paul had never considered loneliness would eventually be an issue for him. He didn't have the time, nor a reason to consider it while she was alive. But he had underestimated the incredible power of that seemingly harmless element of emotion. It was an ongoing issue that never quit. From the time he left the office until he returned the next morning, he sat alone, as he remembered and reconstructed his past with her over and over.

Tonight, however, would be a little different, a change in his routine. Tonight, he would meet the judge and spend some social time outside his house and the office, with a man who was the closest friend he ever had.

An hour later Paul sat with Judge Dimmler in a small bar where they had met many times in the past. Both had chronicled their day's activities and already wasted one bourbon on the rocks, each ordering a second immediately.

"So, how's the office doing now, Paul? Has everything calmed down since the issues involving Ruth and that woman's estate?"

"Yes. In fact, I don't know if you heard, but she is getting married."

"Really? Anyone I know?"

"Yes. The defendant whose motion you ruled on, Ed Hall."

"That motion to suppress? *That* Ed Hall?"

"The same."

"As I recall, he had, at the time, three dead wives. He sounds like an interesting choice for a spouse to me. He has been married three times and not one of his wives survived. I am just not sure personally, I would like those odds, but each to their own I guess."

"She loves him. She doesn't believe he killed anyone. I've talked to her about the risk, but she's hearing none of it. She just really believes he's the right man for her."

"I'll wish her the best of luck and pray she survives. How are you, Paul? I see a change, and a big one, since the last time we visited. How are you doing?"

He looked away. When he reconnected, he said, "Fine, I guess, Judge. I'm not really sure how I should feel. Is this—the way I feel now—normal? Is this the way I should feel—depressed, lost, discouraged? I know the sense of loss must be normal, but it's actually overwhelming. I miss her every waking minute. It made no difference to me *how* sick she was. And certainly, that cliche, 'Well, she's in a better place now,' doesn't impress me either. When she was here, with me, she was in a damn good place *then,* as far as I was concerned."

He turned away, as he said, "I'm angry, I'm sad, disappointed, discouraged…all those things…every day of the week. Life's not much fun right now, my friend, I can tell you that."

"Have you considered professional help? It sounds like maybe it's something you might need to consider to get through this."

"Yes, I have. But I just keep thinking I'll get over it, get through it, get around it, whatever. I know it has only been a matter of months, and I know I *should* feel this way, *but for how long*? How long, Judge? Maybe I should just move on with my life and forget her, but that doesn't seem right either. Should I date? Oh my god, how I hate the thought of that. Should I just continue to live this way? Is that what I should do? What should I do? I've never been down this road before. I have such mixed feelings."

The judge stared at the bottom of another empty glass. He looked up and said, "Want my opinion?"

"Of course. Yes, I do."

"Just take it a day at a time, Paul. I know how overwhelming it has all been to you, but you just need to take it one step at a time. This time of year, was her favorite. I remember. I remember how much she enjoyed spring, early summer, and I know how hard it must be for you to be going through this each day. But, just take it a day at a time. It will get better. You will never forget her, nor will the rest of her close friends, but you just need to get through this one step at a time. Quit looking at the big picture. Quit trying to 'figure it all out' as they say. Just take it a step and a day at a time. I don't think it would hurt to see a professional either."

Paul took a drink and considered what his old friend had just told him. "I'm sure you're right. I just need to relax, remember what we had and move on. Sorry. I was a little over the top. Sorry."

The judge laughed, as he said, "You have absolutely nothing to be sorry about, my friend." He studied Paul for a moment before he said, "You know, there's that benefit on Friday, the end of this week, for the heart association. You remember. Anna and you went with Beth and I a couple of years ago."

"Yes, I remember."

"Well, Beth has a friend that's single, attractive, and easy to be with. Would you like her to line you up—go with us to the benefit? She's a sweetheart. We would both be with you to help if the conversation slowed down."

"No, no, no, I just can't fathom the idea of dating again. That almost makes me sick."

"Come on, Paul. It doesn't have to turn into anything. It's one night…with friends. It would be good for you to get out, have a good meal and see some people you haven't seen in a while."

It was 3:00 a.m. Paul hadn't fallen asleep yet. He had agreed to go out with Beth's friend and together, they had gone to the benefit with the judge and his wife. For him it was a total disaster. She talked all night, nonstop. She talked about weather, politics, politicians, anything, everything. She didn't need a response from him—from anyone. She responded to herself.

She spilled her fifth drink on herself and all over the floor. He tried to help her wipe it up, but because it was all over the floor—where people were trying to dance—they needed the assistance of one of the waiters to help clean it up.

It just didn't work. He told the judge he was sorry, but he was leaving early and asked him to take whatshername home. Once back to the sanctuary of his own home, he watched TV, had a drink, and finally went to bed.

As he thought back, it was therapeutic being around other people in a social context for the first time in a long time, and he did thank the judge for that bit of hands-on guidance. And surprisingly enough, he had looked forward to his date. But the stark reality of his time with her, unfortunately trumped his excited anticipation of being with her.

He was, however, somewhat surprised at his positive attitude as concerned meeting and being with her for the evening. Maybe he could slip back into this dating game somewhat easier than he had anticipated.

Socializing while at the benefit and seeing people he hadn't seen in a while, was also an unexpected pleasure. He would remember that. Maybe he would start socializing somewhat more than he had since Anna's death. However, going out with a woman, any woman, unless he had a basic idea of who the hell she was and what she was all about, at least for now, was no longer a viable option.

Chapter 48

Ed had deferred making this particular phone call as long as he could. He knew how she would feel about what he would tell her, and it would take all of his skill of persuasion to convince her *he* was right. Ed had made up his mind—he hoped he could make up hers.

"Hi. How are you?"

Pat said, "Bored."

"Is that it? Just bored?"

"Pretty much. When can I see you again?"

"I just saw you. Remember. We just met in Murfreesboro, had coffee, went to that little hotel. Am I that easy to forget?"

"Get serious here, Ed. The only life I have is with you. I have nothing else. I have no friends, no job, no family. I have you and that's it."

"I know, but before long we will have each other."

"My sole existence right now centers around you. That is the only reason I'm here, and I am assuming as soon as you sell that stupid house we're out of here, right? That's what you continue to tell me. Is that right?"

He hesitated.

"Okay, what is going on? What has changed? I can't take any more of this Ed. I can't." She started to cry. She yelled, "What the hell is going on? Obviously, something has changed, what is it?"

"Calm down. What I am about to tell you is going to benefit *both* of us in the long run. Just listen. I want to squeeze a little money out of Ruth. She has plenty. She needs to let loose of a little of it. To get that done, I need a partner. I need you to help me."

Patricia said nothing. She had stopped crying, but made no comment of any kind. The phone went dead.

Not a bad start, he thought, not bad.

He punched in her number. She didn't answer. He tried five more times until she finally yelled, "What? What the hell do you want? We had this figured out, Ed. We had a plan. Why can't you stick to it? Why have you deceived me into staying here this long, for one job, and after all this time, tell me you lied to me—it wasn't to do *one* job, it was to do *multiple* jobs. I'm leaving with or without you. Do you understand? With or without you."

Again, the line went dead. Again, he punched in her number, but this time it only took three attempts.

"Listen to me. I *swear* this is it. I swear. But the opportunity has presented itself, and we need to take advantage of it. She is right here, I'm already close to her. All we need to do is seal the deal."

"I thought we had this all planned out and decided when we initially came here. I've been waiting for you, forever. Now, the plan has changed. Now, I have to wait again. I don't know if I can do this Ed, I just don't know..."

"Now look. The job's different than the rest. *The preliminary work is finished*. I just have to clean it up. With your help, I can. We don't have to find a woman this time—we already have her. We don't have to worry about family—she has none, at least none that care. We don't have to worry about her falling in love with me—she's already there. It is just a matter of getting married, getting her money in my name and killing her. This will be the simplest job we have ever done."

Patricia calmed down and was now listening. She hesitated for a moment, then said, "You know, you were charged here in Nashville with murdering that whatshername. You were goddamn lucky those charges were dismissed. What do you think they are going to do with you if another one of your spouse's dies? They will be all over you. You won't be able to piss without a cop standing in line behind you. What are you going to do about that, Ed?"

"*We* are going to do what we've always done! *We* are going to kill my spouse and steal all her money. But this time I'll bury the body, pull the money and we'll leave the country. We might go a little further away than the islands though. We can talk about that as we get closer to the event. I'm not even going to try to make it look legit this time. I am just going to kill her and bury her body in the hills. You can't believe how many places there are to bury a dead body around here. These hills are perfect. I took a trip the other day. Only took me about an hour. I found a dozen places you could bury a body, and even Daniel fricken Boone couldn't find it."

"So, you are going to marry her?"

"I about have to if I want her money. I need to find some way to set our accounts up jointly. There is really no other way."

"When?"

"I'm thinking about a month. It's going to work out fine Patricia, but I need your help to pull this off. Good god, what's another few months. She has about three million the best I can tell. That splits up pretty nicely for each of us. We can just kill her, quickly withdraw the money and get out of town."

She said nothing.

"Come on, Patricia. Help me out here. Actually, help *us* out, one last time."

"What about the house?" She now sounded cold, calculating, more like the woman he fell in love with.

"I think we are close. The broker is to call me later today and I'm hoping we have an offer. I'll let you know."

"Let me think about it."

"Okay. I'll call you later today."

"How are you going to kill her? Do you know yet?"

"Probably just shoot her. I'm not really sure. I may have you do it, if you don't mind."

"If it meant getting you out of here once and for all, I would kill her with a dull knife, chop her body up and feed her to the wolves. It does not matter to me. I just want to get out of here—with you—soon."

"Let's wait and see what happens with the house. I'll call later today."

She terminated the call. All in all, the conversation went much better than he had anticipated.

He punched in Ruth's number. "Hey, what's going on?"

"I'm on a short break. I'm just wrapping up a couple of depos. What about you?"

"Not much. I was just thinking about us. You want to meet somewhere for supper?"

"Sure."

"Good. I'm waiting for a call from my broker. I think the house is sold. If it is, I assume you guys can handle the closing, correct?"

"I can help you, yes. That's great news. Maybe that can all be closed up by the wedding and you can just move in here with me."

"I told the broker we were getting married in a couple of weeks, and if the house was sold, I needed it closed as soon as possible. He was good with that, so hopefully we can get married, close my house sale, and I can move in with you all in the same week. That's my plan anyway."

"I have a magistrate lined up. I talked to him earlier in the day, and he's all ready to go. That was a great idea about having it in my house. There won't be that many invited guests anyway. I am not inviting any family. You know, our date is not far away."

"I know. I'm ready. Let me give you a call after I hear from my broker."

"Love you."

"I love you." He terminated the call. Through the years he had learned how to manipulate—manipulate not only those he tried to deceive, but those with whom he worked. He had both women right where he wanted them. He just couldn't let the opportunity for one last score pass by. The overall plan, the idea he had conceived after Janice's death had come together perfectly. Now all they needed to do was finish it off. He knew the issue with Patricia would be problematic, but he now felt comfortable with her—mentally she was right where he needed her to be.

Midway through the afternoon, he received the call he had been anticipating. His house had sold. An early closing for the buyers would not be a problem. The closing would mark the end of his relationship with Janice, and the planned marriage to Ruth would mark the beginning of the end of his life in Nashville.

He called both women with the same news. They received it with markedly different reactions. Patricia hung up without a word, Ruth was overjoyed—both reactions of which he had fully anticipated, and both fully acceptable within the periphery of the overall scheme.

Chapter 49

Ruth walked into her office and as she sat, she wasn't sure there was an inch of skin on her whole body that wasn't wet with sweat. She had a cold bottle of water in one hand and a cool cloth she was using to wipe off the sweat in the other.

The phone call concerning Sam Harvey had finally come. Two months after his disappearance, based on an anonymous tip, they found Sam's car, with Sam still in it, sitting at the bottom of a lake in Wilson County. He had been shot and shoved into the back seat. All his files were still with him. They were useless. They were in his car when he left the station the last day of his life, and remained there as his vehicle made its final stop at the bottom of the lake.

There was never a doubt she would attend his funeral. She along with many others, both in and out of law enforcement, were in attendance. The church wasn't far from her office, so she decided to walk. The mid-afternoon September sun, along with humidity at its worst, created body-sweat consistent with running a marathon.

The sad fact about Sam's death was that the very man everyone felt was behind his murder, was in fact shot and killed two days after Sam disappeared.

Ruth had planned on being out of the office for the funeral, so she had all of the office work she wanted to complete, finished before she left. As a result, she really had no reason to remain in the office for the day.

It was time to lock up and go home. She never moved. Ruth wasn't necessarily dreading going home, but certainly the enthusiasm she enjoyed early in the marriage concerning her relationship with her now husband Edward, had waned considerably.

Paul had given her time off for a honeymoon, and they had spent a week in the Smokies. The relief from having his criminal charges dismissed, closing his house sale, and Ed's subsequent move to her home, made the week a dream vacation for both of them. But after a couple of months of marriage, she suddenly started to realize she really didn't know this man at all.

Ruth heard Paul walk in the office door and start his short journey down the hallway to his office. He leaned around her doorframe and said, "Hi. How was the funeral?"

"Huge crowd of people, hot and long. I guess that is the response that immediately comes to mind."

"He was a well-liked man, a man of his word and a hard worker. I understand the person they thought was behind this, was killed by one of his own employees a few days after Sam disappeared."

"That's what I heard, too."

He smiled and said, "Well, how's marriage treating you after your first couple of months? Is everything working out as you hoped?"

"Mostly. We have our moments like everyone does, I guess. What was your secret?"

"What secret? I don't have one?"

She smiled. "I mean, how did you and Anna do it? How did you make the marriage interesting and last as many years as you did? I realize you weren't married forever, but still, in spite of all the issues the two of you went through, you were still in love when she passed. How did that work?"

"Hell, I don't know. I respected her, I know that…as she did me. I think that was a lot of it. And we had fun together. I would have rather been with her than anyone I ever knew." He frowned as he said, "Are you having some problems already?"

"No, no. I just think we need to get to know each other a little better. We had a number of problems that needed to be resolved before we married, and now that those are resolved, I think it's time to really get to know each other. But that's not really happening." She looked away. "However, now as I think about it, maybe there's really not that much more of him to know? Maybe *that's* the problem"

"Is he working?"

"No, not yet, and to be honest, I'm really not sure what he's qualified to do. We have enough money for him to just sit at home if he wishes. Or he could be a stay-at-home father if we go that direction. However, the idea of having children right now, is just not in the cards. He seems to have little direction. It's almost like he's waiting for something to happen. Maybe a little time will take care of the problem. I'm not sure. I realize I'm just rambling on here, but I am a little concerned."

"Do you still love him? Is that a problem?"

"No, that's not really a problem. I probably love him more now than I did when we got married. I am… just not sure of him. It seems like he is hiding behind a vale, like he's afraid to open up. It's as if there's an underlying problem he doesn't want to discuss."

"Does he have friends? What do the two of you do in your time away from the office?"

"No, he has no friends or even acquaintances. As for our time together, we read or go boating. We exercise together and, of course, eat out a lot. I don't cook much, and he doesn't cook at all. But that spark I felt prior to the marriage seems pretty subdued right now, especially as concerns what I feel from him."

"Don't worry about it. Just have fun and enjoy life. Everything will work out."

"Thanks, Paul. Time will tell I guess."

Ruth finally arrived home at 7:00 p.m. Ed wasn't there. This wasn't the first time he hadn't been home when she arrived after work. There had been a couple of others times when it had happened since they had married.

She poured herself a drink and sat down in the living room, to consider her options. The money would remain the major issue, not love. For her, money was without doubt the major reason for the marriage, and she needed to keep her eye on the ball.

But, for some reason those two issues seemed to be somewhat changing their order of priority. She had never anticipated loving him would become a factor. She hadn't wanted the emotion to intervene—money needed to remain the focal point. But in the last two months it had somewhat changed. She loved him. She wanted him to love her and only her. She wondered—had her thoughts concerning their relationship, changed. Was money now taking a back seat to her love for him?

This had become much more complicated than she had anticipated.

Where was he? Why was this the third time in less than two months this had happened?

Ruth heard him drive in their driveway. As he walked through the door and into the living area, she said, "Hey, where have you been?"

"Oh, just down the street. I went and had a drink, by myself, just to break up the time until you got home. I didn't figure you would be here until seven or so." He leaned down and kissed her.

"You weren't with anyone else? Just you?"

"Yup. Just me. You want to go out and eat? You want me to try to grill a steak or something here?"

"Let's go out. The last time we grilled, you burned it up. I would rather leave the cooking in the hands of someone that actually knows what they're doing."

"I agree"

Later that night, she lay awake considering all her issues. The money they both brought into the marriage, had been combined into joint accounts at six different banks. She had suggested it. He was surprised, but agreeable. He told her he thought she might have a problem combining their accounts, based on his past problems. She laughed and said they were married, and their funds should be jointly held. They both took appropriate steps to make the necessary changes.

But that was no longer the focal point of the marriage for her. She wanted this to work. For how long, she wasn't sure. If it ended, she certainly wanted to be the one to do it. She wanted to control its direction, its movement.

She had touched him tonight as she had both of those other nights he had been away alone during the day. Consistent with both of those other occasions, he pulled away. Other than those times, they were intimate frequently each week.

Was there another woman? How could that have happened? They had only been married a few months. Was there another woman *when they married?* If there was, why the hell did he marry her?

There were just too many issues and too few answers. She needed more information than she had now. If there was another woman, she wanted to know who and why? Was she *that* horrible as his wife—so bad that he had been married only two months and already found someone else?

Something wasn't right. She could feel it. It was time for some answers. She would talk to Paul. He was her best friend. He would know what direction to take. Regardless of the money, she wasn't about to accept a cheating son-of-a-bitchin husband screwing another woman behind her back. That just wasn't going to work—*ever*!

Chapter 50

Ruth had been waiting patiently in her office for nearly an hour. Even so, it was still earlier than Paul normally arrived at work. But she wasn't going to do anything this morning before she talked to him.

Yesterday, she left the office about midafternoon and drove home. She just wanted to see if he was there—if he was home. He wasn't. His car was gone. She called him on her way back to the office and asked him what he was doing. He told her he was having a cup of coffee, at home, waiting for her to arrive after she left the office.

The early drive home, along with the phone conversation, just confirmed her belief that something was going on. Obviously, it was something he didn't want her to know about.

She heard Hanna walk in a little before eight. Paul walked in shortly thereafter, and as he reached her doorway, he said, "Good morning." He walked in and sat down in front of her desk as if this meeting had been scheduled.

She smiled at him and said, "Okay…good morning to you. What's going on?"

Paul sat on the edge of his chair, eyes wide open, and said, "You will never believe what happened to me last night."

She moved forward in her chair, stared at him intently and said, "Really? What happened?"

"Well, the judge set me up with another woman."

Ruth smiled, relaxed as she leaned back in her chair and said, "Go on."

"I had told him not to—not to ever, ever set me up again with someone I didn't already know, but he did anyway. I wanted to tell him I wasn't going, but he *is* the judge, and he *is* a friend whom, through the years I've been able to trust. Not anymore. After last night, I wouldn't trust him as far as I could throw him."

Ruth laughed. "What happened?"

Hanna apparently heard the laughter, as she was now standing in Ruth's office doorway with a grin on her face. Last night, she had apparently dyed part of her hair a deep purple, and with her pink top and orange slacks, Ruth could have concluded she had been standing too close to an artist's palette when it blew up—way over the top.

"What's so funny back here?"

Ruth said, "Go on, Paul."

"Well, I made dinner reservations for the two of us, against my better judgement, at Etch, downtown. I was to meet her there. She got there on time. I told the man at the door she would be looking for me, so he brought her over to the table as soon as she walked in. Her name was Eulinda. Strange name, but I didn't think anything about it, other than trying to remember it every time I turned around."

"Was she attractive, old, young—go on."

"She was about my age and yes, she was a good-looking woman. As soon as she got there, she ordered a Manhattan. Well, you know how much alcohol those contain. I figured she knew and she could hold her liquor."

"They can put you under the table," Hanna opined. "Been there, done that."

"I could tell she was in trouble after the first one. *She immediately ordered another one*. Holy crap, I could see she was becoming more and more intoxicated as we talked. She downed the second one, and then put her head down on the table. She was completely out of it. That wasn't so bad, but when I heard her start to snore, I knew it was time to make a move."

By then, both women were doubled over in laughter.

"You know, I'm sure it sounds funny to you, but it wasn't the least bit funny to me."

Ruth said, "This is no time for your comments. Go on, go on with the story. What happened then?"

"Well, she couldn't walk by herself, so I helped her to the front door and had the valet get my car. He helped me put her inside, and then he strapped her in. While I sat there, I called the judge and got her home address."

"Did you tell him what was going on?"

"No. I told him I would tell him later. So, we take off, she is slumped over her seatbelt, passed out, completely drunk. I get to her house and tried the front door. It was unlocked—*unlocked* if you can believe that."

"Did you go in?"

Paul started using his hands to help describe the scene. "Yes. I took her to the couch, laid her down and left. But that house has traumatized me forever. It was a complete mess. It looked like she was living in an enclosed garbage dump. It stunk to high heaven. There were dirty dishes everywhere. I couldn't get out of there fast enough. I was afraid to touch anything."

The laughter had subsided, when Hanna said, "You can thank your friend Judge Dimmler for that."

"I have already talked to him this morning. I told him if he ever sets me up again, I'll file a complaint alleging...something...against him with the bar association. It will take them a year to sort it all out. He clearly not only has bad taste in women, but he seems to fancy those that are drunks. I don't know how he was ever so lucky as to have found Beth."

The phone rang. Hanna had stopped laughing, as she said, "I better go answer that."

As Hanna walked down the hallway, Paul stood and said, "One of the worst experiences I ever had. My god, when she started to snore..."

"You got a minute?"

"Sure. What's going on?"

"Shut the door, will you?"

He shut the door and took a seat.

Ruth hesitated, then looked up at Paul and said, "I think Ed is seeing someone."

"Are you kidding?"

"No. He leaves the house while I'm at work. He has lied to me about leaving; he's lied to me about where he goes. Something's wrong. I need to know what is going on. I need to get to the bottom of it before I go crazy."

There was a knock on the door. Paul opened it and found Hanna standing there, smiling from ear to ear. She said, "That phone call, it's Eulinda for you, Paul. And she won't hang up."

Paul said, "You are shitting me. Just get her number. Tell her I am in conference and I'll call her back. If she gives you crap just hang up on her."

"Okay."

Paul shut the door, turned around and said, “How long has this been going on?”

“Since we got back from our honeymoon. It may be nothing, I don’t know. But I need to get to the bottom of it and *now*. I don’t want this type of issue defining our marriage for the next 20 years. Do you know a good private detective? Someone I could trust?”

“Yes. I have a friend who has an office in Franklin. He is expensive, but he’s good. Do you want his number?”

“Yes. I’m not worried about the cost. I just want to make sure he is good at what he does. Apparently, you feel he is.”

“Yes, I do. I have had him handle a number of jobs for me. I’ve always been satisfied with what he has done. Now, explain again, exactly what he’s doing?”

“He leaves the house, mostly during the afternoons, then lies about where he has been. I have caught him. I went home one day, he wasn’t there, and when I called him from right outside the house, he told me he was home. I have never confronted him about it. Those times he’s gone, when he returns home, he’s standoffish; he wants little to do with me. Something is going on and I’m going to get to the bottom of it.”

“It sure sounds like there is another woman.”

Ruth looked down and said, “Yes. I’m embarrassed, I’m hurt, I just can’t believe I didn’t see this before we were married. Bad judgement, I guess.” She looked up, and in a whisper said, “I am not letting that bastard get away with this. If he is seeing another woman, I will take him for all he’s worth in ways he will never figure out until it’s over.”

“Calm down, Ruth. Let’s first figure out what’s going on. Let me get you this guy’s number. His name, by the way, is Randy Blackburn.”

Paul stood and walked across the hall to his own office. Shortly thereafter, he returned to Ruth’s office, and said, “Here is his number. Do you want me to sit in with you when you talk to him? Is there anything I can do to help?”

“No. I will handle it. I’ll remain as objective as I can. I’ll give him a call right now. Thanks.” She then whispered, “Just shut my door when you leave will you. I don’t want Hanna knowing what’s going on”

Paul walked out of her office, shutting the door as he did.

Ruth stared at the number lying on her desk. Was this really necessary? One of the major reasons she originally entered into the relationship was for the money, not love. Was this smart? Should she just forget what the hell he was doing and con him the best she could?

As she punched in the PI's number, she concluded deceiving someone out of a little money was one thing, this was another. This was personal. This had to do with a man she really did care for. She thought the feeling was mutual. He had lied to her concerning something that was extremely important. She needed to know who the other woman was and why he was doing this.

Was she in the picture when they married? Did she spring up *after* they were married? There were so many questions to which she needed answers. She wondered if this Randy Blackburn could answer all the questions she posed—and quickly. She really did hope the answers weren't as she expected, because she was certainly in love with him. But unfortunately, at this point in time, she was now somewhat concerned she just might have made a substantial, significant error in judgement.

Chapter 51

Ruth's call to Mr. Blackburn initially went unanswered—she got his voice mail. He wasn't in his office, but he did return her call the following day. He was out of town, on vacation, and wouldn't be back for a week. He told her he would be in touch as soon as he returned.

She didn't want to wait until next week to get started, but she apparently had no choice. She could seek out another investigator instead of Blackburn, but she trusted Paul's judgement. Ruth wanted to know, and she wanted to know *now*, but she would wait.

Slowly her interest in what Ed was doing had turned to concern, then her concern turned to anger. How dare this son-of-a-bitch have another woman on the side. Of course, she wasn't exactly sure he did, but all signs pointed to that very fact. She assumed the worst.

She felt she had been a good wife. Of course, her original intentions had been more toward removal of money from his pocket to hers, but beyond that, she had done everything she knew how to do to be a good wife. It was failing at that role, without ever having been given a chance to succeed, that incensed her. Ruth had concluded this other woman, whomever she was, had been involved in the picture from day one.

A week later, true to his promise, Randy Blackburn called her on her own cell, not through the office—she wanted none of this to involve the office—and set up a time to meet with her. They would meet at a small bar in East Nashville tomorrow afternoon. She couldn't meet him at the house, and she wasn't going to mix her personal problems with her office practice in any respect, if it could be helped.

She was early and was waiting for him when he arrived. He had described himself to her. There was no question who he was when he walked in the door. He was tall and good looking, with eyes that seemed to stare right through you.

"Based on our phone conversation, it sounds like you might have a problem"

She hesitated, then smiled and said, "I'm actually not sure *what* I have. That's why I need your help."

He ordered a cup of coffee. She had a glass of wine in front of her, and when he ordered coffee, she looked at him quizzically.

"I never, ever drink while on the job. Now, what's going on that might need my attention?"

"Well, it's pretty simple really. My husband and I have been married a few short months, but I believe he's seeing another woman. I honestly don't *know* that he is, but that's my belief. I have a feeling she was in the picture before we ever married. It is all a little confusing to me, which is why I hired you. I need to know."

"Why do you *believe* he's seeing someone?"

"He doesn't work. I do. While I am gone, he leaves the house and goes somewhere else. He stays maybe an hour or sometimes apparently up to a few hours. When I know he's gone, he lies to me either about being gone or about how long he's been gone."

"Did you ever try to follow him?"

"No. I work. I have a very active practice. He is never gone at the same time during the week. I never know when he's going to leave, so I really can't sit and wait for him. I am in court about half the week, and I can't have my hearings continued at the last minute so I can follow him. I need someone to help me. That's why I called you."

"I'm not cheap. I will need payment in advance."

"I don't have a problem with that, as long as you get results." Her demeanor changed immediately. She leaned over the top of the table as she starred at him intensely. "I want to know who he's involved with…what they do…where he goes. I am *not* concerned about the cost. I need answers."

"I understand. How do you want me to handle it?"

"I want you to spend every waking second of each day watching him. The evenings and nights are not a problem. He is home with me. But from the second I leave the house, until I return, I want you to watch him. Make sure of your results. Make sure it's just one woman as I suspect, and not more than one."

"Okay. I understand. When do you want me to start?"

"Today, if you can. I've typed up all my contact information for you." She pulled a small envelope from her purse along with a blank check. "His picture is in there along with other information about us you may need to know. My contact information is also there. I don't want you to ever contact me at home or through the office phone." She filled in the check and shoved it in his direction. "Is that enough for you to get started?"

He looked at the amount, then opened the envelope. As he started to quickly review her information, he said, "Yes, that's more than I would have asked for. If I incur fees that exceed this amount, I'll just bill you at the time."

"That's fine. I must emphasize that you *cannot* contact me at home. In fact, don't contact me at all, until you are sure. I do not want a mistake. When you contact me, I want you to be sure what the issue is—whether it's a woman or even a man. Hell, he might be involved with a man, I don't know. I want to know that, along with where they meet, or whether it's some other issue altogether. When we meet again, I want it to be the *final* time, and I want an *accurate* answer. Okay?"

"I understand."

"Thank you. Thanks for helping me. This is painful as you can imagine, but I need to know."

"I will be in touch."

Ruth had been in court all day. She was tired and discouraged after losing her hearing. Paul and Hanna had both left the office for the day, when her cell rang. Caller ID indicated it was the call she had been anticipating for over two weeks.

"Hi, Randy. Have you got something for me?"

"Yes, I do. Can we meet?"

"Same place as before in about an hour?"

"See you then."

This time *he* was waiting for *her*.

"Sorry I'm late. I had a number of messages to look through after being in court today, and I just didn't want to go back to the office tonight."

He smiled. "You are three minutes late. In my business, that's not considered late at all. You want something to drink?"

As she sat, she said, "Am I going to need it?"

"Probably."

She got the waiters attention and told him she needed a beer—whatever brand he recommended.

"Okay, give me the bad news."

"He left the house a number of times during the past two weeks. There were different places he would go—bars, restaurants for lunch, or maybe just drive around. But on four occasions he did meet up with a woman."

"Where?"

"Always the same place. A little bar up in Hendersonville."

"Did they leave together?"

He hesitated. "Yes."

"All four times?"

"Yes."

"Where did they go?"

He looked at the bottom of his glass, for only a moment, took a deep breath, and said, "There's a little hotel right across the street. That is where they went all four times. They normally stayed about an hour, and then went their separate ways."

"That rotten bastard. I *knew* he was seeing someone. Did you get her name?"

"No."

"Did you ever follow her?"

"No. You told me to tail *him.* That's what I did. I was afraid if I didn't keep track of him each time, once they went their separate ways, he might end up somewhere else that might be important and I would have never known. I never took my eyes off him."

"You did the right thing. That is not what I wanted to hear, but it's what I expected."

"So, what now?"

"I honestly don't know. I need to think about it. I may want you to do a little more work for me, I'm just not sure. I guess who she is, really isn't that important right now—just the fact that there *is* another 'she,' is all that matters."

"I'm sorry, Ruth. I really didn't want to bring you this kind of information. It is never easy, in this type of situation, to bring the spouse this kind of news. But it is what you paid me for, and you were right all along. What's your next move?"

Ruth thought before she spoke. "I'm not sure. I have an idea or two, but I need to think it all through. Where do I stand concerning your fees?”

“You have a refund coming to you. It doesn’t amount to much, but you do have a balance. Do you want me to send it back to you?”

“No, not yet. I may have a few more things for you to do.”

“Okay. I need to meet with another client shortly. I better be on my way.”

He stood to go and as he did, she stood, walked toward him, then gave him a hug.

“Thanks for everything you’ve done for me. I will give you a call later this week.”

He nodded and walked away.

She sat back down and as she did, she downed the rest of her beer, then indicated to her waiter she needed a refill. She needed to consider what she now knew, then determine her next move.

First of all, she needed to hurt him as badly as he had hurt her. Secondly, there was all that money. What move could she make at this point to handle both issues? She needed to formulate a plan, here and now. She wasn’t about to walk through the front door of that house until she had determined her next move.

Chapter 52

The home of Ruth and Ed Hall
One week later

Ed drove in his driveway and touched the remote to open the garage door. As he did, he concluded the frequency of his trips to see Patricia would most likely need to be somewhat reduced. He had the feeling Ruth knew he was leaving the house on a fairly regular basis, which wasn't an issue in and of itself, but she didn't seem to believe him when he told her where he had been. Generating any degree of animosity between them, at this point in time, had not been part of the plan, and, in fact, was clearly counterproductive. They needed to remain close, without issues of any nature, right up until the time he killed her, then stuffed her body in a shallow grave somewhere in the hills.

As the door opened, he noticed her car—she was home. That was unusual for her. It was only 4:00 p.m. She was rarely home before seven or eight.

He walked in the door, through the kitchen and into the living room. She was seated on the couch with a glass of wine. She smiled as he walked in. He said, "What are you doing home so early?"

"Surprised? I figured you might be. I just thought maybe you and I might spend a little quality time together. We haven't done that in a while—just you and I. Maybe we can just talk a little and have a drink or two together here, in my living room. Do you have the time?"

Her living room? Interesting way to start a conversation. "Certainly. Let me get a drink first."

He walked to the bar, poured himself a half glass of wine, and smiled as he sat down beside her. "Is there something in particular we need to discuss? You want me to make dinner reservations for tonight? This is just so unusual for you to be home at this hour. I like it."

"Where have you been, Ed?"

He could tell this conversation was already headed in a bad direction. "Oh, just out. I watched a baseball game at one of the bars, then drove around for a while. I've been thinking about different things I might do—you know, businesses I might get into."

"Alone?"

He smiled, "Yes, alone."

"So, every time you leave here without me, you know, when you are '*by yourself,*' are you alone the whole time you are gone—is that what you're telling me?"

"Of course. Why are you asking me all these questions? Is there a problem? I don't understand."

"Who is she, Ed?"

"Who is who, Ruth? What are you talking about?"

"I have been having you followed. I hired a private investigator. I figured there was another woman. Now I *know* there is."

He stood. "You have what? You've been having me followed? What the hell did I ever do to warrant that? How dare you have me followed!"

"Stop, Ed, just stop. I know there is another woman. I know you meet her frequently. And I know you are involved with her. Now, who is she?"

Ruth stood, walked to the wet bar and poured herself another glass of wine. She never turned around as she said, "Cat got your tongue? Who is she?"

"I really can't believe you had me followed. I can't believe you would do that."

She walked back to the couch, and as she sat, she said, "Well, I did. I know you meet her at a small bar in Hendersonville, and once you are together you go to that little hotel across the street. I know you are never there long, but you stay long enough to get the job done. Then you run home to me. Once you are here, you have a real issue touching me, holding me, and kissing me, every fricken' time you come home after you have been with her. Now, those are the elements of the story as I know it. Finish it off. Give me the remaining facts. Fill in the blanks for me, Ed. Who is she?"

He walked away, looking out the window as he processed the situation. He knew it was no use. He just needed to find the best way out of this situation and then finish what he had planned on doing from the day he married her. He would try once more.

"She is an old girlfriend I had before I met Janice." He turned to face her. "I'm sorry. It has been hard to cut the cord with her. I'll tell her I can no longer see her." He walked toward her, set his glass down, and reached for her hand.

She stood, and walked away, toward the wet bar, as he said, "I'm sorry. I really am. I'll get rid of her."

She again filled her glass, smiled at him and said, "The only thing you are sorry about is you got caught with your pants down, you stupid son-of-a-bitch. You and I are finished. You are *not* going to leave here, time after time, go be with some idiot in a hotel, and then come back to my house, to me and act as if it were nothing. You are not going to do that to me, Ed. Maybe someone else, but not me."

She threw her glass of wine at him, a wild throw that shattered as it hit the wall, while shards of glass filled the air near him.

"Now wait, surely there's something I can do to make this right. Please, Ruth, give me one more chance. I promise it will never happen again."

"We are done, you rotten bastard. One chance is all you get with me. This is my house and I want you out of here—tonight. I don't care where you go or what you do, but I want you out of here."

"Please, please don't do this. Give me one more chance. I'll make it right."

"Go to hell." Again, she smiled as she said, "Oh by the way, since you'll find out soon anyway, I removed all the funds from our joint accounts and put the money in my own account. You have what is left in that one account that's only got your name on it. From what I can determine, there's about fifty thousand in it. But if it would have had my name on it, that money would have also been moved."

He felt the color literally drain from his face. He thought he was going to be sick. Once he determined he still had a voice he said, "You didn't. You didn't really do that did you? You took *my* money and put it all in *your* name?"

"You bet your sweet ass I did. Now since your dick seems to be the president of this party, what does he think about that? Shrivel him up, did it? Cat got his tongue? I'll tell you something else too, you worthless piece of shit. I'm going to find out who that woman is. I am going to investigate the hell out of her. I will know more about her than you do before I'm finished. I will find out, and when I do, she and I are going to have a little talk. I'll figure out what to do with her after I learn about her."

It was over. It was clear they were done. All that remained was staying out of prison. If Ruth figured out Patricia was involved, he had no doubt Patricia would tell everything she knew about everything. She was weak. He had found that out to late. She was a great partner while everything was good, but once it turned bad, he knew she would spill the beans about everything. It was over.

"Just wait. Just wait a minute. I want to show you something. Would you please just wait here?"

"I think you forgot. I am not going anywhere. You're the one that's leaving. Sure, I'll be here."

Ed walked through the kitchen and into the garage. Out from under the seat of his vehicle, he removed his Glock, loaded and ready to use whenever he needed it. He certainly had not anticipated its use now—not this soon. He grabbed the silencer that lie under the seat, screwed it on the end of the barrel, and shoved the pistol into his pants near the small of his back, so she wouldn't see it as he walked in the room.

When he returned, she was seated, on the couch, with a full glass of wine.

He said, "Once again, Ruth, is there anything we can do to resolve this—anything at all. I'll do anything."

"Get out of here—*now*—you bastard."

He pulled out the Glock, aimed it at her, and pulled the trigger twice. Both shots struck her in the chest. She fell over on the couch, clearly gone before her wine glass hit the floor.

As he stood there, surveying the room, he thought about ransacking the whole house, making it look like a burglary gone bad, but that made little sense. He couldn't survive another investigation. It would be obvious who did this. He just needed to run.

He quickly packed a suitcase of essentials and walked back into the living room. As he did, he took one glance back at Ruth. She lay on the couch, eyes wide open, in a much better humor now than when he had first walked in the door.

As he got in his vehicle and backed out the driveway, he punched autodial for Patricia.

"Hey. I didn't think I would be hearing from you again today. It's nice though. I never hear from you twice in one day. What's going on? Isn't she home yet?"

"Listen. Don't talk. Don't say a word until I'm done. Ruth found out about us. She hired a private investigator, and he followed me. He found out where we met, then followed us to the hotel. She was insane. She moved all my money into her own account, so I think I got about fifty thousand left. She swore she was going to find out who you were and investigate you. I couldn't let that happen. I shot her, killed her. It's going to be obvious who did this, so I am heading to the bank to draw out what I have left and leave the country, probably go to Rio and disappear. Can you meet me there?"

She said nothing.

"Hey, wake up. Can you meet me there?"

As he turned onto Gallatin Street, driving toward downtown Nashville, again he said, "Hey, where the hell are you? Why don't you answer me?"

Finally, in a whisper, she said, "She took all your money?"

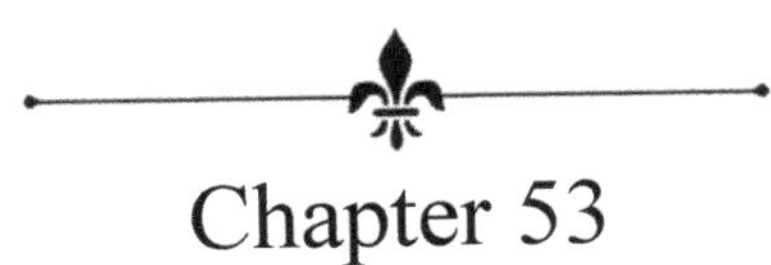

Chapter 53

The office of Paul Thomas
One month later

Paul sat alone, thinking of all the office work he needed to start or complete before the day ended. The volume of work walking in the front door of the office had not changed since Ruth's death. Unfortunately, the number of attorneys available to *handle* the volume of work *had* changed. He knew it was time to at least consider someone to fill that office across the hall, the one that had remained closed and dark since her murder. But he had a problem thinking about someone else sitting in her chair.

He had become close to Ruth, especially within the last few months. He never thought that would have been possible when he first hired her, especially when he was initially made aware of the problem involving Mrs. VanArsdayle's will.

But, while working through that problem, they had become close—father and daughter close. Their relationship had continued to remain strong until her murder.

Law enforcement knew who did it. There was never a doubt in anyone's mind that Ed shot her. No one had any idea where he was, but then again there weren't many they could ask. He had no friends, no family, no one they could go to for information about him. All law enforcement knew was that he withdrew funds in his name, approximating fifty thousand dollars, and apparently left the area. No one was talking about it. All he found out came through rumor and conjecture from members of the bar association that knew Ruth and had a personal interest in her murder.

They searched her office on multiple occasions, from one end to the other, but turned up nothing that might help. They had interviewed both Hanna and him, as they continued to search for a motive. They couldn't come up with any indication as to why he killed her. To Paul, at this point, it made no difference. She was gone and there remained an emptiness in his life, and in his profession, which her death had created.

Hanna peeked around his doorframe. "Morning, boss. You alright today?"

"Oh, I guess. I have a hell of a lot to do, I know that." He hesitated as he looked away. "I miss her. But I guess the only thing I can do about either of those issues is work a little harder, because we are sure as hell not going to bring her back." He looked at Hanna and said, "Should we cut back, or replace her? I don't know which way to go, Hanna. You and I have been together from day one. What do you think?"

"I think I liked it with two attorneys here. It was almost like our own little family taking on the world. I miss her too. She brightened up the office, that's for sure."

The mail came midmorning, but Hanna never even had time to deliver it to Paul. He had appointment after appointment until late in the afternoon, when the work load started to let up. Hanna walked in, laid the mail on his desk, and said, "I haven't had time to bring this to you. Whoa, what a crazy morning."

"You are not telling me anything. What's in the mail?"

"Looks like nothing to me, but you can open it and see." She walked back to her desk as he started opening each envelope which consisted mostly of advertising.

He noticed a letter from Central Bank and Trust which looked like a statement of some type. He had no funds deposited with them, but it was addressed to him, so he opened it. The statement, which was for a period of time ending prior to Ruth's death, showed a cash balance of three million five hundred fifty-five dollars and twenty-nine cents. The account showed titled in the name of Ruth Hall but payable upon death to him.

Paul laughed as he stood. He walked out to Hanna's desk and said, "Call these idiots at the bank and tell them they've made a mistake. I have no money with Ruth anywhere. I wish it were mine, but no such luck."

As he reviewed all the new business he had taken in for the day, Hanna walked back to his office, sitting down in the chair directly in front of him. She was pale in color—her eyes wide open. "You...you're...you're not going to believe this."

"What happened? What the hell is wrong?"

"That money...that money you know...that money in the bank...that million plus."

"Yeah, what about it?"

"It's yours."

"It's whose?"

"It's yours"

He smiled. "No, you don't understand. That is obviously why I had you call them. The statement's wrong. It's not...."

"No, it's *you* that doesn't understand. Ruth went to the bank a couple of days before she was mur...died, and removed the money from a joint tenancy account she had with Ed, and set up a new account, this account, which is payable to you upon her death. She is dead. The money is yours."

"You must be mistaken. She..."

"*Paul, Paul there's no mistake*. I talked to a teller, then I talked to the vice president of the bank. The money is yours, she's dead, it all goes to you."

He leaned back in his chair. "Well, I'll be damned. I can't believe that's what she did. I knew we were close, but not that close."

He thought for a moment, before he said, "No one has or probably ever will do anything concerning her estate. Ed, of course is gone. She was estranged from her family and had been for quite some time. I think she just basically had you and I...and Ed. Her family paid for her funeral and..." He thought for a moment. "I'll definitely want to talk to an attorney...first, as concerns inheritance tax, and secondly as to whether anyone else can stake a claim to it."

"The banker told me it was a legitimate account and couldn't be touched by anyone but you."

Both remained quiet, reflective. Finally, Hanna stood. "Well, that's about enough for me for one day. I am going home. See you tomorrow."

Paul waived goodbye, and closed up the office shortly thereafter. He was a millionaire, at least for now. He was going out and buy one drink that contained the most expensive scotch sold. He was king for a day, and he would do all he could to make sure it remained that way, at least until tomorrow.

During the course of the next week, he received statements from several different banks. They were all set up the same way—the money was payable to him. When all the funds were added together, they contained millions.

He had no idea what had happened. He had no idea what had motivated her to do what she did. He assumed this was all the money the two of them had accumulated, but whatever had happened in that last week to push Ruth to do what she did, he had no idea. And now, with her gone, and Ed on the run for the rest of his life, Paul figured he *never* would know what motivated her to do what she did.

The following week he made an appointment with an attorney specializing in probate issues concerning payment of any inheritance taxes he might owe. He also asked him if there was any way the payable on death status could be challenged in case Edward came back, or anyone else made a claim. He received an emphatic *no*, and was told that no one could ever make a claim to any of the joint tenancy accounts, other than him. He had concluded he never needed to worry about Ed anyway. The cops had a warrant out for him which remained outstanding and would remain outstanding until they caught him.

During the next few months, he made Hanna a wealthy woman, and provided donations to many organizations, the largest amount of which went for ALS research. But he also retained a substantial amount for himself. He never turned on the light in Ruth's office and left it as it was during the final hours she occupied it. He thought of her every day.

Paul did downsize his practice so he could handle a smaller workload. In those few months after receiving all his money, he often went out for a drink with Judge Dimmler, but he never again went out on a first date with a woman he hadn't first researched, notwithstanding the judge's recommendation.

Epilogue

Stoney River Steakhouse,
Nashville, Tennessee
Eight Months later

Paul had represented her before. She had purchased a home and he had helped her complete the transaction. He found out she was single and had been married once, but her husband was long deceased.

She needed some estate planning done. He met with her and determined she had no children. She needed a will. He prepared it for her. She would need to come back in to sign it. He met with her when she returned, and they talked about a little of everything for over an hour.

She wanted to know about him, about his deceased wife. She appeared to be compassionate and interested in her death and in his life since her death.

She was attractive and independently wealthy. She was not pretentious, nor overbearing. He had Googled her. The name was nowhere to be found on the Net, which to him was a point in her favor.

He decided to take the plunge. He would ask her out…on a date…the first one *he* had instigated since Anna had died.

She had two issues going for her. First, Judge Dimmler had not offered her up as a blind date, and second, he had accumulated enough information about her to have come to his *own* conclusion their time together would make for an enjoyable evening.

Tonight, was the night. He was nervous. Paul arrived at Stoney Creek Steakhouse early, fifteen minutes before she was supposed to meet him.

He saw her walk in and motioned for her to join him.

As she approached his table, he stood and said, "I arrived a little early."

He helped her with her chair, as she said, "I understand. I'm just glad you are here. I would hate to show up and then find out you stood me up."

He laughed. "No chance of that."

They ate their way through lettuce salads and prime beef, until they found themselves splitting a piece of chocolate cake and enjoying an after-dinner drink.

Paul said, "You know, I've certainly told you enough about myself, but let me ask a couple of questions about you and your life. As I recall, you told me you had been married, correct?"

"Once. A long time ago. He passed away years ago."

"Was that when you accumulated all your money, or did you work after his death. Your estate plan shows you have a nice net worth."

"No, that came from my husband and I working hand-in-hand."

"Where did you live during that time? Did you make it all in one place or at different locations?"

Patricia Maxwell said, "Different locations. I've lived in California and Colorado along with a few other locations here and there."

"It sounds like you've been around."

"Both my deceased husband and I followed a simple principal in life. Always follow the money—you know—figure out who was making all the money at the time, determine how they were doing it and then…follow their example. We just felt it was in our best interests to just…follow the money, if you know what I mean."

"That's an interesting philosophy for sure. Maybe we can discuss your thoughts in that respect one of these days. Are you ready to settle down now—stay here on a permanent basis?"

"Maybe so, Paul, maybe so. I really do believe there is plenty of opportunity right here in Nashville, but we'll just have to see." She took a sip from her wine glass, smiled and said, "Oh, by the way, I understand you just came into quite a sum of money yourself lately. Is that correct?"

About the Author

JB Millhollin resides near Nashville, Tennessee. He has published a number of novels and continues to write, using the city and surrounding area as a backdrop for his stories. His stories are character-driven and devote a considerable amount of time in the courtroom. If you enjoy his style of writing, stay in touch through his Facebook author page, on twitter (@jbmillhollin), and through his website at www.jbmillhollin.com.